PRAISE FOR
FALLING

· · · · ·

"Summer's big thriller . . . The frenzy for *Falling* is understandable: At every turn, Newman cranks the tension in unexpected ways that still satisfy the thriller lust. Her insider's knowledge comes through in details that not only bolster the book's credibility but also catalyze the plot."

—**Margaret Wappler,**
Los Angeles Times

"One of the most talked-about debuts of the year. Like all good thrillers, *Falling* gets off to a dramatic start and maintains its momentum . . . Newman's various narrative strands resemble high-voltage live wires. One tense predicament replaces another, from poison gas attacks to mutinous passengers to orders to kill the co-pilot or shoot down the plane. The suspense is heightened by the fact that the terrorist is not open to negotiation."

—**Malcolm Forbes,**
Minneapolis Star Tribune

"The summer's buzziest beach read."
—*Los Angeles Magazine*

"Bound for JFK out of LAX, pilot Bill Hoffman has no idea he's about to be given a choice: Either crash the plane or his family will be murdered. The author, a former bookseller and flight attendant, seems to think of everything—every trick, every error, every advantage—in a plot that executes more barrel rolls than a stunt plane on the Fourth of July."

—**Bethanne Patrick,**
Los Angeles Times

"One of the year's best thrillers . . . This novel is like the films *Die Hard* and *Speed* on steroids . . . Newman keeps up an extreme pace from the first page."

—*Library Journal* (starred review)

"Brilliant . . . Incredibly suspenseful . . . With abundantly human characters, natural dialogue, and a plot that unleashes one surprise after another, this could be the novel that everyone is talking about this summer."

—*Booklist* (starred review)

"A superlative debut . . . This tense, convincing thriller marks the arrival of an assured new talent."

—*Publishers Weekly* (starred review)

"High-octane drama . . . Newman's background means *Falling* brings a freshness and depth to the genre. While the story is propelled by the impossible situation Bill and his captive family find themselves in, at its heart is the relationship between the tight-knit crew. . . . It's an eye-opening look into the reality of working on a plane."

—*The Guardian*

"Attention, please: T. J. Newman has written the perfect thriller! Such a cool, high-concept idea: commercial airline pilot forced to make the ultimate life-or-death choice. Newman's background in the air grounds the story in reality, while her writing amps up the suspense to unbearable levels. Terrific and terrifying, a true page-turner. A must-read for summer vacation—but my advice is, don't start this book until you've gotten off the plane."

—**Gillian Flynn,**
#1 *New York Times* **bestselling**
author of *Gone Girl*

"*Falling* is the best kind of thriller (for me as a reader anyway). Characters you care deeply about. Nonstop, totally authentic suspense."

—**James Patterson,**
#1 *New York Times* **bestselling author**

"T. J. Newman has taken a brilliant idea, a decade of real-life experience, and crafted the perfect summer thriller. Relentlessly paced and unforgettable."

—**Janet Evanovich,**
#1 *New York Times* **bestselling author**

"Amazing . . . Intense suspense, shocks and scares plus chilling insider authenticity make this one very special."

—**Lee Child,**
#1 *New York Times* **bestselling author**

"A bullet train of a thriller with incredible tension and personal stakes. The real engine of this stunning and relentless book is how far would you go to save your family? I read *Falling* with my heart in my throat—this is *Jaws* at 35,000 feet. An extraordinary debut and the perfect summer page-turner."

—**Don Winslow,**
New York Times **bestselling author of**
The Force* and *The Cartel

"Heart pounding. Heart wringing. Heart STOPPING! A great book! One of those where you're afraid to turn the next page, but you can't stop."

—**Diana Gabaldon,**
#1 *New York Times* **bestselling author**
of the *Outlander* series

"Think *Speed* on a passenger jet—with the cockpit dials turned up to supersonic."

—**Ian Rankin,**
#1 internationally bestselling author

"Buckle up for a completely original edge-of-your-seat thriller that will keep you guessing until the final nail-biting pages. Save your family or save the hundred passengers who have put their lives in your hands. You cannot save both. T. J. Newman's chilling novel stayed with me long after I finished reading it. This is the best thriller I've read in years."

—**Adrian McKinty,**
New York Times **bestselling**
author of *The Chain*

"A jet-propelled thriller that will have you in its grip from first page to last. A truly astonishing debut and an incredible work of pure suspense."

—**Steve Cavanagh,**
#1 bestselling author of the Eddie Flynn series

"*Falling* redefines the phrase roller-coaster ride. It redefines the term edge-of-your-seat thriller. *Falling* is that rarest of things, a book that is even better than everyone says it is. T. J. Newman has delivered a stunning debut."

FALLING

T.J. NEWMAN

POCKET BOOKS

NEW YORK   LONDON   TORONTO   SYDNEY   NEW DELHI

Pocket Books
An Imprint of Simon & Schuster, Inc.
1230 Avenue of the Americas
New York, NY 10020

This book is a work of fiction. Any references to historical events, real people, or real places are used fictitiously. Other names, characters, places, and events are products of the author's imagination, and any resemblance to actual events or places or persons, living or dead, is entirely coincidental.

This Pocket Books paperback edition April 2023

POCKET and colophon are registered trademarks of Simon & Schuster, Inc.

For information about special discounts for bulk purchases, please contact Simon & Schuster Special Sales at 1-866-506-1949 or business@simonandschuster.com.

The Simon & Schuster Speakers Bureau can bring authors to your live event. For more information or to book an event, contact the Simon & Schuster Speakers Bureau at 1-866-248-3049 or visit our website at www.simonspeakers.com.

Interior design by Ruth Lee-Mui

Manufactured in the United States of America

10 9 8 7 6 5 4 3 2 1

ISBN 978-1-6680-1940-5
ISBN 978-1-9821-7790-4 (ebook)

For my parents,
Ken and Denise Newman

What hath God wrought!

—Numbers 23:23

WHEN THE SHOE DROPPED INTO HER LAP THE FOOT WAS STILL IN IT.

She flung it into the air with a shriek. The blood-ied mass hung in weightless suspension before being sucked out of the massive hole in the side of the aircraft. On the floor next to her seat, a flight attendant crawled up the aisle screaming for the passengers to put their oxygen masks on.

From the back of the airplane, Bill observed it all.

The passenger with the shoe clearly couldn't hear what the young flight attendant was yelling. She probably hadn't heard a thing since the explosion. Thin lines of blood trickled out of both ears.

The blast had thrown the flight attendant's body into the air and then back down, her head of curly brown hair hitting the floor with a thwack. She lay motionless for a second before the plane went into a steep nosedive. Sliding down the aisle, the flight attendant grabbed at the metal rungs beneath the passenger seats. Clutching on to one, her arms shook as she tried to pull herself up against the plane's downward pitch. As she flipped onto her side, her feet floated and dangled in the air. Debris flew all around the plane; paper and clothing, a laptop, a soda can. A baby's blanket. It was like the inside of a tornado.

Bill followed her gaze down the plane—and saw sky.

Sunlight shone in on them from a wide opening that had been the over-wing emergency exit not thirty seconds ago. The other flight attendant had just stopped there to collect trash.

Bill had watched the older, redheaded flight attendant smile, take the empty cup in her gloved hand, drop it in the plastic bag—and then in one explosive moment she was gone. The whole row was gone. The side of the aircraft was gone. Bill widened his stance as the plane yawed left to right, seemingly unable to keep a straight path. *Of course, the rudder*, he thought. The whole tail was probably damaged.

A crack came from above the brunette flight attendant's head as several overhead bins burst open. Luggage tumbled out, tossed violently about the cabin. A large pink suitcase with wheels shot forward, sucked toward the opening. It hit the side of the fuselage as it went out, a chunk of the aircraft's skin ripped off with it. Exposed frames and stringers created a lattice of human engineering against the heavens. Beyond the whipping wires hissing orange and yellow sparks, clouds dotted the view. Bill squinted against the sun.

The plane leveled off enough that the flight attendant on the floor could get to her knees. Bill watched her struggle against a body that wouldn't cooperate. She managed to pull her leg forward only to find her femur sticking out of her thigh. She blinked at the bloody wound a few times and then kept crawling.

"Masks!" she screamed, dragging herself up the aisle

toward the back of the plane, her voice barely audible above the deafening roar of wind. She looked over to a man grabbing at the oxygen masks. He caught one and went to put it over his face but a gust ripped it out of his fingers, plastic and elastic straps flailing.

Gray fog choked the cabin in a swirling haze of debris and chaos. A metal water bottle went flying through the air, smacking into the crawling flight attendant's face. Blood began to pour from her nose.

"He's been shot! My husband! Help!"

Bill looked to the woman pounding her fists against her husband's lifeless torso. Two small circles in his forehead streamed red over his eyes and down his cheeks. The flight attendant brushed the curls out of her face as she pulled herself up on the armrests for a closer look.

They weren't bullets. They were rivets from the plane.

The plane vibrated violently and the floor began to buckle. Bill could feel everything shifting beneath him. He wondered if the airframe would hold. He wondered how much time they had.

The flight attendant continued on, placing her hand in a dark spot on the carpet at the same moment Bill smelled the urine. The flight attendant looked up at the man in the aisle seat. He stared off in a state of shock, the puddle spreading at his feet.

"Ice," someone moaned.

The flight attendant turned. Bill watched the passenger on the other side of the aisle extend her hands to the young woman, holding out a fleshy chunk of something. The flight attendant recoiled. Looking up, the passenger's chin and neck were painted crimson.

"Ice," she repeated, a wave of blood gushing out of her mouth.

It was her tongue.

Bill glanced over his shoulder to the back wall, watching the cord of the interphone thrash in the wind as the flight attendant crawled toward it. He looked to the other side of the galley. The third flight attendant lay crumpled on the floor, a toppled carton of juice next to her. Bill turned his head to the side, watching the glugs of orange mix with the pool of red around her body.

The brunette dragged herself at last to the end of the aisle, packets of sugar and mini creamers crunching against her uniform. She reached a hand forward but yanked it back.

A pair of black dress shoes blocked her path.

The flight attendant looked up. Lying at Bill's feet, broken and bloodied, her jaw hung open but no words came. Bill's tie flapped in the wind. The sound of the engines screamed at them both, willing something, anything, to happen.

"But . . . if you're . . ." the flight attendant stammered, looking up at Bill, betrayal written across her face. "Who has control of the plane, Captain Hoffman?"

Bill inhaled sharply as though to speak, but couldn't.

He looked down the plane to the closed cockpit door.

He was supposed to be on the other side.

Bill leapt over the flight attendant, sprinting down the aisle toward the front of the aircraft. He ran as fast as he could, but the door seemed to move farther away the faster he ran. All around him, people cried out, begging him to stop and help them. He kept running. The door kept moving farther and farther away. He closed his eyes.

His body slammed into the door without warning, his skull bashing against the impenetrable surface.

His hands cradled his head as he stumbled backward. Woozy, he tried to think of how he could breach the sealed cockpit, but not a single idea came to mind. He pounded on the door until his fists went numb.

Hyperventilating, he stepped back to kick at it when he heard a click.

The door unlocked and cracked open. Bill rushed inside.

Buttons flashed red and amber warnings on nearly every surface in the cockpit. A loud, incessant alarm screeched, the shrill noise intensifying in the tiny space. He sat down in his seat on the left, the captain's seat.

He struggled to focus on the display in front of him as the plane's thrashing tossed the numbers about. Red followed him everywhere he looked. Every button, every knob, every display was screaming at him.

Through the window, the approaching ground loomed closer and closer.

Get to work, Bill ordered himself.

His hands stretched out in front of him.

Frozen.

Dammit, you're the captain. You need to make a decision. You're running out of time.

The alarms got louder. A robotic voice repeatedly commanded him to pull up.

"What about asymmetrical thrust?"

Bill turned his head. From the copilot's seat his ten-year-old son, Scott, shrugged. He was wearing his solar system pajamas. His feet didn't touch the ground.

"You could give that a try," the boy added.

Bill looked back to his hands. His fingers refused to move. They just hung in the air.

"Fine, then. Do it the hard way. Dive and use speed to keep a straight line."

He turned again to see his wife now reclined in the chair. Arms crossed, she gave him that smirk. The one she used when they both knew she was right. God, she was gorgeous.

Sweat dripped down his neck as he struggled to move and take action. But he remained paralyzed in fear. Terrified he would make the wrong call.

Carrie tucked her hair behind one ear as she leaned over, placing a hand on her husband's knee.

"Bill. It's time."

He gasped for air as his body shot upright. Moonlight poured through the crack in the curtains to streak across the king-size bed. He scanned the room for the flashing warnings. He listened for the alarms, but heard only a neighbor's dog barking outside.

Bill dropped his head in his hands with an exhale.

"Same one?" Carrie asked from the other side of the bed.

He nodded in the dark.

CHAPTER ONE

GIVING THE DUVET A SHAKE, CARRIE SMOOTHED THE CREASES WITH her hand. A whiff of fresh-cut grass drew her glance to the open window. The neighbor across the street mopped his face with the bottom of his shirt before closing the trash can full of lawn clippings with a clunk. Dragging it into the backyard, he gave a wave to a passing car, the loud music fading as it drove on. Behind her, in the bathroom, the shower shut off.

Carrie left the room.

"Mom, can I go outside?"

Scott stood at the bottom of the stairs holding a remote control car.

"Where's your—" Carrie said, making her way downstairs.

The baby crawled into the room, blowing wet raspberries as she went. Reaching her brother's feet, Elise grabbed on to his shorts and pulled herself up to a stand, her little body jerking subtly as she tried to find balance.

"Okay, did you bring your dishes to the sink?"

"Yup."

"Then you can, but only for ten minutes. Come back before your dad leaves, okay?"

The boy nodded and ran for the door.

"Nope," Carrie called after him, placing Elise on her hip. "Shoes."

The "whoops" baby ten years after the first kid had been overwhelming in the beginning. But as the family of three learned how to be four, Bill and Carrie realized the age gap meant big brother could do little things like watch-the-baby-while-I-get-dressed-and-make-the-bed. Things became more manageable after that.

Carrie was wiping the remnants of sweet potato and avocado off the high chair when she heard the front door open.

"Mom?" Scott hollered, a pinched alarm to his tone.

Hurrying around the corner, she found Scott staring up at a man she didn't know. The stranger on the front porch wore a startled look, his hand frozen on its way to the doorbell.

"Hi," Carrie said, shifting the baby to her other hip as she moved to place herself subtly between her son and the man. "Can I help you?"

"I'm with CalCom," the man said. "You called about your internet?"

"Oh!" she exclaimed, opening the door wider. "Of course, come in." Carrie cringed at her initial reaction, hoping the man hadn't noticed. "Sorry. I've never had a repairman come on time, let alone early. Scott!" she yelled, her son pivoting at the end of the drive. "Ten minutes."

Nodding, the boy ran off.

"I'm Carrie," she said, closing the door.

The technician set his equipment bag down in the entryway and Carrie watched him take in the living room. High ceilings and a staircase to the second floor. Tasteful furniture and fresh flowers on the coffee table. On the mantel, family photos over the years, the most recent taken on the beach at sunset. Scott was a mini-me of Carrie, their same chocolatey-brown hair blowing in the sea breeze, their green eyes squinted with wide smiles. Bill, nearly a foot taller than Carrie, held a then-newborn Elise in his arms, her lily-white baby skin a contrast to his Southern California tan. The repairman turned with a small smile.

"Sam," he said.

"Sam," she said, returning the smile. "Can I get you something to drink before you get started? I was just about to make myself a cup of tea."

"Tea would be great, actually. Thanks."

She led him into the other room, bright, natural light filling the kitchen that opened into the toy-dotted family room.

"Thanks for coming on a Saturday." Carrie sat the baby back in the high chair. Pounding her fists on the table, Elise giggled through a sparsely toothed grin. "This was the only appointment I could get for weeks."

"Yeah, we're pretty busy. How long has your internet been out?"

"Day before yesterday?" she said, filling a tea kettle with water. "English breakfast or green?"

"English breakfast, thanks."

"Is it normal," Carrie asked, watching the stove's pilot light ignite to a full flame, "for our house to be the only one having issues? I asked a few neighbors who also have CalCom and theirs is fine."

Sam shrugged. "That's normal. Might be your router, maybe the wiring. I'll run diagnostics."

From the front room, heavy footsteps made their

way down the stairs. Carrie knew the next sounds well: a suitcase and messenger bag set by the door, followed by hard-soled shoes crossing the entryway. In a handful of strides, he was in the kitchen, polished black dress shoes, crisply ironed pants, suit coat, and tie. Wings above his breast pocket displayed the Coastal Airways insignia, BILL HOFFMAN engraved boldly below. A matching pair adorned the front of the gold-trimmed hat he laid softly on the counter. His entrance felt oddly dramatic and Carrie noticed how much of a contrast his aura of authority made to the rest of the house. She'd never noticed it before; it wasn't like he came to dinner in uniform. And it was probably only because there was another person in the room, a man who didn't know him, didn't know their family. But for whatever reason, today, it was conspicuous.

Bill placed his hands in his pockets with a polite nod to the technician before settling his attention on Carrie.

Lips pursed, arms crossed, she stared back.

"Sam, would you mind . . ."

"Yeah, I'll, uh, get set up," Sam said to Carrie, leaving the couple alone.

The clock on the wall ticked the seconds. Baby Elise banged a drool-covered teething ring on the tray before it slipped out of her fingers, falling to the floor. Bill crossed the kitchen and picked it up, rinsing it off in the sink and drying it with a dish towel before returning it to his daughter's eager hands. Behind Carrie the tea kettle began a soft whistle.

"I'll FaceTime when I get to the hotel to hear how the game—"

"New York, right?" Carrie cut him off.

Bill nodded. "New York tonight, Portland tom—"

"There's a team pizza party after the game. With the

three-hour time difference, you'll be asleep before we get home."

"Okay. Then first thing—"

"We're getting together with my sister and the kids tomorrow morning," she said, and shrugged. "So, we'll see."

Bill straightened with a deep inhale, the four gold stripes on his epaulets rising with his shoulders. "You know I had to say yes. If it'd been anyone else asking I wouldn't have."

Carrie stared at the floor. The kettle began to screech and she shut off the burner. The noise gradually softened until it was only the clock making noise again.

Bill checked his watch, cursing under his breath. Giving a kiss to the top of his daughter's head, he said, "I'm gonna be late."

"You've never been late," Carrie replied.

He put on his hat. "I'll call after I check in. Where's Scott?"

"Outside. Playing. He's coming back any minute to say goodbye."

It was a test and she knew Bill knew it. Carrie stared at him from the other side of the unspoken line she'd drawn. He glanced at the clock.

"We'll talk before I take off," Bill said, leaving the room.

Carrie watched him go.

The front door opened and closed a few moments later and a hush settled over the house. Crossing to the sink, Carrie watched the leaves on the oak tree in the backyard flutter in the breeze. Distantly, Bill's car started up and drove off.

Behind her, a throat cleared. Wiping her face hastily, she turned.

"Sorry about that," she said to Sam with an embarrassed eye roll. "Anyway. You said English breakfast." Tearing open the tea bag, she dropped it in a mug. Steam rose from the kettle as she poured the hot water. "Do you need milk or sugar?"

When he didn't reply, she looked back.

He seemed surprised by her reaction. He had probably imagined she would scream. Maybe drop the cup. Start to cry, who knows. *Some* kind of drama he surely expected. When a woman, at home, in her own kitchen, turns to find a man she's known for a mere handful of minutes pointing a gun at her, a big reaction would seem natural. Carrie had felt her eyes widen reflexively, like her brain needed to take in more of the scene to confirm that this was actually happening.

He narrowed his eyes, as if to say, *Really?*

Carrie's heartbeat pounded in her ears while a cool numbness trickled down from the top of her spine to the back of her knees. Her whole body, her whole existence, felt reduced to nothing but a buzzing sensation.

But that was for her to know. She ignored the gun and focused on him instead, and gave him nothing.

Puckering and cooing, baby Elise threw her teething ring back to the floor with a squeal. Sam took a step toward the baby. Carrie felt her nostrils flare involuntarily.

"Sam," Carrie said calmly, slowly. "I don't know what you want. But it's yours. Anything. I will do anything. Just please"—her voice cracked—"please don't hurt my children."

The front door opened and closed with a slam. Panic seized her throat and Carrie drew breath to yell. Sam cocked the gun.

"Mom, did Dad leave?" Scott called from the other room. "His car's not here, can I keep playing?"

"Tell him to come in here," Sam said.

Carrie bit her bottom lip.

"Mom?" Scott repeated with childish impatience.

"In here," Carrie said, and closed her eyes. "Come here real quick, Scott."

"Mom, can I stay outside? You said I could go—" Scott froze when he saw the gun. He looked at his mom and back at the weapon and back at his mom.

"Scott," Carrie said, and motioned for him. The boy never took his eyes off the firearm as he crossed the kitchen to her, where she deliberately tucked him in behind her.

"Your children may be just fine," Sam said. "Or they may not. But that's not up to me."

Carrie's nostrils flared again. "Who is it up to?"

Sam smiled.

Bill could feel people watching him.

It was the uniform. It had that effect. He stood a little taller.

Bill was many things but the consensus seemed to be that he was first and foremost *nice*. Teachers and coaches growing up, girls he dated, his friends' parents. Everyone knew Bill as the nice guy. Not that he minded. He *was* nice. But when he put on the uniform, something changed. *Nice* wasn't the default description. It still made the list. But it wasn't the only word on it.

Passengers' heads popped up as he bypassed the never-ending line for security at Los Angeles International Airport, but it only took a peek at that hat and tie to dissolve indignation into curiosity. People didn't dress like that anymore. It harkened back to a time when air travel was a rare privilege, a major event. Purposefully unchanged, the uniform kept a certain antiquated mystique alive. It elicited respect. Trust. It proclaimed a sense of duty.

Bill approached the lone TSA agent seated at a small podium set discreetly off to the side of passenger security. Scanning the barcode on the back of his badge, the machine beeped and the computer went to work.

"Morning," Bill said, handing the woman his passport.

"It's still morning?" she said, studying the information printed next to his picture. Comparing it to the information on his badge, she slid the passport under a blue light, holograms and hidden print appearing in the document's blank space. Glancing up, she verified that the face in front of her matched the one on the IDs.

"I guess it's not technically morning," Bill said. "Just morning for me."

"Well, it's my Friday. So the day needs to hurry up."

Bill's badge photo and information popped up on the computer screen. After triple-checking all three forms of identification, she handed back the passport.

"Safe flight, Mr. Hoffman."

Leaving the crew security checkpoint, he walked past the passengers tugging their shoes back on and returning liquids and laptops to their carry-on bags. On his last trip, Bill flew with a flight attendant who refused to retire simply because she didn't want to give up her crew security clearance. She turned up her nose at the thought of having to travel like a mere mortal; waiting in line, liquid restrictions, limited to two carry-ons—which would be searched every single time, not just occasionally at random. Watching a man in his socks being patted down, Bill had to admit she had a point.

Claiming privacy at an unoccupied gate, Bill dialed home as promised. Watching a catering truck outside on the tarmac down below dodge about while rampers in neon vests loaded and unloaded bags from the cargo hold, he listened to the other end of the line ring over and over. An aircraft taxied out to the runway and in the distance, another took off.

He and Carrie didn't fight often. Which was why when they did they were so bad at it. She had every right to be upset. Today was Scott's Little League season opener and Bill had promised him he would be there. He made sure he didn't have a trip on his line for the day of the game and the two days before and after. But when the chief pilot calls to ask you to fly a trip as a personal favor, you don't say no. You can't say no. Bill was the third-most senior pilot flying. When he was a new hire, no one was sure the company was even going to make it. Startup airlines almost never do. But he stuck it out nonetheless. And now, nearly twenty-five years later, the airline was a total success with both passengers and shareholders. Coastal was his baby. So when your boss says the operation needs you? You say yes. No isn't even an option.

He had told Carrie as much. But he didn't tell her that Scott's game hadn't crossed his mind when O'Malley asked if he was available. Or that even if it had, it wouldn't have made a difference.

The phone rang and rang before finally, "Hi! You've reached Carrie. I can't come . . ." Ending the call, he saw a family photo appear on the phone's home screen before he pocketed it.

Catching a glimpse of his reflection in the window,

Bill surveyed his dark, full hair. A betraying gray salted his temples. His eyes, a vibrant, deep blue.

Bill slapped the bell in the middle of the coffee table.

"Eyes. My eyes."

"Final answer? This is for the win."

"She said they're like night swimming. When you can't see the bottom. But it's exciting. So, yes. My eyes. Final answer."

Carrie's jaw dropped.

Bill leaned forward. He could smell the beer on his own breath. "I overheard you say that to a friend on the phone once. I never told you, though. I love you so much, baby." He blew Carrie a kiss.

The wives cheered, the husbands ribbed.

"All right, Carrie," the party host said. "'His eyes.' Was that your answer for what your favorite part about your husband is?"

Her cheeks turned pink. With a giggle she held up a piece of paper, her answer scribbled out: His butt.

The room erupted. Bill laughed hardest of all.

He adjusted his tie. *I'm a good man,* he reminded himself without wavering. His mind flashed to the image of Carrie's look of disappointment as he walked out of the kitchen. He blinked, glancing away to follow a plane as it took off.

CHAPTER TWO

STEPPING OFF THE JET BRIDGE STAIRS ONTO THE TARMAC, BILL squinted under his hand's attempt to shield the sun. Fall leaves and frosty mornings covered most of the country, but in Los Angeles endless summer reigned.

The walk around: the standard aircraft inspection done before every flight. Look the aircraft up and down, check for irregularities, visible signs of a compromised airframe, or any other mechanical issues. To most pilots, it was just another FAA regulation. To Bill, it was church. Placing a hand on the engine's cowling, he closed his eyes. Fingers spreading with a slow inhale and exhale, metal and flesh communed, both warm to the touch.

He would turn eighteen next month, but that day in flight school, Bill knew he'd met a more important rite of passage.

"Now, when we log a flight plan, do you know why we write 'souls on board' instead of 'people on board'?" his instructor had asked.

Bill shook his head.

"We say it that way so that if we crash," he explained, "they know exactly how many bodies they're looking for. Avoids the confusion of different titles like passengers, crew, infants. Just how many bodies, *son. That's all they need to know. Oh!" He snapped his fingers. "And sometimes we carry dead bodies in the cargo hold so they need to know not to count them. So now, after you log in the souls . . ."*

Bill couldn't sleep that night. Lying on his back, watching the ceiling fan spin, he listened to his younger brother snoring softly from across the room. Cream-colored curtains and a warm Illinois summer breeze flirted through the open window, making wavy shadows dance on the wall.

With darkness still painting the room, he dressed and slipped out of the house, riding his bike alongside the cornfields to the town's tiny airfield. Two planes sat on the tarmac; the air traffic control tower, empty and quiet, loomed in the distance. The planes were small single-engine pistons, the types of planes he was learning on. The types of planes he would outgrow, trading them in for bigger engines, greater loads, heavier aircraft. Bill leaned against the fence for a long time staring them down.

Or were they sizing him up? As the stars faded and dawn began to break with pink and orange streaks, it felt as though the questioning had turned.

Could he bear the burden of duty? Could he be the man the job demanded?

Everything looked good. Tire tread fresh, gears greasy, sensors properly positioned, no fractures, no fissures. Catching a movement from out of the corner of his eye, Bill took a few steps out from under the plane. Up in the cockpit, his copilot, Ben Miro, leaned forward with a wave, letting Bill know he'd arrived. Bill dropped his smile when the young man held his Yankees ball cap up to the window. Bill shook his head with a face of disgust. Ben kept on grinning, flashing the captain his middle finger.

Walk around completed, Bill climbed the stairs up to the jet bridge with a look back at his plane. The tail of the Airbus A320, proudly bearing the red-and-white Coastal Airways logo, filled him with pride—and then he remembered Carrie. Punching in the door's security code, he checked his phone.

No missed texts. No missed calls.

His eyes adjusted in the fluorescent lighting as the door shut behind him. Tripping over a passenger's bag, Bill apologized with a surprised chuckle while the man scowled down at him—which was impressive, considering the pilot himself was six foot four. Looking the uniform up and down as the captain stepped around him, the man returned a meager grin.

The line of passengers snaked down the jet bridge onto the plane and Bill skirted through the suitcases and strollers with an accommodating smile. At last he stepped on board with a glance toward the back of the plane through the pink-and-purple mood lighting, the hip airline's iconic nightclub atmosphere.

"I guess we're boarding," he said to the flight attendant standing on her tiptoes to reach into one of the carriers in her galley. Jo turned, her eyes lighting up with surprise as Bill stooped to hug the petite middle-aged woman. Her fluffy black coils tickled his cheek as a familiar vanilla scent rose up from her dark brown skin.

"It's my signature scent," Jo said. "Same as my mama and her mama before that. See, when a Watkins girl turns thir-

teen, all the women in the family gather to celebrate her. No men allowed—just the ladies. We sit in the kitchen. We talk, we cook, we just . . . feel the generations of female."

It was music, the way she spoke. Bill delighted in every dragged-out vowel, hanging on to the hilly cadence and unpredictable word emphasis. He always asked about her childhood because he loved hearing her faded East Texas accent get stronger, as it always did, when she talked about her past. Bill finished his beer, indicating to the bartender they'd like another round.

"I'll never forget Great-Grammy taking the Dr Pepper bottle out of my hand and setting it there on the kitchen counter," Jo recalled, smiling into her wineglass like she was watching the memory play out. "Lord, that woman's hands. She wasn't a big woman, but those hands . . .

"Anyway, she didn't say a word, she just handed me this shiny gold box with this royal-blue bow. I knew what it was, we all did. I remember my fingers sliding that bow off so careful-like, and when I opened that box—there it was. My very own bottle of Shalimar. I smelled it. It smelled like my mama. And her mama. It smelled like what I was and who I would become."

"I didn't know you were on this trip," Jo said.

"I picked it up last night. They were out of reserves so O'Malley asked me to help out."

"Look at you on speed dial with the chief pilot," she said, smiling all the while to the boarding guests.

"See? You understand what that means. Could you please explain it to Carrie?"

Jo raised an eyebrow. "Well, that depends. What are you missing to be here?"

"Scott's Little League season opener. After I promised him I'd be there."

Jo winced.

"I know," Bill said. "But what was I supposed to do? It's not like I'm an absent father. When I'm home, I'm *home*. I'm present, I'm there. I just happen to have a job that means when I'm at work, I'm away. I'll make it up to him when I get back."

He waited for some sort of validation, but Jo just kept pouring her first-class pre-departure beverages. She looked up after a moment.

"Oh, I'm sorry, were you still talking to me? I thought you were explaining all that to your wife. Or to your son. Or to . . . yourself." She picked up the tray of drinks. "You're not wrong, honey. But you *are* working it out with the wrong person."

Jo was right. Jo was always right.

"You want coffee?" she asked over her shoulder on her way to deliver the drinks.

"C'mon. You know the answer to that." Bill ducked into the cockpit.

"Boss man!" Ben said, the men shaking hands as Bill took the left seat. Black and gray buttons and knobs covered nearly every surface in the tiny space. Occasionally, a flash of red or a pop of yellow. Those buttons were the messengers of something gone wrong—the gate-crashers to a quiet flight.

"Sorry I was late," Ben said. "Even on a Saturday, fucking LA traffic."

"It happens," Bill said, reaching for the hand mic in its cradle to the left of his seat. He cleared his throat. "Good afternoon, ladies and gentlemen, welcome aboard Coastal Airways Flight four-one-six with nonstop service to New York's John F. Kennedy International Airport. My name is Bill Hoffman and I have the privilege of being your captain on today's flight. With me in the cockpit is First Officer Ben and we have a terrific in-flight team serving you in the cabin, although they are here primarily for your safety. Jo is up front, Michael and Kellie are in the back. Flight time today will be five hours and twenty-four minutes and it looks to be a smooth ride. If there is anything we can do to make this flight more pleasant, please don't hesitate to let us know. For now, sit back, enjoy our in-seat entertainment system, and as always, thank you for choosing to fly Coastal Airways."

"Did you see Kellie? The new reserve in the back?" Ben asked.

"No, why?"

Ben stopped punching coordinates into the flight management guidance computer to make a few lewd gestures, his hips driving the message home. Bill shook his head with a snort. The days before Carrie, when he too had been a skirt-chasing first officer, seemed like another lifetime. Ben stopped abruptly as Jo entered the cockpit with a steaming cup.

"You want coffee, hon?" she asked the first officer, passing the cup to Bill, not needing to ask to know he took it black.

"No, ma'am, but I will take a drink once we get to the bar in New York."

"Correct," she said with a nod and a finger point. "We're good to go back here, just waiting on two. Y'all mind a visitor while we finish up?"

Bill turned to see a young boy peering out from behind Jo's legs.

"Sure, come on in," Bill said as Jo left, shifting in his

seat to beckon the boy forward. His father crouched behind him, whispering encouragement into his ear.

"He's a little shy," the man said. "But he loves planes. We park by the airport and watch them take off and land all the time."

"The lot by the burger joint just off the north runway? My son and I did that a lot when he was this guy's age. Still do from time to time." Bill made a mental note that he should take Scott after this trip. "Would you like to know what some of these buttons do?" Bill asked the child before starting a tour.

A few minutes later, Jo poked her head in the cockpit as the last two passengers boarded behind her. "All set, Bill," she said, handing him the final paperwork.

"Well, I guess we better get to work. Thanks for coming up. Would you like a pair of wings?" Bill reached into his messenger bag that sat to the left of his seat, producing a pair of small plastic wings. Removing the back with an official flourish, he stuck it to the boy's T-shirt. The child looked down at the shiny wings, his head rising a moment later in a peal of laughter before burying his face in his dad's leg. Bill smiled with a nostalgic pang, thinking of Scott when he was that small, a time that now felt so long ago. The two left to take their seats, the father mouthing his thanks.

Souls on board, Bill reminded himself as he double-checked the numbers on the load sheet. Signing off, he passed it back to Jo, who handed it to the waiting gate agent. A moment later, the aircraft door closed with a heavy thud as passengers ended phone calls and settled in.

"'Before start' checklist to the line, Bill?" Ben said.

Bill's phone lit up. Expecting a text from "Carrie Cell," he frowned at finding a promotional email from his gym instead.

Behind them, Jo pulled the cockpit door out of the magnetic latch that held it open.

"Cabin ready for pushback," she said, waiting. Bill turned in his seat with a nod and thumbs-up. At that, she shut the door and the two men were alone.

Bill turned his phone to airplane mode, shutting Carrie out. She'd known his time was limited; she knew once they took off he wouldn't really be able to talk, what with Ben sitting beside him. It was childish for him to be annoyed. But he was. If she'd wanted an apology she should have called him back on the ground. He'd text her once they were at cruise, but that was the best she would get until they landed in New York.

"Okay. 'Before start' checklist to the line, please," Bill said.

Ben pulled out the laminated checklist. "Logbook, release, tail number . . ."

Reaching up, Bill flicked the FASTEN SEAT BELT sign off. The plane had leveled off and now floated eastward, a mass of humanity hanging in limbo.

"*Coastal four-one-six, contact LA center one-two-niner-point-five-zero,*" the squawk of the air traffic controller rang throughout the cockpit.

"Coastal four-one-six," Bill identified, "LA on one-two-niner-point-five-oh. Good day."

Ben reached to his left and pushed a knob on the lower console control panel. Turning it counterclockwise, yellow digital numbers descended toward the new frequency. The controller who would answer the other end of the line would guide them through his jurisdiction before handing the plane off to the next sector's en route controller. Like that, all the way across the country, the plane's communication to ground would be passed off like a baton.

Bill waited until Ben stopped at 129.50 and pressed the transfer button. "Good afternoon, Los Angeles center," he said into the mic, studying the panel indicating their altitude, direction, and speed. "Coastal four-one-six checking in at flight level three-five-zero."

"*Good afternoon, Costal. Maintain three-five-zero,*" responded the controller. Bill holstered the mic and punched a button on the console in front of him. A green light lit up above the label "AP1," confirming the autopilot had been engaged. Releasing the shoulder straps of his five-point harness and reclining his seat, Bill settled in for the cruise.

"Sir?" Jo said. "Sir?"

The man stared at the seatback TV in front of him. Jo wiggled her fingers in front of the screen, his eyes darting up as he hastily removed his headphones and accepted the glass of wine she held out.

"Sorry," he apologized, returning to the screen.

"Big game?" she asked, passing a seltzer no ice off her tray to the college-aged girl in the first-class seat next to him.

"You kiddin'?" he said, with a thick New York accent. "Game seven of the World Series? Yeah, it's a big game."

"I'm assuming you're rooting for the Yankees," Jo said.

"Since the day I was born," he replied, putting his headphones back on to hear the pregame coverage. Next to him, the girl sent a text to her boyfriend. We land at 10:30. Can you pick me up? She watched his three dots at work, smiling when his text came through.

Four rows back in the main cabin, a man turned the page in his book. The beam of the overhead light irritated the guy in the middle seat next to him who was trying to sleep. Across the aisle, a woman pressed "Send" on her laptop, the email arriving seconds later in her boss's inbox back in LA. The guy by the window squirmed in his seat, wondering how long he could wait before he'd have to ask the row to get up so he could use the bathroom. Behind him, neck arched, mouth agape, a loud snore came from the "passenger of size" who had asked the flight attendants for a seat belt extender during boarding. A toddler ambled down the aisle past them all. His mother held on to his raised hands, steadying the child in the plane's gentle rock.

On the other side of the cockpit door, the pilots spoke with air traffic control, adjusting the plane's altitude or speed when directed. They checked weather reports for updates and surveyed the open expanse in front of them, endless stretches of deserts and snow-covered mountaintops, a rolling procession of the dramatic landscapes of the western United States. But with the plane steadily cruising, they mostly passed the time just like their passengers. Ben read a book on his tablet and occasionally sent a text. Bill chewed a granola bar, working on the computer-based portion of the biannual recurrent training he had coming up in a few weeks.

Bill's laptop pinged with an incoming email. It was from Carrie—but it had no subject or text, only a picture attachment. *That's odd*, he thought as he clicked on the attachment. It wasn't unusual for her to send pictures of the kids or of an activity that he was missing at home. But after the way they'd left things, the gesture felt out of place.

Studying the picture, Bill blinked a few times, even more confused. He recognized the couch and the television behind it. He was familiar with the books and the picture frames. He saw the beer bottle where he had left it the night before after he and Scott finished watching the Dodgers lose game six, and he could envision the tall oak tree in the backyard that left its shadowy outline on the floor of his sunlit family room.

These things made sense to him.

The two figures that stood in the middle of the room did not.

Barefoot, bare-legged, their arms outstretched in the shape of a cross; timid hands opened toward the heavens in a silent plea of helplessness. He knew their faces, but he could not see them beneath the black hoods that covered their heads. He did not need to glimpse his wife's pink toenail polish to know one figure was her, and he did not need confirmation that the other's skinny legs were those of his son.

Bill leaned forward, trying to make sense of what Carrie was wearing. Strapped across her whole torso was some strange sort of vest. Pockets covered it front to back, brightly colored wires protruding from small bricks that lay inside. He'd seen such vests on the news in grainy video footage of suicide bombers making their final martyrdom statements. But in the moment, his mind couldn't process the sight of something so perverse strapped across his wife's body.

His mouth went dry. Steadying himself with a hand on the tray table, his head spun. He closed his eyes for a few seconds, hoping that when he opened them, the picture would be gone. Or that he would wake up and find this was all a dream. Somehow, maybe, he could start over. Or just—disappear.

Opening his eyes, he thought he might be sick.

The picture of his wife, wearing an explosive suicide vest, standing next to their son in their own living room, was still there.

Another email hit the inbox.

Put on your headphones.

With that, an incoming FaceTime call popped up on the screen.

CHAPTER THREE

BILL RIFLED THROUGH HIS SHOULDER BAG LOOKING FOR HEADPHONES. Fumbling the metal end into the tiny hole on the front of the computer, it took him two tries to secure one of the little white buds in his left ear; the side Ben couldn't see. His trembling fingers struggled to connect the call, the cursor confused under his frantic touch. Managing to click the green button, he watched the live video feed of his own face slide into the lower left-hand corner as it connected.

The man who appeared on the screen was gaunt with bushy brows and thick dark hair. His skin was light tan and his lips were pressed into a thin line. Bill guessed the man was in his midthirties—and he was vaguely recognizable, but Bill couldn't place why. The man smiled and straight, white teeth appeared.

Strapped to the man's body was another explosive suicide vest.

"Captain Hoffman. Good afternoon."

Bill remained silent. ATC squawked a direction.

"Coastal four-one-six, roger, Denver center," Ben

replied, leaning forward to change the plane's altitude. "Climbing to three-seven-oh." Twisting a knob on the center dash until the numbers on the altimeter read 37,000, he pulled on the knob to confirm the command and the plane slowly lifted in response. Scanning the horizon for a few moments, he stifled a yawn, turning back to his phone.

The intruder smirked from the computer as Elise's frantic wailing could be heard in the background. "You're not alone. Of course. So how about this. When you have something to say, send an email. I'll respond out loud. Also, in the front of your messenger bag is a privacy shield for your computer. Go get it."

Messenger bag.

The bag he had set next to the cable guy's equipment that morning.

Him.

Jaw clenched, Bill searched his bag. That's how he got in the house and that's how he got something onto the plane. He'd left the room when Bill came in the kitchen, that was when he put it in his bag. What was his name? Carrie had said it at one point. Bill couldn't remember if he introduced himself or not.

Finding a thin, translucent sheet, Bill clipped it onto the front of the screen. He began to type, dizzy with the uncertainty of what else he didn't know. A ping echoed on the other side. Bill followed the intruder's eyes as they read his email:

Where is my family?

"They're fine," the intruder responded. "Now . . ." Bill ignored him, typing as fast as he could.

May I see my family? Please.

"Please! So polite. But no. Let's talk man to man for a minute."

Until I see my family, we have nothing to discuss.

The man read the email with an eye roll. "Your stubbornness is annoying."

Leaning, he beckoned to the kitchen. In his hand, Bill could see what was clearly a detonator. Wireless, with a fitted plastic safety over the red button on top, it was hardly a crude, handmade device.

Carrie and the children appeared on-screen and Bill almost choked. The black hoods had been removed but both his wife and son were gagged and their hands were bound. Elise had stopped crying and Carrie struggled to hold the baby on her hip as her motherly grace was made awkward by the ties and explosive vest. The man brought a chair from the kitchen table over to the desk, motioning for Carrie and the baby to sit. He retook his seat beside her while Scott stood at his mother's side.

"Now," the man said, placing his elbows on the desk with a lean into the camera. "You're a smart man, Captain Hoffman. Or, can I call you Bill?"

Bill stared at the screen.

The intruder smiled. "You see, *Bill*, you probably already get the obvious. Here's the rest. You will crash your plane or I will kill your family."

Carrie's gag muffled a horrified sound that was something between a moan and a gasp.

"If you tell anyone," he continued, "your family dies. If you send anyone to the house, your family dies."

Switching the detonator to his other hand, he reiter-
ated, "It's simple. Crash your plane, or I kill your family.
The choice is yours."

A cold and hollow ache pooled at the base of Bill's
spine. He had prayed the ransom would be money, but
he knew it wouldn't be that easy. The moment he had
seen the picture, he knew his cockpit had been breached.
He knew on some level that the plane itself was in jeop-
ardy. Bill couldn't feel his hands as they moved over the
keyboard.

> I'm not going to crash this plane and you're not
> going to kill my family.

"Wrong," the man said after reading Bill's email.
"One of those things will happen. You choose which."

> Let me repeat myself, son. I'm not going to crash
> this plane and you're not going to kill my family.
> Period.

The face on the screen bristled at the intended dis-
respect. "My name is Saman Khani. Call me Sam. I'd
have introduced myself this morning, but you couldn't
give a shit about the cable tech."

*"Chicago center to Coastal four-one-six, reports of light
to moderate turbulence from Delta two-oh-four-four heavy
thirty miles ahead, just northwest of your heading."*

Bill jumped at the ATC intrusion, surprised that the
rest of the world appeared to have continued on.

"Asleep over there, old man?" Ben laughed, flipping
through his display until it showed the weather radar.
"Coastal four-one-six, roger that, Chicago center," he
said into his hand mic. "We're calm for now but will

maintain as advised. We'll let you know if we need to find smoother air."

"I, uh . . . I think that cell was supposed to weaken around this time," Bill said in an attempt at normalcy. "It's supposed to shift. North . . ." he trailed off with a point at the radar.

"Yup," Ben said as Bill turned back to his computer. "Hey, you mind if we call the back for a break?"

"Huh?" Bill said.

Ben cocked his head. "Okay if I pee? Jesus, you okay?"

"Oh. Sure. I'm fine," he said, glancing at his laptop. "Actually, can you hold on just a minute? I'm right in the middle of something."

"Sure. I'll use a bottle if it gets desperate."

Sam's laugh filled Bill's earbud. "It's like a weird 'bring your family to work' day," he said, Carrie flinching as he laid a hand on her shoulder. An email arrived and Sam opened it, reading aloud: "'I think my first officer would take issue with me crashing the plane . . .' Yeah. I think he will. That's why you're going to have to kill him first."

It hit like a sucker punch.

Ben and he had only flown together a couple times, but he liked the kid. He was a solid pilot. Smart, able to fill in the blanks. His confidence bordered on cockiness, but in the way that was actually an asset in the cockpit. They had sparred about sports teams. Bill had been surprised to learn he was a vegetarian. The young man wasn't married, but surely he had family and friends who enjoyed his easy humor. A girlfriend? Maybe he was dating one of the flight attendants.

Bill was supposed to kill him. Kill him first. Get him out of the way so he could then kill everyone else on board. Nausea simmered in his gut.

Dismissing Bill's typing, Sam said, "I'm sure you're wondering *how* you kill him?"

Bill's fingers paused.

"I mean, ultimately, the same way you kill everyone else. You crash the plane. But he could actually try to stop you. So in your bag—in the bottom of the big pocket—there's a bottle full of white powder. On your last bathroom break before you land, just put the powder in his coffee or tea or whatever. A couple sips, you'll be flying solo."

What's the white powder?

Sam read the email, deliberately ignoring the question.

"Oh!" he said, and raised his finger. "And next pocket back, you'll find a metal cylinder. After your FO is dead—but before you crash, obviously"—he smiled—"shake the can, reach behind you, open the cockpit door. Twist the can open, throw it into the cabin. Shut the door, crash the plane, the end."

Bill blinked numbly at the screen before typing.

What's in the canister?

"You ask so many questions but none of them matter," Sam said, and laughed. "I'm not going to tell you what the white powder is for the first officer. And I'm not going to tell you what's in the canister for the cabin. See, we haven't even gotten to the good part yet because you never ask an interesting question. Like, for example, you could ask: 'Sam, what do you want me to crash the plane into?'"

I won't ask that. I'm not crashing the plane.

"Oh! So that's your choice?" Sam said, lifting the detonator up. "You choose the plane?"

Carrie clutched Elise tighter. The back of Bill's neck prickled.

I haven't chosen anything.

Sam hummed, reading the email. "Well, in this scenario, if you don't make a choice, you will continue on as planned. Which means landing the plane at JFK. Which *is* a choice. So . . ." He adjusted the vest, switching the detonator to the other hand. "If that's what you—"

Bill began typing furiously.

Fine. What do you want me to crash the plane into?

Sam read the email, a smile spreading across his face. Crossing his arms on the table, he leaned into the camera. "I'm not telling you."

Watching the man rock back with laughter, Bill could feel his fingernails almost pierce the skin inside his clenched fists.

"God, this is fun," Sam said. "Look, for now, just keep flying your original flight path. We don't want to raise suspicions, after all. No one except us is to know what's going on—remember? I'll give you more details when you need them. For now, don't worry about what the target is. Just know at some point the plane will be deviating from its path."

Bill typed as fast as his fingers could.

This isn't like driving a car. I can't change course
without creating other problems. Especially if you
don't want anyone to know what's happening. I don't
have time to explain the aeronautical navigational
specifics. Just trust me. I need to know where we're
going.

The captain watched the intruder read the email,
praying the man wasn't also a pilot. What he wrote
wasn't exactly a lie—but it definitely wasn't fully true. If
this guy was a pilot, he'd call bullshit.

Sam blinked a few times, his brow knitting momentarily before he looked into the camera and cleared his
throat, clearly stalling.

"I won't give you the target, but I'll give you the
area," Sam said finally.

Bill watched Sam take in the array of buttons and
knobs that filled the cockpit around him. He'd given
enough preflight tours to passengers who knew nothing
about flying to know the man was overwhelmed. Sam
took a small breath and paused.

"DC."

Bill's head drooped. Of course. It made sense. Washington, DC, was close enough to New York that a
last-minute deviation would be almost impossible to
counter in time. He didn't need to be told an exact
target. It was probably the White House. Maybe the
Capitol Building.

"I won't tell you an exact location just yet," Sam said.
"And I won't tell you what the mystery powder is either,
but I'll give you a hint. I mean, I do need you alive.
So when you twist the canister open before throwing it
into the cabin? I'd make sure you're wearing your oxygen mask."

A toxic gas, surely. Bill looked out the window at the layers of thin, shifting clouds passing beneath the plane. He envisioned the cabin filling with a similar cloud of . . . what? He was being asked—no, *told*—to gas his own plane, his own passengers.

And if I refuse to throw the canister?

Sam read the email, his head tilted to the side while he considered. He looked over to Bill's family.

"Well, let's see. I need them alive until the end of the flight. But . . ." A lock of hair lay across Carrie's face. Sam tucked it behind her ear. "Maybe I don't need them all alive? Or in one piece?"

Bill's knuckles turned white in his grip on the tray table. There was so much he didn't know, didn't understand. He wanted to make it stop; he wanted to scream. He could feel the blood rushing to his face. A line of sweat covered his upper lip. He wiped it off with the back of his hand.

"Bill. Relax," Sam taunted, relishing his visible agitation. "You're working way too hard to figure out a solution when—spoiler—there isn't one. So just let that hero shit go. You *will* make a choice. Your family, or the plane. And if the sacrifice is the plane, throwing the canister is part of the deal. Period." Sam leaned forward, resting his interlocking fingers on the desk, the detonator clutched in his grip. "And Bill? Just so you know? I'm not an idiot. There is, absolutely, a backup plan right there on board. You will, one way or another, make a choice."

Bill felt his face go from red to white.

There is a backup on board.

The innocent souls on board.

Which ones weren't innocent?

Whose eyes watched him and the rest of the crew, reporting back to this maniac? Did they have weapons? A canister full of poison back there already? Would they release it? Would they kill the crew, then rush the cockpit—kill Ben themselves—then force Bill to make his choice? Bill couldn't keep up with his thoughts as they raced from one sick scenario to another.

What are your demands?

Sam read the email and held his hands open. "What do you mean? I just told you."

You told me the conditions. But what do you want?

He laughed. "Bill, what are you not getting? I don't want anything. I don't want money. I don't want a prisoner exchange. I don't want political leverage. This isn't 1968, man. This is not 'Take me to Cuba.' It's not QAnon looking for kids in a pizzeria or whatever other bullshit your white supremacists believe. And it's not some crazy seventy-two virgins in paradise jihad shit either. It's got nothing to do with that."

He leaned into the screen.

"All I want is to see what a good man—a good American man—does when he's in a no-win situation. What does a man like you do when he has to choose. A plane full of strangers? Or your family? See, Bill, it really is about the choice. You. Choosing who will survive. *That* is what I want."

Bill didn't move. The man laughed.

"I love how that freaks you out! Knowing I can't be bought. Or negotiated with. It terrifies you to know I want not a thing in the world except exactly what is happening."

The men stared at each other. Bill raised his hands to type a question. His hands shook.

Why? Why are you doing this?

Bill hit the delete button until the sentences erased. If this man was going to answer that, Bill knew it would be on his own terms. He typed another question, but deleted it too. His fingers moved frantically. He wanted to understand what he was dealing with so he could figure out how to fix it.

Elise whimpered. He looked up at his daughter.

Bill knew he would get nowhere if he continued on and that he was only wasting time. He needed to get to work.

He typed, this time hitting "Send."

How did you know I would be working this flight?

"You mean, how did I make sure you would be working this flight?" Sam said. "Turns out your chief pilot Walt O'Malley is quite the little pervert. He had no problem guaranteeing you would work the flight—so long as the pictures of the little boys on his hard drive didn't become public."

Bill's heart burned at the betrayal. His boss, his colleague. His friend. They'd worked together for twenty-three years. This was rotten all the way up to the system chief pilot.

His thoughts slid out of control, nothing to hang on to, nothing to stop them. He was powerless in his own cockpit. Helpless as a man and as protector of his family. Threats at home, and threats on board. He was terrified of the other ways he could discover he had been duped.

Closing his eyes, Bill thought he might be sick. With a deep breath, he stretched his hands wide and then clenched his fists, repeating that motion while narrowing his mind's eye to the image of the blood coursing through his hands. Gradually, his pulse slowed.

Why did you choose me?

Sam paused after reading the email, turning his gaze to the camera that connected them. "You arrogant prick. You think this is personal? You're just a means."

It will feel personal to the 149 innocent souls on this aircraft you want to kill.

"Well, of course it will. Death always feels personal, Bill. It feels damn fucking personal. But you know what the crazy thing about death is? It's *not* personal. Everyone dies. No one escapes it. It's the only fair thing in the world. Sometimes you're young, sometimes you're old, sometimes you deserve it, sometimes you don't. But what the fuck is that, anyway? Death doesn't just happen to 'bad' people, death doesn't give a shit." He shook his head, muttering to himself. "Fucking innocent souls . . ."

His gaze settled on Scott. "Look at your son, Bill."

Bill refused. Seconds ticked by.

Sam slammed his fists on the desk. Carrie clutched Elise with a sob.

"*Look* at your *son.*"

Scott stared squarely into the camera. Silent tears

rolled down his cheeks, his knuckles white in a defiant clench. He was trying, trying so hard, to be brave. The gravity of the man he would grow into perched precariously on the trembling legs of a young boy. Father and son, the man and the one becoming, stared at each other through a small lens.

"Captain Hoffman," Sam mused softly, "is your son good? Does he deserve this?" Sam shook his head sadly. "You speak of innocence as if it meant something to the world. But we're all just a means to someone else's end."

Sam leaned back, crossing his arms across the explosive suicide vest.

"The choice is yours. I already made mine."

Bill heard someone close the door to the lav out in the cabin. He thought of Jo and the rest of the crew going about their work. He thought of the passengers who were just trying to get where they needed to go. He envisioned the people in DC; senators and members of Congress discussing legislation while their aides passed them paperwork. Security guards smiling down at schoolchildren on a field trip. Families reading plaques in front of statues and paintings. Just regular people living peaceful lives. He thought of his daughter, Elise, who hadn't taken her first steps yet. His son, Scott, who just wanted to play.

For the first time, he allowed himself to *really* look at Carrie.

"I thought you hated cats," Carrie said.

"I do," Bill said.

Carrie smiled, watching him massage her purring cat, Wrigley. She extended chopsticks full of pad Thai and Bill leaned over on the couch to accept, a little bit of chicken falling onto her bare legs stretched out across his lap. A black-

and–white Humphrey Bogart walked across the TV as Bill popped the chicken into his mouth.

Across the apartment by the door, his company badge lay on the floor next to his unopened suitcase. A pile of black— shoes, socks, pants, belt—lay in a heap facing the wall with red lacy panties on top. Buried under his uniform jacket, ungraded essays littered the floor, her red pen waiting on the kitchen table until tomorrow sometime after he'd left. Looming in the distance through the window, the Sears Tower seemed to wink its approval. Bill picked up every O'Hare trip he could find. Chicago had become his favorite layover.

"Do you believe in love at first sight?" Carrie asked, watching the movie.

"Yes."

He'd answered quickly and her face turned pink in return. Audrey Hepburn sipped espresso, talking about the Paris rain. "Oh?" Carrie said, popping another bite in her mouth. "How so?"

He turned, confused. "Well, you."

She froze mid-bite, swallowing. "Oh?"

"When I first saw you at the barbecue. The moment you walked into the yard. Yes."

"Yes . . . what?" she said. Love was a topic they hadn't discussed.

"Yes, I knew I wanted to sleep with you."

She punched his arm.

"No," Bill said, shifting on the couch to face her. Bogart and Hepburn sat side by side, driving down the road. "I mean, yes, but . . ."

Carrie raised an eyebrow.

"Look, the first time I saw you, I knew I wanted you. I didn't just want you, though. I had to have you. It was . . . animal."

"Keep digging."

"Okay," he said, and sighed. "Humans are hardwired for one thing, right? Survival. It's our primary drive. And on a subconscious and instinctual level, we are attracted to, and desire the things, that will serve our survival best. Yes? So when I first saw you, I'm saying my body at a cellular level screamed YES. Voilà. Love at first sight. I'm not saying I was just a guy looking to get laid. I'm saying . . ." He glanced at the screen, trying to figure out how to translate. "Jesus, Carrie. I'm here petting cats. And picking up shitty Chicago trips. And I'd consider moving here if you wanted me to. But the part that's weird is that I want to do all that.

"Carrie, I miss you the second I walk out that door. I fly as fast as I can so I can get to the hotel so I can call you. I mean, the company has to be catching on to the amount of gas I'm wasting. I love that tiny freckle in your left eye. I love it that you say you have a substance-abuse issue with peanut butter. I love knowing—and god knows why—that you believe Buzz Aldrin should have been the first man on the moon but Neil Armstrong pushed him out of the way at the last second. The fact that you sweat profusely when you're nervous but not at all when you're hot? I love that. It's weird. But I love it."

She laughed, a tear falling. He wiped it away and licked his finger.

"My body knew. You're it, Carrie. So, yes. I believe in love at first sight."

Her chin trembled, desperately clinging to caution.

"I use your pillow," she said with a laugh, wiping her face with her sleeve. "After you leave, the next night. I sleep with the pillow you use. It's too fluffy and it hurts my neck. But it smells like you."

Taking the plate out of her hand, he set it on the coffee table. Lying beside her, his arm wrapped around her waist,

he breathed in the smell of her coconut shampoo. He in his
boxers, she in her sweatshirt, the two lay silent for a long
time listening to the movie playing behind them.

"Bill?"

"Hmmm?"

"I thought you hated cuddling."

Carrie looked at Bill through the camera lens. A tear
slid down her cheek, caught by the gag in her mouth.

You are not going to kill my family. And I am not
going to crash this plane.

He pressed "Send" on the email and lowered the
screen halfway.

"All right," Bill said to his copilot, "I'm gonna go out
too. Mind if I go first?"

"By all means, age before beauty," Ben said as Bill
pressed a button, a muffled ding ringing on the other
side of the door.

"You beat me to it," came Jo's voice through the
cockpit speaker. "I was just about to call. Break time?"

"Yes, ma'am," Bill said, adjusting his seat backward.

"Okay, ready when you are." The call clicked as it
disconnected.

"You have control?" Bill said.

"I have control," Ben replied.

Bill's hands trembled slightly as he unbuckled his
harness and stood up. Leaving the cockpit felt like
another layer of abandonment. He tried—and failed—
to block out the image of his family on the other side of
the screen. Bound. Gagged. Helpless. Waiting for him
to do something.

Adjusting his uniform, he closed one eye and looked

out the door's peephole to make sure Jo was blocking. There she stood, cross-armed, facing the cabin, her feet firmly planted. If anyone was going to rush the cockpit while the pilots were coming in and out for their bath-room break, they were going to have to make it through her first. All five feet and forty-six years of her. Most flight attendants executed the post–September 11th security procedure with a slight eye roll. If a terrorist really wanted to bust through the open door, one little flight attendant wasn't going to stop him. But Jo took it seriously. Years ago, the first officer they were flying with jokingly called her his "one-hundred-pound ter-rorist speed bump." He found out the long-winded way what a mistake that was. Jo understood that in placing herself in front of that door, she was declaring: over my dead body.

And Bill knew she meant it.

After the door closed behind her she turned on her heels, dropping her smile the instant she saw Bill's face. When he didn't speak, she did.

"Well?"

"What?" he replied.

Pursing her lips, she crossed her arms, shifting her weight to one side.

"What?" he repeated, scanning the cabin over her shoulder, his brows pinched.

If you tell anyone, your family dies. If you send anyone to the house, your family dies.

He couldn't risk it. He couldn't tell Jo.

But he had to get someone to his family, he had to get someone to the house. He couldn't orchestrate that from the cockpit, where he was being monitored every second. And there was an unknown threat back here in the cabin with Jo and the crew. How could he not warn them? And the gas. The cabin needed to be ready for an attack if it came to that.

Bill knew he wouldn't crash the plane—but he might need to pretend he would. Throwing the canister was a part of that. If he refused to throw the gas, Sam would assume his choice was to save the plane. His family would die.

A hollow dread seeped out of his heart, filling his body. Unless someone on the ground could get to his family, he was going to have to gas the cabin. Which meant the crew needed to be ready. They needed to protect the passengers . . . from him.

"Bill?" Jo's voice sounded a mile away.

If you tell anyone, your family dies.

Bill looked at the rest of the plane, at the one hundred and forty-four strangers sitting in the passenger seats. One hundred and forty-four potential threats. Rage coursed through his body, intertwining with fear. What else didn't he know?

Jo's eyes, full of concern, refused to look away. "Bill?" she said with a little more force.

If you tell anyone, your family dies.

How could he go back up to the cockpit and leave his crew exposed and vulnerable?

Jo placed a gentle hand on his forearm and squeezed. Her warm touch sucked out his breath like an electric shock.

He needed help. His family needed help. He couldn't do this alone.

"Jo," he whispered. "We have a situation."

CHAPTER FOUR

JO STEADIED HERSELF WITH A HAND ON THE GALLEY COUNTER.

Bill had tried to make this look like a typical conversation during a typical bathroom break, casually walking her into the galley. Once out of eyesight, he'd cleared his throat and told her everything.

Jo stared up at him, mouth agape. The slow shake of her head wasn't a denial. It was a realization that from here on out, nothing would ever be the same.

"Repeat everything you just said."

"No," Bill said. "We don't have time. Look. My cockpit, my communications—it's all being monitored on the FaceTime call. I'm wearing headphones so Ben can't hear, but when . . ."

The captain's voice trailed off, each word getting softer and farther away. Jo gazed into the cup of coffee she'd poured for the elderly woman in 2C that sat on the galley countertop cooling. Coffee she had poured in what now felt like a different lifetime. Her life before Bill told her of their situation.

Steam billowed in balletic swirls and twirls as little bubbles rose to the coffee's dark surface, reflecting the fluorescent purple glow of the overhead light. She observed all this abstractly; the graceful steam, the sing-song lilt of a far-off voice, the flowing movement of light and shadow. A gossamer, dreamlike state was the lens through which she viewed reality and, while Jo was not a sleepwalker, she distantly wondered if this is what it felt like.

"I had to take the risk," Bill said. "He said he'd kill them if I told anyone. But you and the crew have to . . ."

Bill's voice was talking about something or other. A family? What family? Hers? No, Michael and the boys were home. Safe. She looked at the tiny bubbles and envisioned herself inside one. Unnoticed by her crew-mates, by the other passengers, she would slip into it quietly, the bubble cocooning her in its completeness. Nothing would come in, nothing would leave. She'd sit down, hug her knees to her chest, and just observe everyone else carrying on without her. She could feel the silence of the bubble, the weightlessness of her body as she bobbed on the surface of the coffee. Maybe she could be poured down the drain, tiny and hidden, slid-ing away on her secret escape. She would be along for the ride, unable to steer and not wanting to. The cor-ners of her lips tugged into an inappropriate smile. She couldn't help herself. There was just so much relief in being so small.

"What did you just say?" Jo said suddenly, cutting Bill off.

Bill looked confused, as if he didn't know what he had just said either.

"I . . . I said I don't know how to get someone to my house. I can't just call the FBI."

"No," Jo said. "But I can."

• • •

Tossing the yellowed houseplant into the trash can under his desk, FBI agent Theo Baldwin wondered how long it had looked like that.

"Those things need water, Theo," Agent Jenkins said, on his way to the break room.

"Noted," Theo replied, opening the file on the top of the stack. Scooting his chair in, his phone lit up with an incoming text. Checking the sender, he hit the button on the side of the phone, the screen going dark.

Across the room in a fishbowl of an office, his new boss paced behind her desk with a phone pressed to her ear. The door was shut, but Theo didn't need to hear what was said to know it wasn't an enjoyable conversation for the other end of the line. He looked away quickly when she caught him watching.

Theo liked coming into the office on a Saturday. It was quiet. He could get boring paperwork out of the way quickly so he could focus on more interesting cases. Having read the first page, he turned to the second but soon went back to the beginning after realizing he hadn't absorbed a single word.

Tossing his pen on the stack of dead-end, low-level case files, he rubbed his eyes.

Who was he kidding? He didn't have more interesting cases to get to. Being at the office on a Saturday was a thinly veiled attempt at brownie points. No, not even that. It was a pathetic attempt at redemption. He'd been with the bureau for close to three years, but that modest seniority didn't matter anymore. Six months back, the clock had started over.

It shouldn't have been a big deal. It was as standard a drug raid as possible. Their intelligence was airtight:

they knew exactly who was in the house, where they were located, what they had done, what they would be charged with. It was practically over before it even started.

But by the end of the night, the crack house was riddled with bullet holes and Theo's reputation as the rising star of the bureau was just as shot. He tried to justify his breach of protocol only once. After that, he wisely kept his mouth shut and his head low. Acting on a "hunch" was as respectable as saying a green fairy whispered in his ear. Five disciplinary meetings, a two-week suspension without pay, and a questionable professional forecast meant the only thing Theo could do was punch the clock, stick to the rules, and hope in time all would be forgiven.

He took a sip of coffee and doubled down on the paperwork.

"Should we be worried," Jenkins said, coming out of the break room with a bag of chips, "that we're the only assholes with nothing to do on a Saturday?"

Theo's phone lit up again. He didn't see it.

"I think," Theo said, leaning back in his chair, "we're the only assholes who are dedicated to their jobs."

"And I think we need to get laid," Jenkins said through a full mouth. "Let's go get a drink. Tell hot chicks we're FBI agents."

Theo's phone glowed yet again. Picking it up, he saw seven unread texts from his aunt Jo. His stomach dropped, immediately going to the worst. His mom, Jo's sister. Something happened. Or maybe Aunt Jo's sons, who were more like his brothers than cousins.

"Well? We going?" Jenkins said, leaning against his cubicle.

Theo stared at his phone. It was too unbelievable, he

had to read it all twice. If anyone else had sent the messages, he would have had doubts.

But Theo knew his aunt Jo.

Grabbing his badge and pushing his chair back, he paid no attention to the toppling stack of files, unfinished paperwork fluttering to the ground.

Bill shut the door quietly and slid the lock to the right, the fluorescent light in the lav brightening as he did. He stood there for a moment, frozen, as though he had forgotten what he'd come there to do. The flimsy plastic door squeaked in protest as he leaned his forehead against it. His tie dangled forward from his neck.

This was not a scenario he had ever anticipated. This was not a threat he had considered and discussed with his colleagues. There was no page in the manual to reference, no protocol to put in place, no checklist to run. All his training seemed embarrassingly naive, now. Safeguards and redundancies were devised for *actual* attacks on the flight deck.

Bill turned to the mirror, taking in his reflection. He felt like a guy in a pilot's costume. It no longer looked right on him. He looked at the gold wings on the front of his shirt and wondered something he never had: Was he worthy of wearing the uniform? Had he ever been?

He peed and pressed the button, wincing at the loud suck of an airplane flush. The sink was just as hostile, icy water assaulting his shaking hands as they wrung out their options.

This would be his only moment alone. This was when he needed to figure it out. Figure out how to fix it. He leaned his face closer to the mirror as though looking for the answer on the other side.

He found nothing.

Grabbing a few paper towels, he entertained an irrational thought of annoyance: the audacity of needing to pee. Couldn't his body make an exception right now? Didn't it know there was no time to waste on the unnecessary?

The faucet leaked. One by one, drops of water fell into the sink. Rhythmically, one after another like a drum. A pause. Then one random drop. Then another. There seemed no pattern to the flow.

Bill watched the water drip, his pupils dilating as the pieces in his mind moved closer together. His hands stopped shaking. His breathing slowed. He stood up straight.

It was a Hail Mary of an idea. But it was an idea.

Sliding the lock to the left, Bill went back to work.

Theo's boss stared at the phone for a long time before tossing it across her desk. It landed to the side of her nameplate, ASSISTANT DIRECTOR MICHELLE LIU reflecting brightly in the screen's glow. Running her hands across the crown of her head, she slicked her thick black hair into a tidy ponytail. Forcibly pulling it taut, her arms came to rest, crossed, across her body.

"You're serious," she said.

He nodded. "Unfortunately."

She began to pace behind the desk. Liu had been at the Los Angeles field office for three months already, but it had been a relatively calm three months and Theo hadn't had a real opportunity to see her act under fire. He knew she'd been with the bureau for twelve years and that the reputation of her short temper preceded her. But what he didn't know was why she seemed angry about the situation he'd brought her. Or maybe she was pissed at him? He couldn't tell which.

"You know it's not just us," she said. "Homeland Security. The Department of Defense. Metropolitan Police Department. FAA. TSA. NORAD. The White House." She paused. "Theo, if we go—the president will be in the Situation Room."

He could feel his heartbeat in his ears. "I say we go," he said.

She scoffed.

"You want me," she said, eyes narrowing, "to raise the alarm on an impending terrorist attack on Washington, DC. You want me to send Hostage Rescue into a suburban LA neighborhood in broad daylight. And all of this, based off intel you and you alone got in a text message. From your aunt."

Theo didn't respond but he didn't look away either. He felt his face flush as he watched Liu chew at the inside of her cheek. He knew he was being sized up.

His test scores were off the charts and his ambition unmatched—but surely Liu had been told the full account of the night of the raid. An "intuition first, intelligence second" kind of agent was a liability, not an asset. That's what he'd overheard her say to another agent, and though he couldn't know for sure, he'd sworn she'd glanced at him after she said it. Keeping him buried under paperwork until she could get a better bead on him seemed to be her tactic so far.

But now this.

Maybe that's why she seemed so angry.

"Look," he said, "I know this situation is . . . insane. I'm asking you to trust first and verify second. Which, coming from me, is a lot to ask. But I know my aunt. Believe her."

"*Her*? I don't know her."

"Fair. But what's her motivation for faking this? She has everything to lose. Her job, her reputation. Liu. This is real."

"And if it's not?"

"And if it is?" he said a bit too forcefully, quickly adding, "Ma'am, you're taking a risk either way. But only one option ends with people dying."

She continued to pace. Theo glanced at the clock on the wall.

"Ma'am, with all due respect—that plane is midair. The pilot and the passengers are running out of time. So is the family."

Closing her eyes, Liu took a deep breath, swearing on the exhale.

"Code it," she said. "FBI SWAT move in immediately, we'll consult with HRT en route. Get everybody in. And Theo?" she said, stopping him as he left the office. "Don't forget. You've already got two strikes."

Jo flipped through the passenger manifest scanning the logistical snapshot of everyone on board. She was just finishing poring over the last page when Bill came out of the bathroom.

"Anything?" he asked.

She picked up her phone, checking to see if Theo had replied. "Not yet. And no passenger is also a Coastal employee." Opening the drawer under the coffeepot, she laid the manifest on top of her lipstick and book, closing it with a metallic click. Bill had asked her to check if anyone on board was traveling on company privileges. Perhaps they had another internal mole on board? Maybe that was the backup? But it was a dead end.

Jo knew assumptions were dangerous in a situation like this, though. Bill crossed his arms and stared into the dim cabin, his eyes narrowing toward the back galley.

"Do you trust the other flight attendants?" he said.

"Absolutely. Well, I mean, our third, Kellie, is junior as hell. We just met. She was assigned the trip off airport reserve. But my intuition says yes."

Bill nodded. "Okay. Then we go with that."

"Do you trust Ben?"

"Completely. But that's my intuition."

Jo nodded. "Then we go with that."

"Wait to tell the other two until after the break. And *don't* mention it to Ben when he comes out."

"I thought you trusted him?"

"I do. But how can he help me?"

"Plus—we don't know how he feels about *you.*"

"Exactly. If he thinks I'm going to kill him . . ." Bill trailed off and cleared his throat. "Look, I just can't risk him taking this into his own hands. I can't risk my family like that." He glanced at the cockpit door. "Dammit, I gotta get back up there."

"Okay, but wait. What about the passengers?" Jo said.

Bill and Jo looked out, scanning the tops of the heads in the cabin. Everyone was reading, sleeping, watching TV. Nothing felt amiss, nothing felt off. No one was watching them, no one seemed to care about what they were doing.

They knew better.

"The passengers can't know, Jo. We can't tip off whoever is on board to make sure I make a choice. I mean, they're going to know something is up because you guys are going to have to figure out a way to protect them. But they can't know about the whole situation. DC?

No. And they can't know about my family. They cannot know about the choice. They'll assume I'll choose my family. There's no way they'd trust us."

She didn't reply.

"You know I'm not going to crash this plane. Right?"

One of their first layovers together had been in Seattle some twenty years ago. The whole crew was heading back to the hotel after happy hour downtown when a drunk walking by muttered a racial slur. As the only Black member of the crew, Jo knew it was meant for her but she didn't say anything. Bill, on the other hand, let the man know exactly what he thought. The next day, the first officer had to fly all three legs because Bill's broken fingers kept him from fully grasping the joystick.

Delays, mechanicals, unruly passengers. She'd passed him a million leftover first-class meals and poured him twice as many cups of coffee. On September 11th, she was one of the first people he checked in with. When his father died, she sent flowers. Their families exchanged Christmas cards every year. After more than two decades of flying, Bill wasn't a coworker. He was a friend, he was family. Jo *knew* Bill.

"Yes," she replied. "I know you're not going to crash this plane."

But something deep in Jo's gut stirred as she said it.

Her phone vibrated against the metal countertop. Reading the message, she smiled.

"The FBI is on their way to your house."

Grabbing her shoulders, Bill kissed her forehead, tears of relief filling his eyes.

He picked up the phone to call the cockpit but paused before pressing the button. "The FBI will take care of my family, and we'll take care of the plane. I'll try to communicate, but no guarantees. You guys may be on your own back here. But eyes open. You know you're not alone."

Jo nodded.

"Most likely," said Bill, "I'm going to have to play along. I will do everything I can to not throw that canister. But I may have no choice. Assume a gas attack *will* come from the cockpit unless the FBI gets my family first. He will kill them if he thinks I chose the plane."

"Okay."

"The cabin needs to be ready, okay?"

"It will be, captain."

"Jo, dammit! I might be the captain, but once that door shuts, you're on your own. Do you understand? This is *your* cabin." His eyes burned with urgency and, transfixed under his gaze, her confidence swelled. "You have my word that I am not going to crash this plane. But how I accomplish that I haven't figured out yet. As far as back here goes, it's up to you all to figure out how to get this cabin ready for an attack. Understood?"

Jo nodded silently as Bill rang the cockpit to give Ben the cue to open the door and let him back up. She turned to block. The pilot and the flight attendant stood back to back, one facing away, one facing toward the cockpit.

"I trust you, Jo. We have control of this aircraft."

The door opened and closed behind her and Jo was alone. Alone in *her* cabin.

CHAPTER FIVE

"NO CHANGES?" BILL SAID.

"No changes," Ben replied.

"I have control."

"You have control."

Ben unbuckled his harness as his seat adjusted back. Ducking, he stepped over the center console. Adjusting his pants and tucking his shirt in, he closed one eye to peer out the cockpit door's peephole to make sure Jo was still blocking. Behind him, Bill readjusted his seat and buckled his harness, control of the aircraft shifting from first officer back to captain.

Bill knew he had a window of less than five seconds. Less than five seconds while the computer screen was still down and Sam couldn't see him. Five seconds when Ben was distracted and wouldn't ask Bill what he was doing. Five seconds to press and release the correct reception knobs. Five seconds to enable the radio's backup frequency. Five seconds to twist the volume on Ben's headset all the way off so he wouldn't hear the secondary channel. A line of gray knobs with white stripes lined up on the center console by his knee waiting for his command.

For the whole flight, those five seconds were his only opportunity to engage the one thing he could think of that might possibly help him out of this hell.

"Door opening," Ben said. The door opened and shut with a slam a moment later.

It was done. He didn't even need all five seconds.

But his plan would have to wait.

Bill opened his computer.

Carrie rocked Elise slowly, her cheek laid gently on top of the baby's sleeping head. Scott stood beside her, his eyes now dry. Neither looked into the camera.

"Welcome back," Sam greeted. "Here you go."

An email pinged in Bill's inbox.

"Hello there," Jo said through a convincing smile, turning at the sound of the cockpit door closing and locking. "How's it going up there?"

"Same shit, different day. Living the dream," Ben said, stepping into the lav.

"You want anything to eat or drink?" Jo asked before he could shut the door.

"Just coffee, thanks."

"How do you take it?"

"Two creams, one sugar."

The lav shut and locked. Immediately, Jo grabbed the full pot of fresh coffee and quietly emptied it into the trash. Putting a new coffee bag in, she would wait to press the BREW button until she heard the toilet flush. She wanted to buy Bill as much time as she could.

•   •   •

"What is this?" Bill asked, reading the email. Alone in the cockpit, he was able to speak out loud without headphones and emails, and he did so quickly, knowing the conditions were short-lived.

"It's a statement you're going to record yourself saying," Sam replied.

Bill continued to read, shaking his head. "But . . . what are you going to do with it?"

"I'm going to send it to the news networks. Later. After the crash," Sam said.

Bill's high school history teacher had once showed the class grainy black-and-white films of American POWs in Vietnam reading forced confessions after having been beaten and tortured by their captors. Later that night, Bill was shaken awake by his wide-eyed little brother only to find his bed soaked and his voice hoarse after the prisoner's hollow gaze had followed him to his dreams.

"I'm not reading this," Bill said.

Sam glared into the camera. "Carrie," he said, peeking into his mug, "my tea is cold. Would you please make me a fresh cup?"

Looking back and forth between Sam and the camera, Carrie tried to determine if it was a trap. Scooting her chair back, she said something to Scott that was garbled behind her gag. He seemed to understand, awkwardly maneuvering his napping sister into his arms as carefully as he could. He and his mother moved slowly, mindful of the explosives around her body. Carrie went to the kitchen, which was behind the computer, out of Bill's view. Panic choked him at the sight of his children alone with their captor.

He wanted to scream at Scott to run. Take his sister and go to a neighbor's house for help. Get away from the man, away from the explosives—and just as he was about to say that, Sam reached under his vest and pulled out a gun. He pointed it casually at the children. Scott wrapped his arms tighter around Elise.

"Bill," Sam said, "have you ever heard the story of the tiger and the crow?"

Behind the galley curtain, Jo stared down at the bright screen of her phone, sending rapid-fire texts to her nephew without a proofread.

> No, the FO doesn't know and we are NOT telling passengers

> Rest of the crew doesn't know yet, will tell after break

> No clue on what todo about gas. we'll figure out something.

> Don't know what it is. Assuming it's bad. Really bad.

> have hazmat meet plane at JFK

In the lav, the toilet flushed. Jo pressed the button on the coffeepot. She knew that meant four minutes minimum, but she'd stretch it.

> i'll text when i can but things are going to get bsuy. for you too.

> I love you Theo.

"That wasn't a rhetorical question," Sam said. "Have you ever heard—"

"No," Bill said.

Sam smiled and leaned back in the chair. "There once was a tiger who was the king of the jungle. One day, a crow circled overhead, landing on a branch. 'Tiger,' he said, 'please show me what your king eyes see.' The tiger brushed the bird away, his powerful paw nearly taking a wing. 'Be gone!' he said. 'I'm the king of the jungle. You're too stupid to know what I see.' So the crow flew away sadly.

"The next day, the crow circled overhead again, saying, 'Please, tiger. Surely you must see such amazing things. Please, tell me what your king eyes see.' But the tiger laughed, puffing out his broad chest at the poor little bird. 'Why should you see what my king eyes see? You're too small. Be gone!'"

"Dammit, we're wasting—" Bill said through gritted teeth. He stopped short, taking a breath as he clenched and released his fists. In a calmer tone, he said, "Look. Let's just talk for a second—"

"So the next day," Sam continued, "the tiger lay relaxing on a tree branch. Suddenly, it broke, dropping the king of the jungle into the raging river below. Helpless, he floated downstream. The crow appeared overhead. 'Help!' the tiger cried out to the crow. 'Help me!' The crow looked down at the tiger struggling in the water. 'How could I help you, king of the jungle? I'm too stupid and too small.' But then—"

Sam paused as Carrie appeared, a steaming mug in hand. The tea bag label hung off the side, twirling in her movement as she set it on the table in front of Sam, retaking her seat.

"Then!" Sam continued with a gleeful smile, tucking the gun away in his vest. "The crow swooped down and plucked the tiger's eyes out of his skull. The king of the jungle was defenseless as the water came up over his mighty head. 'Now,' the crow said as he flew away, 'I will see what the king of the jungle sees.'"

Silence fell over the room and filled the cockpit.

"If you think—" Bill said.

Grabbing Carrie's arm violently, Sam stretched it across the table, his chair smacking the floor behind him as it fell. Elise awoke with a scream.

"You're missing the moral of the story, Bill," Sam said. Carrie winced. Bill could see Sam's fingers digging into her skin. "The moral of the story is that I *will* get what I want. It's your choice what is sacrificed along the way. Make the video."

Grabbing the mug of tea, he emptied it onto Carrie's soft flesh, her muffled screams behind her gag mixing with her daughter's.

The screen went black as Sam disconnected the call.

Bill clutched the sides of the computer. Panting, he stared at the blank screen. He had no idea how long he sat like that, staring into nothingness. The sound of the lav opening and closing in the cabin behind him broke his stupor.

Ben would be back soon.

Jo was opening a little creamer as Ben came out of the bathroom, the ebony skin on her fingers speckled with fine mists of cream, an unavoidable reality of a pressurized cabin at altitude. Wiping her fingers on a napkin, she swirled the cream and sugar before pointing at the machine.

"Coffee was cold so I'm brewing you a fresh pot. Almost done."

The first officer glanced at the cockpit door.

FAA and company protocol said in and out quickly, but the FAA didn't have any eyes on board today. Jo's stalling was a bet on the pilot's youth and cockiness finding him more rebellious than rule stickler, and to her relief, he leaned casually against the galley counter.

"You going downstairs tonight?" he asked.

"Nah," Jo said. "Tomorrow in Portland, sure. But night one I slam-click, catch up on my sleep. You know I've been with my husband for nineteen years? You'd *think* I'd be able to sleep through his snoring."

"Another reason why I'm single."

"Uh-huh. That's why," Jo said, watching Ben look for the younger flight attendant in the back.

"So do you commute?" she asked.

"No, I live in Long Beach."

"Oh, I lived there when I first moved to LA. Where were you before Coastal? You've been here . . ."

"Three years in January," Ben said. "I was at a regional out of Buffalo." He glanced at the glowing BREW button.

"Almost done," she said with a small wink, placing one hand on her hip and the other on the coffeepot handle. "So tell me—"

Behind her, Jo heard her phone vibrate against the counter.

Bill's foot tapped compulsively. Staring out the window at the rows of cornfields below, he hadn't blinked in almost a minute. Carrie's scream as she was scalded with nearly boiling water echoed through his head. Darker thoughts of what could happen to the children bubbled up uncontrollably.

"Dammit," he muttered, reopening Sam's last email.

Taking his phone out, he swiped left to open the camera. Toggling to the video function, he flipped the camera around so his own face filled the screen. Holding the phone out, he brought it alongside the computer so he could read the text like a teleprompter. The image of his face on the screen shook. Breathing deeply to steady his hand, he pressed the red record button.

Jo poured into the mug, watching the coffee swirl with the cream, dark and light combining to a shade of tawny. Taken by the relief of the everyday task, she almost didn't see Ben reach for the interphone to call Bill and head back up.

Acting before she had time to think, Jo yelped in pain as coffee poured all over her hand. The mug slipped out of her fingers, cracking against the metal countertop, covering everything with coffee. She jumped back to avoid the splash.

"Whoa!" Ben said, slamming the phone back in its cradle. "You okay?"

Jo laughed with a grimace. "Besides embarrassed? I think so." She shook off her hand, examining it under the light. "Well, your coffee is hot and fresh, that's for sure. Honey, grab me some paper towels?"

With Ben busy in the bathroom, she glanced down quickly at her phone. The text was from Theo. Almost to the family's house. Dropping the phone in her pocket, she bit her lip, covering a small smile.

"Ah, thank you," she said, taking the paper towels. "Let me just mop this up real quick."

• • •

Bill watched the seconds tick on the recording video. He cleared his throat.

"My name is Captain Bill Hoffman and I am guilty," he said into the camera. "Guilty of abuse, manipulation, and exploitation. I am guilty of repressing an entire community of people whose only true desire is sovereignty and dignity. I am guilty of deserting and betraying a close ally after they sacrificed eleven thousand of their own soldiers in the defeat of ISIS, simply because I asked them to. I am guilty of looking the other way as chemical warfare was waged on innocent civilians."

A bead of sweat trickled down the side of his face. He wiped it away.

"The crash of Flight four-one-six and the chaos and death it will bring are the tiniest glimpse of the pain and suffering the Kurdish people have unfairly endured because of me. Today, poison will fill your lungs, and panic will overcome your senses as you suffocate, gasping for cool relief that will never come. The putrid scent of decaying flesh will fill your nose as your precious American skin festers and rots to the bone. Eyes, burning and bloodshot, will bulge from your skulls, wide with terror, as you see your sins played out across your own bodies. You will cower in the empty promise of your privilege and realize that you are not special. That you too will die. And in your last horror-filled moments, you will remember that thousands of innocent Kurdish men, women, and children have gone before you, dying the same tortured deaths—and all because of you. You and your ignorance. Your indifference. Your unwillingness to be inconvenienced by caring. So now, you and I will pay.

"This pitiful restitution cannot come close to the

justice the Kurds deserve, but it is the best I can do. So on behalf—"

His voice began to quiver.

"On behalf of America . . . and on behalf of my family . . . I come before you with Kurdish blood on my hands and ask the Kurdish people for forgiveness through my sacrifice and the sacrifice of Flight four-one-six."

The intercom buzzed throughout the cockpit and he pressed the red button to stop recording. Bill stared at his frozen face on the screen in front of him. He pushed a button on the center console.

"Yeah," he said, his voice flat.

"Ben here," came the first officer's voice. "Ready to come up."

"Hold on," Bill said. "ATC's talking."

On his phone, he opened his email, attached the video to a new message, entered Carrie's email address, and pressed "Send." Laying the phone next to his computer, he lowered the laptop's screen so he could let Ben up—but paused.

Thinking better of it, he reopened the computer and went to his email there. He clicked on the "Sent" folder, wanting to make sure the email went through. Instead, he found that the last sent message was from nearly twenty minutes ago, before the bathroom break. The email with the video hadn't been delivered.

"Shit," he whispered, refreshing the browser.

Nothing.

Jo tapped her finger on her wrist, staring out at the cabin from her blocking position. She could tell Bill was stalling.

In the back Kellie crossed the galley.

"I think she's single too," Jo said suggestively over her shoulder.

Ben was busy texting. He looked up, clearly having no idea who Jo was talking about. "Huh?"

Jo nodded toward the back.

"Oh! She is?"

"Uh-huh. Want to stay out for a bit and I'll call her up?" Jo suggested, hoping her tone came off as casually as she meant it to.

Bill knew Ben was standing on the other side of the door waiting while Jo blocked. It had already been a long break—he assumed Jo had stalled as best she could—and if he didn't open soon it was going to start looking suspicious. Both to Ben and whatever other eyes were watching them. He refreshed the browser again. The "Sent" folder stayed the same.

Jo watched Kellie flip her hair to the side with a laugh. The young woman picked up a magazine and walked it over to the other flight attendant, the curves of her tight uniform impressive even a full length of a plane away.

Ben glanced at the flight deck door, then back to the blonde.

"I don't know, it's been long enough of a— Oh. Hey, Bill. Yeah, I'm ready."

He hung the phone up with one more glance down the aisle as Kellie ducked out of sight.

"Next break, for sure, Miss Matchmaker." He winked at Jo as the door opened and he disappeared up front.

· · ·

"You get lost out there?" Bill said.

"Jo can talk, man."

Bill opened his computer. At the top of the "Sent" folder sat the email with the video.

Jo heard the door close and lock behind her. Turning with a deep exhale, she quickly picked up the interphone and looked through the plane to the back galley.

Everyone was in their seats except a young lady coming up the aisle from the bathroom. Taking her seat, she became one of the mass; tops of heads occasionally swaying in unison with the plane's movements like sheep packed tightly into the bed of a truck. Jo looked out at these strangers and wondered what twists of fate had brought them all here, now. People didn't pay to leave their comfort zone unnecessarily. Every person on board had a reason for being here. She wondered who was being shepherded to visit friends, who was going to a wedding. A funeral, a work trip, a vacation. Going home.

Hijacking a plane.

But with 144 passengers on board, surely not all of them were a threat. So knowing what she knew, was it fair to keep the innocent in the dark? Telling them would be a risk to Bill's family, of course. But didn't these families on board deserve more?

There it was again. That faint murmur in her gut. She had ignored it the first time, but this time it was stronger, unavoidable.

Jo knew Bill wasn't going to crash the plane. Her trust in him was bedrock. No, that wasn't the problem.

The problem was, she was afraid he couldn't trust *her*.

The terrorist would kill his family if they told the passengers. That was clear.

But how could the flight attendants not tell them? How could they not give these innocent people every advantage they could to protect themselves from their own peril? Keeping it from them, making choices for them, taking away their autonomy. It didn't sit right. It didn't seem fair.

Stop.

Jo shut out the line of reasoning by ripping the interphone off the cradle. They would protect the passengers, they would figure it out. But they would do it without telling them. She couldn't betray Bill like that.

She watched the other two flight attendants in the back galley. Kellie was holding a tray with drinks on it. She laughed at a joke from her coworker before walking off to deliver the drinks. Jo envied their ignorance.

When she pushed a button, a green light lit up in the back with a high-low chime. Jo watched her colleague cross the galley and pick up the phone.

"Housekeeping."

"Hey, Daddy," Jo said. "Look, we—"

She stopped herself. Not over the phone. She needed to tell them in person.

"Grab Kellie and come up here. We need to talk."

CHAPTER SIX

CAREFUL OF THE SUICIDE VEST, CARRIE BROUGHT HER ARM CLOSER to her face.

The skin was wet but unscathed.

The old tea bag, the one from Sam's first cup, sat in a puddle on the desk. The rest of the old, chilled tea soaked the front of Carrie's shirt and pants. Her own screams of terror echoed through her head, haunting her by how unnecessary they were.

When Sam grabbed her arm, her hands had still been tingling with warmth from the hot mug she had just given him. She knew how hot that water was. She expected incredible pain. So when the liquid hit her skin, her thermoreceptors went wild, sending shock-waves of reaction throughout her body. It was only momentarily, but it took that second for her brain to register the temperature sensations as *cold*, not hot. By the time she'd figured out Sam's sleight of hand, the call with Bill had already been disconnected. The last image he had seen was his wife being tortured. Or so he thought.

Please don't do anything stupid, Bill. I'm fine. Stay strong. Don't give in. He didn't hurt me. Babe, please. Don't give in.

It wasn't so much a prayer. More a plea she hoped he would somehow intuit.

The family computer made a noise.

"Did he do it?" Sam said from the kitchen. Carrie looked over at the screen. Her inbox had a new message with a large attachment. She nodded.

"Smart man," Sam said, walking back to the family. "How about some entertainment?" Opening the email, he started the video. Her husband's face appeared on the screen while his voice filled the silence of the family home. Carrie listened, but she couldn't look.

Instead, she watched Sam.

Taking a sip of the fresh tea Carrie had brought him, he winced, blowing into the steam. Tossing the old tea bag into the now empty mug, he brought it to the kitchen, placing it in the sink like an overly courteous houseguest.

Sam returned with a dish towel, wordlessly mopping up the desk before taking her pale, slender arm in his hands. Wiping it dry, he worked the towel in one hand, while the other held on to the detonator. He looked down at her soaked jeans. Blinking, he turned away, placing the towel in her bound hands. He disappeared into the downstairs bathroom, but returned moments later with a tissue. Scott bounced his sister softly, the baby finally quiet after crying herself into exhaustion. Snot ran down the boy's face onto the gag in his mouth. He had cried nearly as hard as Elise when Sam grabbed his mother's arm.

Walking over to the boy, Sam placed the tissue over his nose.

"Blow," he said. Scott blew and the man folded the tissue, wiping the child's upper lip.

Bill's voice, breaking with emotion, was unavoidable. Carrie turned.

"On behalf of America . . . and on behalf of my family . . . I come before you with Kurdish blood on my hands and ask the Kurdish people for forgiveness through my sacrifice and the sacrifice of Flight four-one-six."

The video stopped and Carrie stared for a long while at the frozen image of her husband's face. Looking away, she found Sam watching her.

She held his gaze. A charged energy filled the distance between them as they tried to read one another. Carrie could tell her reactions, or lack thereof, were not what he'd expected. What she couldn't tell was whether that was a good thing or not. He didn't seem angry or hostile, not with her or the children. No, he seemed . . . curious. That was as close as she could place it. He seemed to be putting her together like a puzzle, like he was gradually discovering what piece fit where.

"When I told your husband it wasn't personal, I meant it."

Her lips hugged the gag without moving.

Meandering through the kitchen, Sam seemed to consider the space at a sort of clinical distance. He opened the silverware drawer, closing it before repeating the step with the one that held the cooking utensils. Pausing at the fridge, he tilted his head to the side while looking at the pictures and children's artwork. He studied Scott's report card with an approving glance over his shoulder before leaning in to examine the family calendar. He pointed at today's date.

"'Internet repair. 11:30 a.m.' Well, here we are," he said, and laughed. "By the way, your internet's fine. I put

a jammer on the side of your house a couple nights ago.
Clearly I already turned it off. Oh, I'm also the person
who makes the technician appointments. That was me
you talked to on the phone the other day. Your appointment also never made it officially on the books. Plus,
today's my day off. CalCom also thinks my name is
Raj." He smiled, clearly pleased with himself. "So what
I'm trying to say is—there's no reason for suspicion. No
one is coming to help you."

Carrie didn't react. She just listened, giving a small
nod to express her understanding. His smile slowly dis-
solved. She wondered what kind of reaction he wanted
from her.

He continued on his personal tour of the kitchen
and, upon reaching the sink, stared out the window
for some time before turning to lean back against the
counter, arms crossed.

"Carrie," he said, "do you know where Italy is?"

At first she didn't bite. Then hesitantly, she nodded.

"And how about Australia?"

Reluctantly, her head went up and down. He nodded
too, looking down at the floor. For a long time he didn't
say anything. Finally, he looked up.

"I will let you and your family go, I swear to god," he
said. "Carrie, I will walk out the front door and never
come back—if you can point Kurdistan out on a map."

Carrie could sense an undertone of hope beneath his
deadpan expression. But the longer she sat unmoving,
the fainter it became. He shook his head with a cluck,
tapping the detonator against his arm.

She tried to speak but the words came out as unin-
telligible sounds against the gag. Sam considered for
some time, then walked over, bending, his face hovering
in front of hers.

"I won't regret this twice. Understood?" he said.

He untied the gag and the saliva-covered clump of fabric dropped into her lap. She stretched her jaw.

"How many," she said finally. Hoarse, she cleared her throat. "How many kids do you have?"

Sam stared at her. "What?"

Carrie lifted her chin at Scott. "No one wipes a child's nose like that unless they've done it before."

A smile flickered briefly across Sam's face. He considered her for a long moment before walking back to the sink, to his tea, to staring out the window.

For some time no one spoke. Sam finally gave in, choosing his words cautiously.

"I don't have any children. I had siblings. I'm the oldest of six. I was eighteen when the youngest was born and I was planning to leave home not long after that. I was supposed—" Sam stopped himself. "Plans. I had plans."

He took a sip of tea. Elise cooed. He regarded the baby with a forlorn glance.

"Four days before I was supposed to leave, my father died. My mother was disabled and while she could do most things, she would need help. Five young kids, Ahmad was only four months old—" He stopped and shook his head.

Ahmad. Carrie made a mental note of the name. The youngest sibling. The deepest wound.

"I couldn't leave. I knew I couldn't." Sam shrugged. "So I didn't. I stayed. For seventeen years I took care of my mother and I helped raise my siblings like they were my children. The younger ones barely remembered our father, if they could remember him at all. I *was* their father."

Sam stared into his tea like he was staring into

another world. Carrie didn't intrude; she waited for him to come back on his own. When he did, his voice was soft and sad.

"And then I left," he said, and told her nothing else.

"What—if I may—" Carrie said cautiously. "What happened to them?"

Sam cocked his head.

"You speak of them in the past tense," Carrie said. "What happened to your family after you left?"

Whatever had happened to them, whatever memory or image it brought to mind, it hit Sam with such force that he actually took a step forward. He looked to Carrie, tears filling his eyes.

Carrie's jaw dropped and she managed to stammer, "I-I'm sorry. I . . . I didn't mean to . . ."

She'd crossed a line. Glancing at Scott and Elise, she worried about what Sam might do if he snapped.

Sam folded his arms across his chest in a way that appeared defensive and almost wounded. In any other situation, she might have felt the motherly urge to comfort him. He seemed exposed in a way that came off as unfair.

"I—" he began weakly.

The high-pitched whine of a braking vehicle came from the front of the house. Sam grabbed the gun off the counter and pointed it toward the hall to the entryway. His eyes were wide and he breathed through his mouth. Any softness or vulnerability Carrie had glimpsed only a moment before was gone.

Sam walked to the far side of the kitchen and stood across from Carrie, who was seated at the computer in the family room. "Can you see out the front window?" he asked.

"If I stand over there," she said, pointing her bound

hands toward the end of the family room. He motioned for her to move.

As she crossed the room, she heard the sound of a heavy engine rattling to a start. Reaching the far wall, she peeked her head out to see the left side of the picture window in the living room. Tall shrubbery covered their front yard, but she could glimpse the top of the brown UPS truck as it pulled away from the neighbor's house across the street.

"It was a delivery truck," she said, turning back to Sam. His eyebrows were pinched together tightly and he didn't seem convinced. He thought for a moment and then pointed the gun at the children. Carrie's breath caught in her throat.

"Go close the curtains," he said, motioning to the living room. "Make it quick."

Carrie's heart pounded as she ran into the living room. She shut the curtains tight and then hurried back through the darkened room toward the kitchen. She'd been out of sight for mere seconds, but the relief she felt at finding the children in the same spot, unharmed, was overwhelming.

But she hid it all. She reminded herself that Sam would get nothing from her. He watched her walk coolly back to her seat at the computer and his scowl deepened. There was a deep confusion to his look. He watched her for a moment longer before speaking, his voice crisp. The gun was still pointed at the children.

"I'm not sure I like how calmly you're handling this."

CHAPTER SEVEN

JO STEADIED HERSELF AS SHE WAITED FOR THE OTHER FLIGHT ATTEN-
dants to come up front. She had tried to sound so non-
chalant when she called them. Poor things had no clue
what was about to hit them.

"What is this? Are we praying? What's going on
here?" Big Daddy said, startling Jo with his silent approach. His badge may have said "Michael Rodenburg,"
but everyone at Coastal knew him as Big Daddy—and
everyone at Coastal knew Big Daddy. Five foot three,
not 115 pounds soaking wet; he'd been in the airline's
first flight attendant class and was one of only a handful
still flying who had an employee number with only three
digits. Coastal Airways was his third airline since starting his career a lifetime ago (the exact year of which he
never exactly specified). He was a never-ending source
of flight attendant folklore, the authenticity of which no
one dared question. Passengers and crews either loved
him or hadn't a damn clue what to do with him. But
either way, Big Daddy could get away with murder.

"Where's Kellie?" Jo said.

"She's coming."

"Good. Listen. Things are about to get . . . interesting. Okay? I'll explain once she gets here, but you and I are the seasoned ones. We're gonna have to hold it tight, because I don't know how Kellie's going to react."

"React to what?" Kellie said, her approach unseen from behind the galley curtain.

"Listen, baby girl," Big Daddy said, clapping his hands. "Training is over. Shit is about to get real. But no matter what Jo says, just remember: planes can fly—no problem—with only one engine, and if at least seventy-five percent of the people currently on this plane walk off alive? I consider that a success."

"Not helping," Jo said, eyebrow peaked. "All right, look. We're facing something that . . . I . . . Look, we're going to have to . . ." She sighed. "Guys, this is a new one."

Ignoring their looks, she soldiered on, ripping the Band-Aid off as quickly and clearly as Bill had with her. Neither moved a muscle or visibly reacted as they listened silently to the situation at hand.

Once Jo finished, Kellie's wide eyes shot back and forth between her and Big Daddy like she was watching a tennis match, the seconds ticking on as the two senior members of the crew simply stared at each other with mutually raised eyebrows and pursed lips. During their preflight briefing, Jo had asked how long she'd been on-line. Kellie had said a little over a month. Jo realized the poor girl probably hadn't even had her first medical yet, not even oxygen.

"I'll cover service, don't worry about that," Kellie offered.

The other two stared.

"What . . . do you mean?" Jo asked.

"Like, while you guys handle all the crisis stuff. I'll get all the food and drink orders."

Jo and Big Daddy shared a glance. Jo spoke softly. "Honey, listen. The usual things? The drinks and the food and the smiling? You know that's not what we're here for, right?"

"Sure, but it'll still have to get done," Kellie said. "So I'm saying I'll take care of all that so you guys can focus on, like, this other stuff."

Jo watched the young flight attendant put on plastic gloves and shake out a trash bag.

"I'll collect trash and just, you know, do service stuff," Kellie said. "Probably better I'm out of the way anyway. I'm so new, I'd . . . I'd just be in the way, I'm sure."

Jo wrapped her fingers around the young woman's forearm, pulling her back in as she tried to leave. A heavy tear slid down Kellie's cheek, plopping onto her red dress just above her wings.

"Kellie," Jo said. "That's not our job. Service is just something we provide."

It had been decades since Jo's initial training, but that didn't matter. The five weeks of training flooded back in Technicolor vividness as though she'd been in Kellie's class last month. Relentless studying followed by written tests. First aid and self-defense. Drilling, over and over, the evacuation of hundreds of people from a burning aircraft, or from a water landing. She and her classmates, breathless and sweating, had screamed commands until they were hoarse, orchestrating survival. They'd learned about the different kinds of fires and the different ways to fight them. Hazmat, heart attacks, hijackings. Federal regulations and federal air marshals. Turbulence. Terrorists. And all of it in a pressurized metal tube, thirty-eight thousand feet in the air going six hundred miles per hour. Five weeks of training and in only one of those days did they go over food, drinks, and hospitality. Jo watched the junior flight attendant struggling to breathe, knowing that this was the moment when Kellie understood what her job *really* was.

Kellie looked to the back of the aircraft. Her head whipped right and left. She looked at every exit. Shifting her weight, she pulled against Jo.

"Sweetheart," Jo said. "Where are you gonna go?"

Kellie stared at the back of the plane with no answer.

Big Daddy cleared his throat. Closing his eyes, he flared his nostrils through a deep intake of air. "Okay," he said, his eyes fluttering open. "I'll say this much. When this is all over and we're walking off the plane in Kennedy? Someone is going to have to pull my bag because I will be pushing *that* big boy"—he jabbed an emphatic finger at the liquor cart—"off this plane and directly into my hotel room."

Turning to Kellie with a look that said *How about you?*, Jo waited.

"I'm not ready for something this big," Kellie whispered. "I'm not even off probation."

Jo tried not to laugh. At a moment like this, the poor girl was worried about getting in trouble with her supervisor. "I know, honey. It doesn't feel fair, does it?" She shook her head. "But it is what it is."

The three stood in silence for a moment, processing. Kellie wiped her tears, accepting the napkins Daddy handed her. Blowing her nose, she rubbed her lips together and cleared her throat, attempting a smile. The others politely ignored her quivering cheek.

"I'm a whisky girl," said Kellie, her youthful cadence making most statements sound like questions. "So I call dibs on a few Jack and Gingers."

"Well, all right, then," Jo said, nodding in approval. "Jack and Gingers for you, a whole bottle of that first-class Chardonnay for me, and, I'm assuming, the rest of the cart for Daddy."

"Preach," Daddy confirmed.

"But in the meantime?" Jo said. "We have to prepare this plane and the one hundred and forty-four passengers on it for an airborne chemical attack and emergency landing. Okay? Now, I have an idea—"

"Excuse me?" came a voice from behind, making them jump. It was the man at the window in row two, aircraft left. "I was wondering what snacks—"

"No," Daddy said, "we're busy. You finished your chicken a half hour ago, your blood sugar is fine." Sliding the galley curtain shut on the dumbfounded man, Daddy turned back to the crew. "What?" he said in response to Jo's face. Rolling his eyes, he poked his head out into the cabin.

"Wink. Just kidding," he said coyly. "Jo has popcorn, potato chips, almonds, gummy bears, and little squares of chocolate."

With chips and ginger ale in hand, the passenger regarded the three flight attendants with suspicion before returning to his seat. Big Daddy closed the curtain behind him.

"Okay," he said. "The end with that nonsense. The whole plane is cut off. Jo. What's your idea?"

Jo thought about all the problems they faced. The gas attack. Washington, DC. Bill's family. The unknown mole on board. There was so much going on, but most of it was entirely out of their control. They couldn't afford to waste time and energy worrying about it all.

"Okay. So," Jo said. "There's a lot going on, but the problem *we* need to focus on is the attack here in the cabin. We have no idea what it is, so we're just going to assume it's worst-case scenario and plan from there."

"Sarin nerve gas," Daddy said. "Ricin. VX. Anthrax. Cyanide. My god, what if it's botulinum?"

"C'mon," Jo said. "That's chemical warfare–level stuff. There's no way these people got their hands on something like that."

"Um, they've managed to hijack a domestic commercial flight in a post-9/11 world. I don't think we should count anything out."

"So say it is one of those," Kellie said. "What can we expect will happen? Like, to us. If we breathe it."

"I mean," Daddy began, flourishing his hand, "we're talking shortness of breath? Muscle paralysis? Abdominal pain, vomiting, and diarrhea? Loss of consciousness? Foaming at the mouth? And, uh. Well. Death."

Jo pinched the bridge of her nose. "Short answer: we don't want to breathe it. So," Jo said, crossing her arms, "here's my idea. The passengers will need clean oxygen—"

"The PSUs," Kellie said.

"Yes!" Jo said. "Exactly. Everybody on board has oxygen right above their heads. We just need to release the masks."

Opening the compartment below her jump seat, Jo extracted the small metal slat affixed to the inside. The manual release tool was essentially an expensive version of a paper clip bent open into a straight line. She held it up and they all gazed upon the smallest, most inconsequential piece of emergency equipment on any aircraft. Its only purpose was to release the masks above the seats—manually, row by row—in the unlikely event that an automatic release didn't happen. None of them had ever used it or thought they ever would.

"We have to assume the attack will happen right before we land, just before final descent," Jo said. "But we need to be ready early. Honestly, as soon as we can. We don't know how much passenger resistance there might be, and it's going to take some time even if it goes perfectly. Which means we need to start dropping the masks soon."

"So what are you going to say in your announcement?" Kellie said.

"My announcement?" Jo said.

Kellie opened her hands. "What, we're just going to, like, start dropping masks? And . . . hope they don't notice?"

"Well, see, now that's where we need to plan and come up with something. Because we obviously can't tell them what's going on."

The other two stared. Daddy raised his hand.

"Josephina—quick question. *What* in the actual fuck?"

"We can't tell them anything. The terrorist will kill Bill's family if we do."

"And that is truly awful, and I'm sorry. But what about these people? We're just going to let them run blind into an attack while we know damn well it's on its way?"

Jo shook her head. "It's not just Bill's family. There's a backup, remember? Back here. With us." The tone of her voice was rising with her anxiety. Taking a breath, she glanced around the curtain to survey the cabin. Two people were waiting for the bathroom in the back. A man stood in the aisle bouncing his baby. Nothing seemed off.

"Look," she said. "We need to keep this contained. We can't let anyone know anything is going on."

"Okay," Kellie said. "So again. We're gonna drop the masks and smile and nod? Like it's totally something we normally do on flights?"

Jo sighed and dropped her head. "I know. I *know*. Look, I don't have an answer to everything. The only thing I know for sure is that we need those masks out, and that's final. We must give these people what they need to survive. Let's just start there, okay?"

Daddy raised his hands in surrender and Kellie nodded. The engines hummed, far in the back a baby cried, and someone in first class shut an overhead bin. The three flight attendants stared at the floor amid the ambient noise.

With a tiny gasp, Daddy covered his mouth, a glint of *Eureka!* gleaming in his eyes.

"The FAR!" he said. "How the hell did we forget Federal Aviation Regulation four-point-two-point-seven? It clearly states that in the event of an Oxygen Release System fault in the flight deck, flight attendants are required to manually release all cabin oxygen masks from the PSUs so that in the unlikely event of a decompression, passengers will have access to oxygen."

Kellie blinked. "I didn't know that FAR. I mean, if that's what we're supposed to do, then obviously—"

"He made that up," Jo said.

Big Daddy curtsied.

"You want to lie to them?" Kellie said.

"Do it all the time," Daddy said. "Guess they're still not teaching that in initial."

"No, he's right," Jo said. "Fooled you, it'll fool them. I think they'll go with it. We just need the masks out. Let's cross that bridge first, then we'll figure out what to do next after that."

"Okay, fine. Let's get this over with," Kellie said. "But I'm not making the announcement. You guys can do the talking."

"We're *all* doing the talking," Jo said. "No one's making an announcement."

"What?" Daddy said.

"We're trying to be covert, remember? Bill's still on the video call and the FO doesn't know anything's happening. He *can't* know anything's happening."

"The pilots can hear our announcements?" Kellie asked.

"Sort of. They can always hear when we're making an announcement, just not clearly. But if they want to, they can switch the audio and listen in. They just don't usually. So the less attention we attract, the better. We have to make this seem like a nonevent. Not just for us back here, but for the sake of Bill's family."

Jo thought of Carrie. Over the years, enough company picnics and Christmas parties had turned into the families getting together on their own. The women weren't best friends, but a happy hour here and there kept them in touch. When Scott was born, Jo gave Carrie a bunch of her son's hand-me-downs and she loved the pictures she got of the baby in her boy's old favorites.

Shaking the flood of images out of her head, she refocused.

Theo would take care of the family.

Bill would take care of the plane.

They needed to take care of the passengers.

CHAPTER EIGHT

TAPPING HIS PHONE AGAINST HIS LEG, THEO WATCHED THE TRAFFIC on the 405 part to let their procession through. Three unmarked SUVs and one windowless mobile command center was about as subtle as the FBI could get.

"Lights and sirens off once we exit the freeway," Liu said to the driver. "Ladies and gentlemen, our suspect has no idea we're coming. That is our one and only advantage. This is the Hoffman family."

Liu turned and held up a tablet displaying a photo from social media, and the SWAT team's combat helmets bobbed up and down. "Mother's name is Carrie, children are Scott and Elise, ten and ten months respectively. Mom is strapped with a suicide vest. The wireless detonator is held by our suspect, who is also wearing a vest. So what do we know about him? Male, estimated early thirties. He works for a cable company and his full name is something that starts with 'S' but he goes by Sam."

Theo felt Liu glaring at him. He checked his phone

to see if there was anything new, or more helpful, from his aunt. Nothing.

"This is an exploratory mission only, understood?" she continued. "We are establishing a perimeter and conducting reconnaissance. All our intelligence is being passed on to HRT, who we are consulting with and who is preparing to deploy as we speak. If tactical force is deemed necessary, we wait for them unless we have no other option."

Theo adjusted his bulletproof vest. He already felt out of place, but once the HRT arrived, that feeling would intensify. Theo was just a field agent. He wasn't SWAT and he definitely wasn't a member of the Hostage Rescue Team, the elite tactical unit of the FBI trained to deal with extreme high-risk situations. The only reason he was along on the mission was because he was an intelligence liaison between the plane and the ground. Liu had made certain he understood that.

Exiting the freeway, the vehicle's sirens and flashing lights ceased. The sudden silence only heightened the feeling of anticipation felt by Theo and his fellow agents.

"Location, please," Liu said into her comm set that connected all the units. Someone in the van sent the digital map to her tablet, which she studied with increasing disapproval.

"It's a shit location for us," said a voice in all of their earpieces. "Suburban neighborhood in Playa del Rey just off Manchester. The house is at the apex of a three-way street, flanked by houses on all three sides. There's very little back or side yard for us to work with."

"The front is too exposed. We can't all go," Liu said. "Alpha will approach head-on, straight up Eighty-third Street. Bravo and Charlie units, I want your vehicles behind on Eighty-second and east on Hastings. Comms, post up where Eighty-third meets Saran. Once you're in position, report and stand by for my order to advance on foot. Everybody got it?"

The unit leads affirmed, voices heard in all four vehicles through every headset. The vehicles split up to assume their positions and Liu, Theo, and the agents in Alpha unit continued down Lincoln, stopping behind traffic at the red light, waiting to turn onto Manchester.

Theo looked out the window at a family leaving a restaurant. HACIENDA DEL MAR according to the faded sign. A teenage boy held the door open behind him, his mom following, a to-go container in hand. The father worked at his teeth with a toothpick while the younger sister trailed after them all, dancing more than walking out of the restaurant. The light turned green and the vehicle rolled forward, the scene receding behind them. Theo wondered if the Hoffmans ever ate there. It was just up the street from their house. Maybe just yesterday they looked like that family, leaving the restaurant blissfully unaware of what was to come.

"Bravo unit in place," said a voice a few minutes later. Soon, Charlie and the command center reported the same.

"Alpha unit is turning onto Berger now. Stand by," Liu said. The SUV slowed, pulling to a stop on the right side of the street.

Liu muttered an expletive. Theo rubbernecked for a view and understood immediately.

"We can't see shit," Liu said. "We're going to have to move in a lot closer than we thought. Front yard has a couple trees and some shrubbery. Only enough to conceal two, maybe three agents."

"Standby, Bravo might have a break," they heard a voice say.

Bravo unit was behind the house on Eighty-second and could access the Hoffman backyard if they went through the neighbors'. On the Hoffman property, there appeared to be several large trees and a small structure, a sort of shed or workshop, for hard cover.

"Good," Liu said. "How many agents covered and concealed?"

"Four, maybe five."

Liu nodded to herself. "Bravo unit, go."

"Affirmative. Moving out," said a voice.

"Charlie," said Liu. "What you got?"

A breathless voice came over the line. "We're in the back, headed west on foot, ma'am. Civilian sweep clear. Will assess side yard entry once in position."

Liu affirmed and then no one said anything for the next few minutes as Bravo and Charlie units moved into position. Over the shrubs, Theo could see the top of the home's front window, but because of the glare from the sun, he couldn't tell if the shades were drawn. If open, there was no way to approach from the front without being in direct line of sight, which meant in direct line of fire. The kill zone.

"Bravo unit is in position," a hushed voice said in their ears. "But we have zero visibility. Every window in the back is covered."

"Roger," Liu said. "Stay in position. Charlie unit. I want—"

"Comms to Alpha," a voice interrupted. "We've got an issue. A civilian pedestrian is headed east on foot, seems to be alone, seems to be going door to door."

Theo leaned forward, looking left. A man with a clipboard appeared, walking up to the front door of the house two down from the Hoffmans'. After knocking, the door was opened by a little old lady seemingly confused by his presence. She shook her head and went to close the door, the man barely getting a flyer in her hand before it shut in his face. Walking back down the drive, he stopped to punch around on his phone before beginning an animated conversation, tapping the volume up on his Bluetooth ear piece. The bottom of his clipboard said the same thing the side of his bag did, both in obnoxious blue-and-red letters: "CAMPBELL FOR CONGRESS!" The man made for the next house, the house next door to the Hoffmans'.

"Motherfucker," Liu said. "We gotta stop him."

Ordering Charlie unit to hold their position, she turned to face the Alpha team. Theo realized every agent except him was in full tactical gear, the words FBI SWAT written in bright yellow across their backs.

"Rousseau," Liu said.

"Ma'am?"

"Out of your gear, now. You're intercepting."

Agent Rousseau blinked at the director. Removing his gear would take minutes. He frantically began to strip his protective suit, checking the politician's progress. The man had already knocked on the next-door neighbor's door and no one was answering. Bending, he slid a flyer into the mail slot.

"We have to stop him," Theo said, pressing his hands against the glass. "He can't go up there, it's way too dangerous."

"I've got five agents already inside the inner perimeter. We have no idea what we're dealing with. And you want to blow our cover?" Liu said. "Rousseau! Let's go!"

Theo watched the agent wrestle with straps and ties. There was no way he would make it in time. Not a chance. Theo looked around the van, at the agents who were idly observing their colleague taking off his gear.

Theo couldn't believe it. The politician would be ringing the Hoffmans' doorbell before Rousseau was halfway done and none of the agents seemed to get that.

Either they didn't get it—or their order to sit and wait blinded them to the urgency.

Theo looked down at his own gear, his one bulletproof vest.

Ripping the Velcro, he slid out of it, discarding it on the seat as he jumped out of the car. Liu pounded against the glass with a string of muffled expletives, but Theo ignored her, sprinting toward the Hoffmans' house.

CHAPTER NINE

JO STUCK THE END OF THE MRT INTO THE TINY HOLE AND JABBED upward. The ceiling panel flopped down on a hinge and four oxygen masks tumbled out with a perverse jack-in-the-box-like swing.

"Why is this necessary again?" a woman on the aisle asked the flight attendant. The man next to her at the window didn't hide his skepticism, arms crossed, his ginger ale and chip bag now empty.

"Honey, I don't make the rules. I just follow them," Jo said. "A sensor up front told the pilots that the system that drops the masks automatically may not be working. When that happens, FAA protocol requires . . ."

Jo had started at the first row of first class, Daddy at the over-wing, Kellie in row eighteen. Row by row they went, informing the passengers of the regulation, dropping the masks, fielding any questions, and then quickly getting out so they could repeat the process with the next row back.

Stay calm, stay confident, Jo told them just before they started. The crew would set the tone. If this wasn't a big deal to them, it wasn't a big deal at all. They weren't manipulating the passengers per se, they were artfully managing a perception that was in the plane's best interest.

As a career flight attendant and mother of two, Jo knew there wasn't much difference between the roles.

Get the masks out. That was step one—the most important step. Get the masks out and available so the passengers could protect themselves when the time came.

Step two: manage the inevitable confusion and resistance.

Step three: deal with whatever "backup plan" might pop up after steps one and two.

Step four: fight and survive the actual attack.

Step five: evacuate the plane upon landing at JFK.

The crew decided to focus on step one, which, in light of everything else, felt manageable.

Dangling yellow masks began to fill the plane as the three flight attendants made steady progress. When she finished with a row, Jo would do a quick visual sweep of the cabin before moving on to the next. She didn't know what she was looking for; it wasn't like someone in a ski mask was going to hop out and tell her to put her hands up. Still, she assumed something would seem off. But nothing did. She already felt hunted and the false sense of normalcy made the tension worse.

Every row jumped as the compartment popped open even though they knew to expect it. The passengers thanked Jo after the masks dropped as though she had just set their warm chicken entrees in front of them. They were confused and nervous, understandably.

But ultimately, they complied.

Jo had assumed it would go like that. After all, a flight is just a random sample of the general population, a classic bell curve. A few assholes and a few exemplars, but primarily, a whole bunch of sheep.

Jo would often sit on her jump seat during take-off and assess the group assembled for that particular flight. She would consider who would be an ABP—Able Bodied Person—willing to assist in an emergency. She would find her hot spots, those passengers already showing a proclivity for noncompliance. But she would also wander to the realm of questions like, *Okay, if something were to happen, who's gonna be the comic relief? Who's gonna be the drama queen? Who's the rebel? Who's the hero? Who's the coward?*

"I knew it," Jo said to herself, watching a woman storm up the aisle. Her husband stayed behind holding a squirming baby.

"I have a child," the woman said to Jo in a way that was somehow an accusation.

Jo glanced over the woman's shoulder. "And he's adorable. Congratulations."

"This is not funny," the woman hissed. "The kind of emotional trauma my baby is being put through with these, these—*things*—everywhere"—she gestured at the masks—"will scar him for life."

Jo tried not to look down at the young couple holding their own child who was roughly the same age as the woman's. "Ma'am, I'm sorry you find this upsetting. Unfortunately, policy dictates—"

"I don't care what the policy is."

"Well, I'm afraid the FAA does. This is for your baby's safety."

"*I* will decide what is safe for my baby," the woman said, leaning in to examine Jo's name bar. "Jo what?"

"I'm sorry?"

"What is your last name, Jo? I *will* be writing in."

96 T. J. NEWMAN

Jo shifted her weight. "Just to make sure I understand, ma'am. You're going to write the airline to inform them that this crew not only knows FAA and company policy but also enforces it?" She paused. "Watkins. W-A-T-K-I-N-S. Would you like my supervisor's email too? I can write this all down for you if it helps. I really want to make sure this information gets to the right people."

The woman curled her lip. "How dare you think—"

"Ah, shut up, lady," the man in the window seat next to the young couple said. "She's just doing her job."

"Don't you tell me to—"

"Your kid is still shitting his pants. He doesn't even know where his nose is."

"My child—"

"Ma'am," Big Daddy said, sliding himself between the woman and the row. "Your darling baby boy is back there wondering why his mother is yelling at people. Please go back to your seat and inform him of the great news—Coastal will be giving you a bunch of free miles for this truly harrowing personal trauma you and no one else has had to endure."

"I will have—"

"At-a," Daddy said, holding up his palm. "One more word and authorities are meeting the aircraft."

"But—"

"Karen, I swear to god," he said.

"My name is Janice."

Daddy wrinkled his nose. "But is it?"

Narrowing her eyes, she stormed off in a huff, the husband looking rightfully fearful as she sat back down.

"Don't worry," Big Daddy said just loud enough for the rows within earshot to hear, "I'm not rewarding that behavior. The only thing she's getting is a dysfunctional teenager. Jo, the plane is FAA compliant in the back," he said with a salute.

"Perfect. Thank you," Jo said before leaning in, lowering her voice. "Anyone raise suspicions?"

"Maybe one guy," Daddy said, barely even a whisper. "Aisle seat, aircraft right, two rows behind me. Buzz cut."

Jo nonchalantly shifted her weight to see around Big Daddy. She quickly flicked a look at the man.

"The tall guy?"

"Tall?" Daddy said. "When he went into the bathroom he had to duck."

"What's suspicious about him?"

Big Daddy shook his head. "It's just a hunch. Kellie and I actually commented on his weird vibe before any of this started."

Jo nodded. "We'll keep our eye on him. Send Kellie up. I'll check the manifest so she can Google him and see what comes up."

Daddy headed to the back while Jo finished the final few rows, which went smoothly. She was just releasing the last set when Kellie came up behind her.

"I didn't know you had Rick Ryan in first," Kellie said, eyes trained on the front of the plane.

Looking over her shoulder, Jo saw the kid who had been sitting at the window in row two leaning up against the lav, scrolling on his phone. He wasn't really a kid. Probably somewhere in his midtwenties. But the beanie, hoodie, and tattoos gave off an odd arrested development. Jo assumed he was considered hip and fashionable by those who knew what hip and fashionable were.

"Am I supposed to know who that is?" Jo said.

"He's got like ten million Instagram followers," Kellie said.

"Why?"

Kellie shrugged.

"But what's he famous for? What does he do?"

"I actually have no idea. He just is?"

Seeing the two watching, he waved them over.

"Don't you dare ask for an autograph," Jo whispered to Kellie as they walked up. "Mr. Ryan, did you need something?"

"Yeah," he said. "You want to explain this?" He held up his phone and the women squinted at the bright light in the dim cabin. It was a selfie of himself wearing the oxygen mask. Kellie leaned forward to read the specifics. Twelve hundred likes, two hundred and forty-three comments. He had posted the picture only six minutes ago.

"Shit," Kellie muttered under her breath.

"Explain what?" Jo asked. "Sorry, kids, I'm lost."

"I posted this on Instagram. Said what was happening. And now everyone's like, *Dude, that's not real.*"

Jo stared. "What's not real?"

"This FAR stuff," he said. "People are saying it's bogus. Like, airline people."

Jo's stomach dropped. She glanced at Kellie, who didn't appear to have anything to say.

"Mr. Ryan," said Jo, not entirely certain of what she would say next. Suddenly a chime sounded through the cabin; a call button, row ten.

"I'm sorry, Mr. Ryan. We have to get that but we'll be right back to explain."

"What do we do?" Kellie whispered as they left him up front. "Shit, shit, shit."

"Calm down," Jo whispered back. "We were going

to have to tell them something anyway. We just need to figure out what that something is and craft the message first. It'll be fine, we just need a little time." Jo sounded like she was in total control but as she went to turn off the call light in row ten, she saw that her hand was shaking. "Yes, sir?" she said to the man in the middle seat.

"Yeah," he said, pointing at the TV in the seatback in front of him. "I'd like to know about this?"

Jo angled her head to where she could see the screen. He was watching the news, and on the screen was Rick Ryan's—apparently—now viral picture. Looking up, she saw his mask-covered face on many screens, the number increasing as passengers switched channels. Almost instantly, his face seemed to be everywhere. Growing murmurs of doubt and dissent filled the cabin, the energy shifting.

"Well?" the man asked, pointing at the TV. "What aren't you telling us? What the hell is going on?"

A rumble of support went through the cabin.

Jo turned to look at Kellie, who was looking back at her, and it was suddenly clear to both of them that they were totally, completely, and utterly screwed.

Jo opened her mouth to speak. Not because she knew what to say, but because she had to say something.

"Okay, everybody. Listen—"

A loud triple high-low chime bleated through the cabin, cutting her off. Jo and Kellie whipped their heads to the back to see the flashing amber light above the lav, aircraft left.

Smoke alarm. Fire in the bathroom.

CHAPTER TEN

THE POLITICIAN WAS HALFWAY UP THE HOFFMANS' DRIVEWAY BEFORE
Theo could even get to the cross street. Theo whistled,
but the man jabbered into his earpiece, oblivious to
anything outside of his own world.

Theo knew he couldn't just rush up behind him. The
man would be caught off guard and no doubt a loud
scene would follow. Plus, if the door opened to the man
and Theo was seen rushing the house at the same time,
the whole operation would be compromised.

The politician dropped out of sight, disappearing
behind the tall shrubs in the front yard. Theo raced
across the street and up the lawn of the house to the
right of the Hoffmans'. A short white fence cut across
the yard and he cleared the low hurdle easily, something he hadn't done since his high school track and
field days. Dropping into the courtyard in front of the
house, he saw the drapes on the front windows were
wide open. Theo prayed no one was home.

The politician knocked on the Hoffmans' front door
as Theo grabbed a chair from the set of patio furni-

ture and ran it over to the fence dividing the two yards. Standing on the chair, his head and shoulders just cleared the fence.

The man had his head down with his back to Theo, probably looking at his phone. Theo waved his arms uselessly. He looked for movement in the house, but the windows were all covered.

"All right, talk to ya later," the politician said into his earpiece, turning back to the door. Theo was now in his periphery and he waved his arms even more wildly. This close to the house, he didn't want to make any noise, but the man still wasn't noticing him. The politician reached into his bag, the clipboard catching on a strap, a stack of flyers fluttering to the ground.

Theo pivoted on the chair and scanned the yard. Down the fence to his left was a large basket full of pool toys. Sticking out the top was a neon-pink pool noodle. *Perfect.* Theo ran to grab the toy.

Jumping back up, Theo dangled the bright piece of foam into the Hoffmans' yard. The politician had picked up the flyers and was lifting the flap of the mail slot, which was now at eye level in his crouched position. The waving flash of color in his periphery caught his attention and he snapped his head to the right, freezing at the sight of Theo on the other side of the fence.

Theo held up his badge and pointed at it, repeatedly mouthing the letters *F-B-I* until the man nodded slowly. The politician was still crouched and unmoving and the flyer began to tremble in his hand. Theo held a finger to his lips. The man closed his gaping mouth. Pantomiming his fingers walking down the path and away from the house, Theo returned his finger to the front of his lips, praying the man got it. The man nodded to indicate he did.

Slowly, the man stood from his crouched position, letting the flyer fall into the house as he did. The hand that held the flap of the mail slot released and the metal slat retracted with a slap against the house.

A concussive blast slammed Theo backward. A roiling orange fireball shooting up against the sky was the last thing he saw as his feet went over his head. Slamming into the side of the neighbor's house, he crumpled to the ground.

CHAPTER ELEVEN

FORGET THE OXYGEN MASKS, FORGET A CHEMICAL ATTACK. IF THERE was a fire on board, the plane would crash regardless.

Jo made her way to the back, ignoring every extended hand and questioning look. An uncontrollable fire was the only thing that turned her cold with fear anymore. Well, until today. That was when it hit her: *This was the terrorist's backup plan.*

Her pace quickened.

The illuminated toilet sign outside the lav shone green, meaning the bathroom was unoccupied, or at least unlocked. Scanning the door as she approached, her eyes narrowed in the dim cabin, searching for any sign of smoke escaping through the crack at the base of the door or the ventilation slats directly above that. Nothing. Inhaling deeply through her nose, she braced for a burning smell to assault her—but none came.

Taking those final steps, Jo mentally reviewed the location of the emergency equipment. Primary halon extinguisher and fireproof gloves: under the L2 jump seat, right next to the lav. Secondary extinguisher: under the R2 jump seat, aircraft right.

God help them if they needed more than two.

Reaching the door, Jo leaned slightly toward it, listening. Nothing but silence. She extended her non-dominant arm and cautiously placed the back of her left hand on the surface of the door. It was cold. Replacing it nearer to the bottom, she found the same. Confirming a third time up top, the whole surface was cool to the touch.

Getting a visual on whatever was happening on the other side of the door was the last line of defense.

Taking a breath, Jo blinked a few times, steeling herself for the worst.

She twisted the handle and cracked the door open only a sliver in an attempt to introduce as little oxygen as possible. Leaning forward as close as she dared, Jo looked in.

She threw the door open wide. Nothing. Besides some toilet paper on the floor, nothing was amiss. She opened the trash flap, looked inside, smelled deeply, and was about to repeat the steps with the toilet when she heard her name.

Turning, she found Kellie and Big Daddy blocking the passengers' view of what was going on. Kellie looked annoyed. Shaking a canister, Daddy held it out to Jo as she came out of the lav.

"You're welcome, please don't hurt me," he said.

Jo ripped the can of dry shampoo out of his hand.

"*You* set off the fire alarm?"

"I think what I actually did was save you two from that angry mob."

"Daddy, I swe—"

A high-low chime sounded and a red light lit up

above their heads. Jo tore the phone off the wall. Her eyes burned holes through Big Daddy but her voice was chirpy as she talked to the pilots.

"False alarm, boys."

Bill's scalp tingled with relief as the blood rushed back down his body. When the continuous bleat of the smoke alarm sounded in the cockpit accompanying the flashing red button and SMOKE/LAV/SMOKE panel readings, both pilots assumed an upright position of defense that practically gave them whiplash. Ben's dinner still covered his feet.

Bill had assumed it was the terrorist's contingency plan. He'd assumed there was an attack happening in the back. He had actually unbuckled his seat belt as though he was going to abandon his seat and rush into the cabin to help. Ben noticed it and gave Bill a quizzical look, but continued with the checklist and protocol for the emergency. Which was what Bill *should* have done.

"What set it off?" Bill asked into the mic, clearing his throat in an attempt to cover the tremble in his voice.

"A woman spraying dry shampoo," Jo told the pilots. Ben rolled his eyes, dropping his head into his hands.

"You can let her know we're both wide awake up here now."

"Us too," Jo said. "Sorry for the scare. You guys need anything?"

Bill looked to Ben, who shook his head. "I think we're all set. Thanks, Jo. Are, uh, do you guys need anything?"

"Nah, we're good. Nothing new to report back here,"

she said with meaning, her tone indiscernible to anyone but him.

Bill bit his lip. He wanted to scream into the microphone and demand an update from her nephew. There had been no contact from his family since Sam hung up on him, and in the void of information, horrifying possibilities filled his mind.

Bill thanked his lead flight attendant and disconnected the call. He heard himself say to his copilot, "I have control and communications, ECAM actions," and he saw his hands press the correct buttons on the dash in front of him until the flashing words of alarm disappeared with each procedure, wiping the slate clean. Some hardwired aspect of his conditioning was taking over. He was on autopilot—but still in control.

Barely.

"No more stalling," Jo said, pulling the two flight attendants deep into the galley, away from the passengers. They'd massaged the truth, told a few fibs, set off a goddamn smoke alarm. Now they needed a real plan.

"The masks are out," Jo said. "But we're not going to survive this on cute and clever alone. We need to decide—now—how we're going to handle this, and what we're going to tell them."

"Agreed," Daddy said. "I say we go with this: the truth."

"Absolutely not," Jo said, as a painful image of Scott as a baby in her son's onesie came to mind.

Daddy clasped his hands under his chin like he was praying. Or perhaps he was keeping himself from slapping her, which is what he looked like he wanted to do.

"Joleen," he said with a clenched jaw. "Walk me

through how this plays out in your head. Because one hundred and forty-four people blindsided by an attack from the cockpit does not end well in the movie I'm watching. I'm seeing an angry mob. I'm seeing the mob turn on us. I'm seeing them take things into their own hands. I'm seeing them try to storm the flight deck."

Jo pointed to the front of the plane at the locked, Kevlar-reinforced, bulletproof cockpit door.

"You know no one breaks that down," Jo said.

"You and I know that," Daddy said, "but they don't and they'll try anyway. If we keep these people in the dark and something attacks them, there's literally no chance it ends well for any of us."

"But there's a backup on board. If they know we know—"

"If they know we know?" Daddy repeated, his voice rising. "Jo. The plane is filled with masks. We're refusing to answer questions. There's a viral picture all over the internet. I think the cat's out of the bag."

"But Bill's family—"

Daddy slapped the galley counter and the women jumped. "And what the fuck do you think we're flying here? Cargo? There are *people* on this plane, Jo. And every single one of them is someone's family too. You don't get to say their lives aren't as important as Bill's family."

Jo's lip trembled in the stunned silence that followed Daddy's outburst. She knew he was right. She'd known it the whole time. That was the little nudge of dread in her gut. She knew it would come to this, it had to. But it made *her* responsible. If they told the passengers the truth, it felt as though she was making the choice for Bill. Like she was choosing the plane over his family. The weight of the betrayal to not only Bill, but to

Carrie and the children, was crushing. She would live the rest of her life knowing their deaths were on her. Jo struggled to breathe against the choking lump in her throat.

"Jo, think about it. Bill told *you*," Daddy said. "He told us. He wasn't supposed to do that either, but he knew he had to. He knew we had to know. It was a risk, a calculated risk. Just like telling the passengers will be. But we have to. There's no other way. It's Bill's duty to take care of the airframe. It's our duty to take care of the passengers."

Bill's command floated around in her head: *This is your cabin.*

"This is our cabin," she said softly.

Daddy nodded.

No one said anything for a few moments and in the silence Jo knew they'd reached an unspoken agreement.

Jo buried her face in her hands for a few breaths. She took one final inhale.

"They don't need to know about DC."

Daddy put a hand on her shoulder and gave a little squeeze. "Agreed."

"And am I wrong," Kellie said, finally contributing, "or should we also *not* tell them that the oxygen only lasts for twelve minutes?"

Jo and Big Daddy both nodded vigorously.

"I say we don't tell them anything that is totally out of their control," said Daddy. "Nothing about DC and nothing about the oxygen running out."

Something connected in Jo's mind. "That *is* the truth, Daddy. That's exactly it. What you just said about things being out of their control. That's what they need to know. They need to know there is literally nothing they can do."

The hum of the engines accentuated her point, a steady, incessant reminder of where exactly they all were, and what exactly the situation was. When the passengers boarded the plane, they placed their lives directly into Bill's hands. And once the plane was airborne it became a choice they couldn't go back on. *Bill* would decide what happens to the plane. That's what they agreed to. So now the only thing the passengers could do was trust that the captain would uphold his end of the bargain and land the plane in one piece.

"What, they'll want to storm the cockpit?" said Jo. "Even if they could, to what end? No one else can fly the plane."

She waited for a retort.

"To take down the terrorist? Guess what. He's not here!" Jo wiped her mouth, the full realization of how little they controlled sinking in. "Our best chance of surviving this is to trust Bill. The passengers need to understand that. Hell, the whole world needs to understand that. Because you're right, Daddy. This isn't just us anymore. Thanks to that picture on the internet, it's not just the terrorist and whoever the hell his backup is who know what's going on. The whole world does. So *everyone* needs to understand that trusting Bill is the only way this plane makes it out alive."

Big Daddy and Kellie nodded in agreement. They were all on the same page. They knew what they were going to say.

But one problem still lingered: How?

They couldn't make a PA. But the plane was too big for them to just stand in the middle and yell. If they went row by row, the confusion and misinformation that would spread by that kind of disorganized communication would stoke a sense of panic. If they had any hope of a unified passenger response to the situation, it would only come as a result of an articulate, streamlined message. But Jo had no idea how they could accomplish that.

Kellie made a strange squeaking noise with a little gasp. When she didn't say anything else, Big Daddy snapped his fingers in front of her face. "Grasshopper. Do you have something to say?"

Kellie studied the floor. Looking up to Daddy, her face opened into a sort of bewildered and childlike surprise. She smiled broadly. "Actually, yes. Guys, I know exactly how we can tell them."

CHAPTER TWELVE

THE NOISE IN THEO'S HEAD WAS A HIGH-PITCHED TRUMPETING SOUND, rolling up and down the scale. A full-body ache intensified as the sound grew louder. A horn blared. Behind his eyes was a throbbing so intense that the feeling became a color.

Confused by a wet, earthy smell, he realized he was facedown on the ground. Cool blades of grass tickled his lips when he opened his mouth. Breathing was almost impossible. He let his mouth gape open and hoped that would be enough.

Why was he in so much pain and where was he? And wherever he was, how did he get there? He had so many questions but none of them seemed to matter. Wasn't it enough to just lie still? Dissolving into a cloud of pain until the questions disappeared—yes—that seemed like what he should do.

Theo.

He heard a person say that word and wondered at the sound. *Theo.* What did that mean? He heard the person repeat it, closer this time. It reminded him of something. He felt like he should know the answer to this question.

He opened his eyes but quickly closed them. The light that flooded in felt like it would split him from the inside out.

Lying there, he examined what was in the darkness of his closed eyes, the hologram-like outline of what he saw in that brief moment when he'd let the outside world in. People running toward him. A fire truck with its hose extended. A swing, dangling from a burning tree.

The noise was a siren. The fire truck was here for the house. The explosion. The politician. The family. Aunt Jo. It all rushed in at once.

His pain disappeared like it was never even there.

"Don't move," one of the SWAT agents said to him. Theo rolled to his side anyway. Pushing himself up would be impossible, though. He couldn't move his arm.

"You're beat up, man. Let the medics look at you. Jesus," the agent muttered at the sight of his left arm, which hung at an awkward angle, unquestionably dislocated.

"I'm fine. What happened? The agents, are they—"

"Liu had them hold after you went in," the agent said. "They're okay."

"And the guy. Did he get out?"

The agent's slow head shake told him everything he needed to know.

Theo buried his head in the hand of his good arm. He'd never lost anyone. Not a suspect, an innocent bystander, a fellow agent—no one. The politician alone was devastating enough. What if Liu hadn't ordered the other agents to stand down? What if they had advanced to back him up, and then this had happened? It was the first time the job had taken a tragic turn, and it easily could have been worse.

Theo sat stricken. In training they warned agents about this sort of reaction, teaching them instead how to detach, compartmentalize, not be emotionally connected to the mission. As if there was a switch to simply turn off the human part of a person.

"We got here as fast as we could," the other agent said. "And you did more than any of us to get to him and the family. This isn't on you. Okay? Theo? Theo."

Theo looked up and nodded. Not in agreement, but just so they could move on. "Help me up."

Sitting on the end of the ambulance, Theo heard the paramedic drone on but he wasn't listening. He watched the firefighters try to put out the blaze ravaging the Hoffmans' house, the home where they ate family dinners and watched movies. Where the baby took her naps.

"This is going to hurt really badly. Are you sure you don't want drugs?"

Theo nodded.

Trick-or-treaters would get candy from their front door. At Christmas no doubt Bill would put up lights.

"Here we go, on the count of three. One, two—" Theo's jaw clenched with the pain, but he didn't make a sound as the medic relocated his arm back into his shoulder socket. He opened his eyes and watched the house burn.

It wasn't a house. It was a tomb. They were dead. Carrie. Scott. Elise. An innocent man who was simply at the wrong place at the wrong time. All dead.

He was supposed to save them. He failed.

Liu approached the ambulance and Theo swore he saw concern flash across her face, gone as quickly as it came.

"You're lucky to be alive," she said, looking him up and down. She turned to the medic and asked, "He'll be fine?"

The medic nodded. "Probably has a concussion and he'll want X-rays on the arm. Other than that, superficial injuries."

"Great. Could you give us a minute?" she asked the medic. He nodded and scurried away.

"You were right," Liu said, her voice cold and flat. "But you put all of us—and the mission—at risk."

Theo kept eye contact, but didn't respond.

"Go home."

Theo shot to his feet. "No. I know I didn't—"

"Not a chance," Liu spat at him, taking a step forward so he had to sit back down. "You were on thin ice to begin with. You're way too close to this to keep going. You're emotionally compromised and that makes you reckless. It makes you dangerous. Go to the hospital and then go home. You're done."

Theo didn't know if she meant the case or his career. Either way, he didn't say a thing.

An agent approached and Liu shot the man an annoyed look. He held up his phone. Liu leaned forward.

"Jesus fucking Christ," she said, seizing the phone from his hand for a closer look. "How much damage?"

"It's viral. All the news stations have it," the agent replied.

"Does it mention the family?"

Apparently, there was a lot of discussion on social media regarding FAA regulations, and a lot of speculation as to the real reason the masks were out. But there was no mention of Washington, DC, the Hoffman family, or a poison gas attack on the cabin.

Liu turned the phone toward Theo. He squinted in the bright light, his concussed head still fuzzy. It was a picture of that pseudo-celebrity Rick Ryan wearing an airplane oxygen mask.

"The fuck is your aunt up to?" Liu said.

"Well, I'd ask her, but I'm off the case."

Liu's eyes narrowed to slits. "You're going to play it like that, huh?"

Theo stared at her without blinking. Leveraging access to his aunt so he could stay in the game was a risky career quid pro quo. But Theo knew he was probably toast at the bureau anyway and at that moment he couldn't have cared less. The only thing that mattered was helping Aunt Jo.

The two stared each other down. Slowly, Liu leaned over until her face was an inch from his. "If you step one foot out of line, if you disobey a single order," she said, her voice a whisper, "your badge is mine at the end of this. I promise you, Theo. You will never work in law enforcement again." Tilting her head slowly, she said, "Is that understood?"

He tipped his head. "Yes, ma'am."

The director rubbed her eyes and began to pace. Several agents arrived and Theo held up a finger to keep them from coming closer. Liu ignored them anyway, turning toward the burning house with an exhale, resting her interlaced fingers across the top of her head.

"We need to find out if the captain knows his family is dead," Liu said, finally. "That changes everything."

Turning quickly, she addressed the agents directly.

"Is the media here?"

"Yes, ma'am," one of the agents said. "Nobody's spoken to them yet."

"Good. Official line is this: investigation's ongoing, but the explosion is due to a gas leak." The agents nodded. "Has Coastal Airways released a statement on the mask photo? Have they acknowledged any issue with the flight?"

"No."

The FBI had informed the airline, the FAA, and Air Traffic Control of the situation—but requested they wait to close the airspace, ground planes, and shut down airports. A panicked public response to this kind of threat would be colossal, and if the FBI secured the Hoffman family, it could all be avoided. All the agencies—including officials on the ground in Washington—were ready to enact evacuation and defense protocols at a moment's notice, but they agreed the most prudent option was to give the LA FBI time to find the family.

"And yet," Liu said, "we didn't secure the family. So now we have a dead family and a pilot under duress whose mental state we can only guess at. Plus a dead civilian who had nothing to do with this. Have we ID'd him and contacted his family?"

An agent strode off, saying he'd get on it. Liu sighed, and ran a hand down her face.

"Theo, get in touch with your aunt. I want to know what's happening up there. I need to know if the pilot knows about his family. And I need to know what his intentions are at this point."

Theo nodded, taking out his phone.

"I want Bravo, Charlie, and comms out of here," she continued. "Our presence looks fishy and I want to avoid questions if we can. Assemble somewhere not far, we may need to move. But I want us out of camera shot."

She paused, looking at the house.

"Now that the family's dead, we don't know what we're looking at. It's probably more of a case for the FAA, Homeland Security, ATC, and East Coast FBI. But we have a lot of pieces to pick up and we don't know anything for sure."

Liu took out her phone and Theo watched her out of the corner of his eye. There was a hesitation to the way she punched the buttons. He knew she was about to make the call back east. The call to let them know she had failed. The family was dead and the threat was not pacified. He knew that, after the call, massive evacuations would begin at the most important and symbolic institutions in the country. Those in power would be sheltered and innocent civilians would be forced to flee. Pandemonium and terror would run rampant in the nation's capital, and *she* was the one who had to make the call.

Theo now understood why she seemed so angry in her office. However this situation went down, it went down on her.

The fire captain approached the group and Liu stopped punching buttons. She pocketed her phone and her shoulders seemed to relax a little.

The fireman took off his hat, wiping his brow with the back of his arm. Sweat dripped off his face onto his fire suit.

"The fire should be out within the hour."

Liu thanked him. "When will it be safe for us to go in for recovery?"

He cocked his head. "Recovery?"

"The bodies. When can we recover the bodies for identification."

His eyes narrowed, confused. "The man on the front porch was the only victim. There were no other human remains, ma'am. The house was empty."

CHAPTER THIRTEEN

THE EASTERN HORIZON GLOWED A DEEP SHADE OF SAPPHIRE, THE RICH blue fading as the sun dragged itself deeper beneath the world behind the plane. The view from the cockpit was like looking over the calm surface of a lake; the stars, a reflection of the city lights below.

Feeling detached from everything else in the world, Bill listened to the sound of dead air in his headphones. Nothing.

Ben peered around the cockpit with a puzzled look. "What's that clicking?"

Bill stopped to listen. The men stared at each other in the silence.

"Oh, sorry," Bill said, holding up his pen. He clicked it a few times. "Nervous tic. Drives my wife nuts."

Ben chuckled and turned back to his tablet.

Bill looked at his computer, then his phone. He'd lost count of how many times he'd done that. Still no word from his family. Just then, his phone lit up with a text.

Gary Robinson iMessage.

Bill's shoulders released with his exhale. He couldn't care less what his neighbor wanted. He ignored it.

Checking his watch, Bill played the game.

It was a game Carrie came up with when they'd first started dating, back when she was still living in Chicago. She told him the world was sublime when they were together. But whenever he'd leave to fly a trip, she was miserable. She'd find herself thinking of how many time zones separated them, and that made it feel like Bill was even farther away. So she made up this game where she would think of where he was or what he was doing as opposed to just what time it was there. The clock would say it was eight p.m., but instead she would think, *Dinnertime. He's probably somewhere over the Rockies. It's a full moon tonight, and I bet the snow on the mountains is absolutely glowing.* And somehow, Bill wouldn't feel as far away.

Bill thought it was silly. He was as firmly left-brained as she was right, so the soft reimagining of the way things were just didn't compute. Loneliness can bend a man in unexpected ways, though, and late one night, alone in Honolulu, Bill couldn't sleep. Carrie was four hours away. It was seven in the morning her time. He envisioned her stretching in bed, wearing that old, oversized IWU baseball T-shirt she slept in. He knew she would get up and make coffee right away, NPR playing in the background. She would choose the pink mug with the words "Ooh la la!" written in cursive under the Eiffel Tower. It was her favorite. Just cream, no sugar.

Rolling over, he'd tucked a pillow under his arm and drifted off to sleep.

He'd played the game ever since.

He looked at his watch. Five thirty-seven in LA. At this time, Carrie would be . . .

It was like staring at a blank piece of paper. He couldn't fathom what Carrie was doing and every attempt to imagine it led him back to the image of her screaming in agony as a man tortured her in their own home. He closed his eyes, searching in the dark for a world where this didn't happen. A world where he turned down the trip, where he chose to be a father and a husband over a pilot. A world where his family was simply going on with their day.

A lump formed in his throat as he remembered.

Five thirty-seven in Los Angeles. They should have been at Scott's baseball game.

His phone glowed. Pat Burkett iMessage. Bill frowned. Another neighbor? Why were—

He rushed to open the messages.

> Hey buddy are u flying? Were u home? Let me know if I can help

> Hi Bill, Pat here. I saw you drive off this morning, I think you're flying? Do you know where Carrie and the kids are? Are they ok? Oh my god this is just insane. Please check in. Steve and I are here for anything you guys need. Please let us know how we can help.

Help with what? What were they talking about? Hot panic seared through his veins. His thumbs hovered over the tiny keyboard, the cursor blinking in wait. He had to be careful.

> Hey Gary. I'm flying. What's up?

Gary would give him facts. Pat would give him gossip. Three dots on the other side of Gary's text popped up. That was fast.

Wow. Ok. This is hard man. Have u heard about ur house?

Bill couldn't feel his fingers as he asked the neighbor what he meant by that.

It exploded. They're saying gas leak. Where are Carrie and the kids?

Bill stared at the message so long without moving that his phone went dark. It slipped out of his fingers, falling into his lap. He didn't move.

Carrie. Scott. Elise. His whole world. Gone. He envisioned their house from the inside. The kitchen table, where they read the paper while Scott crunched Rice Krispies. The nursery, where he rocked Elise back to sleep. The living room, where they decorated the Christmas tree. Their bedroom, where Carrie's body tucked into his at night. He tried to place that world on fire, blown to bits. He tried to fade his family out, to make them disappear. His mind wouldn't let him. There was just no way. It couldn't be.

Carrie, wearing the suicide vest. Gagged. Holding Elise. Next to Scott.

A wave of nausea washed over Bill as he realized that was the final image he would ever see of his family. A lifetime of love and joy, and he knew he would fixate on that final shot for the rest of his life. This was his fault. Bill had failed as a husband, as a father, as a protector.

He was going to be sick. Bill was grasping for the trash bag when a picture of his wife popped up on his computer with the words "Accept FaceTime call from Carrie Cell." Bill stared in disbelief before clicking on the green button.

His eyes darted back and forth across the screen,

willing the call to connect. *Please let them be alive. Please, God. Show me my family.* His face slid out of the way as the call went through. In the center of the screen appeared his family. All three. Alive. He pinched his leg as hard as he could to keep from weeping.

Carrie and Scott were still bound, but no longer gagged. Sam was by their side, holding the detonator. Both he and Carrie were still covered in explosives. Carrie was holding Elise, so he couldn't make out the condition of her arm from the boiling water, but she appeared to be all right.

They were alive. Bill felt dazed with relief. He forced himself to focus.

Where were they? It was incredibly dark; besides a soft light off-screen to their left, the glow from the phone reflecting off their faces was the only light in the space. It was also small. They sat close together and by their posture, Bill thought they might be on the floor, not in chairs.

"Tsk, tsk, tsk," came Sam's voice through the earbud in Bill's left ear. The voice sounded closer than it was, the way a voice was amplified when it was in an enclosed space like a car. "You shouldn't have done that, Bill."

Bill furiously typed out a response. Done what? Did you get the video? I did exactly what you asked.

Sam received the email with a chuckle. "Oh, no. I got the video. No," he said. "I said you weren't allowed to tell the flight attendants."

Bill's stomach dropped, but he tried to keep a poker face while deciphering that statement. How did he know he'd told the crew? Did that mean he knew about Jo's nephew and the FBI? Was that why they left the house? Why he blew it up?

Sam's voice was confident. "I knew something was off after you sent the video. Something just didn't feel right. And sure enough . . ."

Sam swiped around on his own phone for a moment before holding it up to the camera. Bill squinted to see what was on the screen. It appeared to be a picture of a passenger in a Coastal Airways first-class seat, the cream-colored leather and pink mood lighting a contrast to the panicky yellow cup of the oxygen mask covering his face.

Bill closed his eyes, piecing it together. They released the masks with the MRTs. Brilliant. But none of them, clearly, took into account the passengers' use of the internet.

With a sinking feeling it dawned on him that, actually, they might have—but they couldn't cut the internet because Bill needed to talk to his family. Yet one more way that he was destroying anyone and everything around him.

"I assumed you'd be that arrogant, though," Sam said. "That's why the family and I proactively took a little road trip."

Road trip.

Okay, so they were in a vehicle. Bill tried to remember if he had seen a cable van parked outside their house when he left for the airport that morning, but he had no recollection. Or maybe they were in Carrie's car, the massive SUV they bought last year after finding out they had a baby on the way. The back two rows folded down flat—they could easily be in the back of that.

"I mean," Sam continued, "I don't know who else knows now besides your flight attendants. But whoever you sent to your house, I hope you didn't like them too much. You know what? Here—hold on."

The screen jiggled as he handed Carrie her phone to hold, his free hand punching buttons on his own. Carrie looked down at his screen, watching whatever he was looking up. A voice started speaking, and Carrie gasped.

". . . I'm here in front of the home, which, as you can see, has been completely destroyed in the explosion. Authorities are saying the cause was a gas leak and they have not told us if anyone was inside at the time of the blast. Luckily, only one home seems to have been . . ."

Sam held the video up for him to see. Bill fought the urge to cover his mouth. The reporter stood on their street, yellow caution tape stretched out behind her. Beyond it was their home. What was left of it.

Bill stared at the wreckage and grew cold with a newfound realization.

There was no chance this man was bluffing. He knew exactly what he was doing, and there was no doubt in Bill's mind that he *would* kill his family if Bill did not comply.

Carrie began to cry. Not loudly, but not quietly either.

"Really?" Sam said to her. "You've been so strong. Surprisingly strong. You're going to fall apart now because of a house and maybe a few people?" He shook his head. "How are you going to live with yourself after a whole plane full of people die so you and your kids can live?"

Tears rolled down Carrie's face as she looked up at the ceiling.

Sam laughed. "That's assuming Bill chooses you guys over the plane." He shrugged. "Maybe I shouldn't assume. Let's check in. Have you made your choice, captain?"

Bill typed angrily, watching the man receive and read the email with an eye roll.

"I will not crash this plane, you will not kill my family, blah, blah, blah," Sam said. "What is it with American men? Why do you guys always see yourselves as the hero? Why do you always want to do things the hard way?" He sighed. "Fine. Have it your way."

Sam started typing on his phone, the detonator hugged between his fingers and the device. Carrie looked up at Bill. She looked as terrified as he felt.

"Bill," he said, still working on his phone. "I told you that you *would* make a choice. I told you that there were things in place on board that would ensure it. I also told you that you weren't allowed to tell anyone. Now, I assumed that threat would be enough—but I also know you're a privileged, arrogant prick who thinks he can get away with whatever he wants. Turns out I was right. So, I'll level with you. I can't kill your family right now. I need them. I'll leave that final choice up to you. But you *did* break the rules, and guess what? Actions have consequences. You sent authorities to your house, so I blew it up. You told your flight attendants"—he looked up from his phone, his fingers paused, and stared into the camera—"well, we'll get to that."

Goosebumps spread up Bill's arms and wrapped around the back of his neck with an icy prickle.

Sam resumed his typing. Seemingly finished, he laid the phone down with a smug smile. "Your refusal to cooperate has forced my hand. It's time for Plan B."

Bill could feel his heartbeat in his throat. He strained to listen to the sounds coming from the cabin, waiting for muffled screams. An explosion. Panic and chaos. Something. Anything.

But all he heard was the hum of the engines.

And then, there it was.

So loud he almost jumped.

The unmistakable cock of a single-action hammer.

Bill turned slowly toward his copilot.

"Sorry, boss," Ben said, extending the barrel of the gun.

CHAPTER FOURTEEN

THEO AND THE OTHER AGENTS STOOD ACROSS FROM THE HOFFMAN home, which was disintegrating into little more than a smoldering pile of rubble. Lone structural beams rose up from the foundation here and there. Embers glowed inside withering timbers. In the haze of the late-fall golden hour, the house took on an odd quality of aliveness. Like a felled beast, her wounded form exhaled its final breaths: black smoke rising and dissolving into the atmosphere.

A heavy crack sounded from somewhere in the rubble. Everyone turned to see the house shift, a charred piece of a wall crumbling into the foundation. Liu never moved.

"What about cars?" she asked the fire captain.

"Garage was empty."

Liu chewed on the inside of her cheek. "Two-car family. One brought Bill to work. The other . . ." She cracked her knuckles. "Check the database and put out a citywide alert on their cars, priority on whatever seems like it would be the family car. A minivan or an SUV."

The agent standing next to Theo nodded and walked away, punching buttons on a device.

"Did you find any cable equipment?" Liu asked, turning back to the fireman. "Or anything that seemed out of place in a family home?"

The fire captain looked at the house and back. "Ma'am, that fire was completely catastrophic. I don't know what to tell you. That house is a dead end."

Liu nodded her thanks as he walked off.

"Ma'am?" came a voice through Theo's earpiece. "We've heard back from CalCom. There was no record of a service visit for the Hoffmans today. They also don't have any male employees with a name that starts with the letter S. And all company service vehicles are accounted for."

Watching Liu's jaw clench, Theo wondered if the rest of the agents also felt the impulse to take a step back from her.

"Tell me you got something," she said to the two agents walking up.

"Nothing," one of them said. "Two neighbors have video surveillance, but none of the camera angles cover the Hoffmans' property."

"So," she said, "we don't have a name, location, or description of our suspect."

No one challenged her.

"If the captain knows this guy blew up his house—and let's assume he does—he's got to be getting scared. This guy isn't a hack. I mean . . ." She gestured toward the house. Turning back to the team, she said, "I want to know more about the captain. Who is he, and why should we trust him. Our priority is the family. But we got a whole plane full of people to think about as well, not to mention Washington, DC."

Liu glanced down the street to where the media had assembled. Looking around the group of agents in full SWAT gear, her gaze landed on Theo. With a sinking feeling, he knew where this was headed.

"You," she said to him with a nod at the reporters. "Deal with them."

Five media vans lined the street on the other side of the yellow caution tape that surrounded the perimeter. The satellite dishes on top of the vans all angled the same way, the side doors opened to expose similar control panels.

This wasn't Theo's first time acting as spokesperson for an investigation—but it was his first time lying about one.

"Gas leak?" one of the reporters said, clearly skeptical. "Then why haven't you evacuated the rest of the neighborhood?"

"OG&E is assuring us it was an isolated event," Theo said, trying not to squint. The lights from the camera were a lot to handle with a concussion.

Another reporter didn't wait to be called on. "But the FBI was already on scene when the explosion happened. Why?"

"We were responding to a report that a cable worker might have cut a gas line. We were here in an abundance of caution."

"But SWAT? And—" The reporter pointed at Theo's injured arm, tucked against his body in a sling.

"I'm feeling pretty lucky," Theo said, glancing over his shoulder at the house.

"Was anyone else hurt? Was anyone home at the time of the explosion?"

Theo immediately flashed to the politician.

"The investigation is ongoing, and I'm not at liberty to comment on that," he said, trying hard to keep emotion out of his voice. He spoke quickly before anyone could lob another question. "Ladies and gentlemen, thank you very much. I'm sorry we don't have more information at this time. When I get something new, you'll know." Turning, he ducked under the yellow tape.

"Agent Baldwin?"

One of the reporters stood off to the side. The others were heading back to the vans. Theo walked over casually, trying not to attract attention. He recognized her from CNB broadcasts. Vanessa Perez. She'd always struck him as a professional who told the news with integrity, not someone who just wanted her face on TV.

"Gas leak?" she said.

Theo didn't say a thing and neither did his expression.

"Gas leak," she repeated, nodding. "Absolutely. But."

She extended her hand, a business card tucked between the index and middle finger. "Just in case that changes."

Remaining unreadable, Theo pocketed the card without a word and walked away.

"Liu wants you," Agent Rousseau said as Theo approached.

"Maybe I'll get fired twice today," he said, looking around for his boss. Seeing her alone and on a phone call down the street, he headed that way, checking his phone as he went. Thank god the fire captain had told them the house was empty before Liu called Washington to evacuate and Theo could send a text to Aunt

Jo telling her the family was dead. Misinformation like that could have been disastrous. His phone showed nothing new from his aunt and he opened the message thread to make sure all of his texts said "Delivered." He had no choice but to wait. She was probably busy preparing for the gas attack, he realized with a chill.

The situation he was living through was surreal enough. But at that exact moment, his aunt was facing a trauma of another magnitude. Jo had been flying forever, and from the stories she'd told over the years, he knew all the crazy stuff she'd seen. But this? Never had her stories come anywhere close to this.

When Theo was six, his mother put him and his two little sisters in the car one night and drove away from their father and the only home he'd ever known. He didn't understand what was going on, but something told him they would never be coming back. He still hadn't gone back to Texas, to this day. That night his mom drove all the way to California, where her only sister lived—Aunt Jo. She was pregnant with Wade at the time; Devon would be born two years later. By then, Theo and his family were settled into the house four doors down from Aunt Jo's, his new world consisting of two back doors that were never locked, constantly opening and closing. He was the eldest of the five cousins and since he didn't have a father figure, he took it upon himself to fill the role. Even Uncle Mike, Aunt Jo's husband, seemed to regard him as a peer, not a child.

Every night, the kitchen in one house or the other would fill with the sounds of family; a hot sizzle coming from the stove, a soda being cracked open after a mom said it was okay, a tale being told of what had happened that day at school or at work. The best stories were always Jo's. She was a natural raconteur, always knew how to paint a scene just so. Her tales would begin like they were no big deal and not two minutes later, forks full of spaghetti would hover over plates, forgotten.

Theo couldn't wait to hear how he and Jo would recount this day to their family. This one would be replayed for the rest of their lives. They would get it to the point where it would become a bit, both of them sharing their viewpoint as the saga unspooled. Legendary.

He nodded to himself, confirming that happy future.

"Theo!"

An agent raced up to him with the news that the LAPD had spotted the Hoffmans' SUV at a vacant strip mall not far away.

Theo pumped the fist of his good arm. "I'll grab Liu."

She had her back to Theo, unaware of his presence. He wasn't going to wait for her to finish the call to tell her the good news. This was too important—she'd want to be interrupted. Coming closer, Theo could overhear her conversation.

"Yes, sir," she said, pausing. "I understand and agree. But this is Washington, DC. This is potentially the White House. We're talking about the safety of the president of the United States. I think we need to start thinking very seriously along the lines of secondary protocol."

Theo stopped in his tracks.

In a situation like this, there was only one contingency plan, one line of secondary protocol.

If the FBI didn't save the family, they were going to shoot down the plane.

CHAPTER FIFTEEN

BEN'S FEET KICKED UP BROWN DUST THAT CLUNG TO THE THICK, midsummer air. He wiped the sweat off his brow with the sleeve of his shirt, squinting against the setting sun as he ran as fast as he could. His chores had taken longer than he expected—he didn't even have time to eat dinner—and his stomach rumbled as he hurried, but he didn't care. He was late. He just hoped he wasn't too late.

Nearly every storefront he passed was closed early for the day, the homes above them dark as well. No cars were out, so he ran in the middle of the road. No people were out either. Almost everyone in their northeastern Syrian village was already at the cafe. Ben picked up his pace.

Rounding the corner, he saw the cafe's lights spilling out into the twilight along with the patrons who couldn't find a chair inside. The shop was packed wall to wall and excited chatter rang through the crowd. The scene was thick with anticipation, as it always was on the rare occasions when something different happened in a place this small.

Ben pushed his way into the cafe, plunging through the crowd, a smack on the back of the head from Auntie

Sarya not even slowing him. A single oscillating fan stood off to the side, slowly sweeping over the packed room and back again—and at the front of the room, Sam blocked the view of the TV with his outstretched arms, his fingers spread wide. Arguing with all the might a nine-year-old boy could muster, he pleaded with the village barber to wait until Ben got there before they started the movie. Someone threw a cashew, hitting Sam in the face. Everyone laughed, including Sam, who picked it up, ready to lob it back into the crowd when he spotted Ben. Jumping up with a hoot, he declared that they could now start. More nuts sailed his way in return.

The crowd simmered to a hush as the barber slid the VHS tape into the player. Sam and Ben took their seats cross-legged on the floor with the rest of the kids. They didn't say a word, just sat with their jaws hanging open while Ben tried to catch his breath.

Someone turned off the lights and the glow from the TV became the only illumination in nearly the whole village. Words in English no one could understand filled the screen, while odd percussive '80s music, foreign to their ears, played in the background. Then, two words appeared:

TOP GUN.

Everyone in the room cheered.

For the next two hours, no one moved. They were transfixed by the strange world they saw on the TV. Palm trees and sun. Motorcycles and beautiful blonde women. Men in uniform. Aviator sunglasses and volleyball.

Airplanes.

When the movie ended, everyone dispersed, chatter and excitement carrying them off. Off to the restaurant, off to their homes, off to begin what they would be doing for a long time: discussing.

Sam and Ben stayed frozen in place, eyes glued to the

*TV while everyone around them moved. It wasn't until the
last credit rolled off the screen that they turned to each other.*

*They shared a look that neither of them understood.
Hours later when the sun was rising and the whole plan
was laid in front of them, they would get it. By morning,
they would have it all figured out.*

*They would start saving their money. They would
learn English. They would get to America. And they would
become pilots. They had no idea how. But that didn't matter. They would figure it out. They knew, more than they
had ever known anything, that this was their destiny. To
go to America. To be comfortable, unbothered, and happy.
To play on California beaches and date beautiful women.
To fly airplanes.*

*But as the cafe owner shooed them out, they didn't know
any of that, yet.*

They just knew that everything had changed.

"Coastal four-one-six, slow to mach seven-five for
metering."

Somewhere, in some en route control center miles
beneath Flight 416, an air traffic controller watched a
small dot track forward on the radar in front of him.
His tone felt casual, like it was just another direction on
a day like any other.

Ben switched the gun to his left hand, reaching for
his mic with the other.

"Roger wilco. Slow to mach seven-five, Coastal four-
one-six," he said, his voice as calm and even as the controller's. "I gotta hand it to ATC," he said to Bill. "They
deserve Oscars for the show they're putting on. I mean,
if you sent the FBI to your house, the FAA has to know
what's up." He laughed and told Bill to unplug the lap-

top's headphones and take the privacy screen off after he finished adjusting the plane's speed.

Bill had heard the controller, but it was only sound. Ben spoke too, but his words held no meaning either. It was just noise that bounced around the cockpit. Bill didn't know anything anymore. He only knew the barrel of that gun. He didn't move.

Rolling his eyes, Ben reached forward. He twisted a knob counterclockwise and the yellow numbers on the dash began to descend. When they reached the ATC directive, he pulled the controller up and the plane's computer set the new speed. "Talk to ATC. Fly the plane. Crash the plane. Do I have to do everything today? This is your leg to fly, you know."

Bill continued to stare at the gun. His mind flashed to a few hours earlier when he passed—no, breezed—through crew security at the airport. Ben would have met the same screener not long after. But the first officer's abuse of the system was the least of Bill's problems at the moment.

Bill looked to his laptop. There was a strange new listlessness to Carrie's expression. She seemed to be staring at something that wasn't there, her focus scattered and undefined. Sighing as though that was that, she locked her eyes on Bill. The hair on the back of his neck stood on edge.

Something in her had changed.

Unclipping the privacy screen, Bill tossed it and the headphones on top of his messenger bag. Elise's whimpering filled the cockpit.

"How do you two know each other?" Carrie asked Sam.

The tone of her voice was too familiar and Bill was suddenly wildly uncomfortable with not knowing what had happened when he'd lost contact with them. He felt a whole new level of alpha male protection, one rooted in envy and possession. It was animal, not rational, but it snapped Bill back into focus.

He watched Carrie and Scott glance up at something out in front of them before dropping their gazes a few moments later.

"Bendo is my brother," Sam said. "Well, good as." Pointing at the camera, he said something in a language neither Carrie nor Bill understood. Ben laughed in response and replied in the same foreign tongue. The warmth of their reunion felt unfair, like ticker tape falling on the losing team.

"Well, Ben is my brother too," Bill said, his voice shaking. He stared at the wings on the first officer's shirt before pointing back at the cockpit door. "They boarded this plane in good faith. They put their lives in our hands. Our duty is to respect that responsibility."

Sam began to talk but Ben stopped him with his hand.

"Why?" Bill continued, his voice rising. "Why not just shoot me and crash the plane? If that's what you wanted, you didn't have to involve my family."

"This isn't what we wanted," Ben said.

"Then what do you want?" Bill pleaded. "I don't understand what you want. I don't understand why you're doing this."

Ben looked out the window in front of him, considering the question, the hand holding the gun drooping slightly.

"Where we come from, our people have a saying. 'No friend but the mountains.' It means our fate is one of betrayal and abandonment. That we only have each other. No one else cares. We can only count on ourselves."

Ben looked to Sam, his eyes misting above a forlorn smile.

"We tried not to believe that," the first officer continued. "We wanted so badly to believe it could be different, it *would* be different. We bought into hope. Into the American Dream. Freedom, hope, belonging—that's all we wanted. For ourselves and for our families. And tell me—why is that wrong? To want that kind of life? Why shouldn't our lives have that kind of dignity? Why don't *we* deserve it? We played by your rules, we did what you wanted, we were everything you asked us to be. And you betrayed us! You ask me how I could betray this profession—well, how could you betray millions of people who only want a decent life of their own?"

Bill tried to think of a good response, but came up empty. He didn't really grasp what Ben was talking about. Finally he said, "What does any of that have to do with my family or the passengers on this plane?"

Ben spread his arms wide and laughed.

"Keep going. Keep reacting exactly as we knew you would. Because that's exactly it! That's exactly why we're doing this! You people *never* think it has something to do with you. All around the world, shit happens. And you just carry on. Because it doesn't have to do with you. You never get involved unless you're forced to. So?" He motioned around the cockpit. "Here we are. You're finally being forced to face the truth."

"What truth?"

"The truth that people are only as good as the world lets them be. You're not inherently good and I'm not inherently bad. We're just working through the cards life dealt us. So putting you in this position, dealing you these cards—what does a good guy do now? It's not about the crash, Bill. It's about the choice. It's about good people seeing they're no different from bad people." He looked from Bill to Carrie. "You've just always had the luxury of choosing to be good."

Bill's face flushed. He didn't fully understand what Ben was talking about, but he recognized the anguish he saw burning in his copilot's eyes. It was the same hot rage that coursed through Bill's body every time he looked at his helpless, captive family.

"But what about people who have no choice?" Bill said. "The passengers on this plane, the people in Washington, DC. How do their innocent deaths prove your point?"

"What about the innocent deaths of my people?" Ben spat back. "Why are their lives of less worth, why are their deaths less tragic? No one cares when they die horrible deaths. It's time your people shared the same meaningless ending. I want America to mourn in the way we've had to mourn for our whole lives."

"An eye for an eye isn't justice," said Bill.

"Neither is inaction. Nothing will change if nothing changes."

"But nothing will change if you do this either. America won't bow to a vigilante terrorist."

"We never wanted you to bow! We just wanted to be seen!"

Ben panted in the silence that followed his outburst, the gun trembling in his hand. Bill faced forward in his chair. Ben turned his head away to look out the window. Sad attempts at a physical de-escalation in the cramped space.

Bill dropped his hands to his side, defeated. He didn't know what to do. Everything felt hopeless. He stared at his family, mentally removing them from this madness, trying to remember how simple their lives seemed as recently as last night.

Bill had grilled hamburgers. They had eaten with the TV on, volume low, watching the game. Scott spilled his milk at one point. Elise had cried and so Carrie ate her sweet potato fries standing up, bouncing her until she stopped. Bill remembered thinking he needed to take out the trash when he threw the milk-soaked paper towels in the bin. He had forgotten to do that before he left this morning.

A distant noise was beeping in his earpiece. Bill barely noticed it, lost in the blissful memory of normalcy. But the faint, irregular sounds eventually pulled Bill away from his reverie. All at once something clicked in his mind as he strained to listen, trying not to breathe.

But now there was only silence. His mind was playing tricks on him.

He looked over to Ben, who showed no sign of having heard anything unusual. If there *were* any sounds, they would come through the backup frequency, which was only audible in Bill's earpiece. Ben was in his own world anyway. He was inspecting the gun, his thumb running over the handle.

Suddenly, there it was. Bill's eyes widened. There *was* a noise.

It wasn't his imagination. Someone had heard him and they were talking back.

CHAPTER SIXTEEN

"ALL SET?" JO SAID.

Big Daddy tossed an almost-empty bag of cheap plastic Coastal Airways headphones on the forward galley countertop with a thwack.

"All set," he said.

"Every passenger?"

"Every single one."

"And you had them all turn on their TVs? And turn to the news?"

"Yes, Mom."

"Did it go okay? Were they receptive?"

Daddy stared at her, deadpan.

Reaching the galley, Kellie passed between them, tossing her nearly empty bag on top of his.

"Okay, these people do *not* like us," she said, her eyes wide. "Holy shit are they angry."

Daddy nodded in agreement. "He needs to finish whatever it is that he's doing—now—because we need to give these people some information."

The flight attendants looked across the galley to

Rick Ryan, who continued to swipe and tap on his phone.

Jo said, "As soon as he's finished—and thank you, Mr. Ryan, for assisting—we'll go. In the meantime, let's talk specials." She handed Daddy the manifest and Kellie looked over his shoulder. "Miraculously, we don't have too many. Two infants and one wheelchair. Thank *god* no unaccompanied minors. You do have a language in eighteen delta, though. Last name Gonzales, so I'm assuming Spanish? Do either of you speak Spanish?"

Kellie shook her head.

"Un poquito," Daddy said, poring over the list. "That'll be a fun briefing."

"Kellie, while Daddy's doing his briefs, break down your galley. We need it final-descent secure, now. There won't be time later."

She nodded.

"Gimme just a minute," Rick Ryan said. "I'm almost done."

The crew waited. They each had a thousand things to do to get the passengers ready for whatever was coming, but they couldn't do any of it yet. *Hurry up and wait.* Even in a crisis, the unofficial motto of aviation held true.

"Do you remember," Daddy broke the silence, "way back in the day, what they taught us to do if the plane was hijacked?"

Jo smiled. The memory seemed quaint. "Talk to them. Appeal to their emotions. Level with them. Give them what they want. Basically? Do whatever you gotta do to get the plane down safe."

Back then, the tactic was to gain the hijackers' empathy, so the company had instructed the flight attendants to keep pictures of their children or family on them at all times. Jo had the boys' baby pictures tucked in with her badge and she remembered Big Daddy kept a picture of his cat. He'd told her his plan was to distract the terrorists with his pussy.

"Then 9/11 happened," Daddy said, his voice trailing off. "And everything changed." He leaned back against Jo's jump seat. The cockpit was right there and he ran the backs of his fingers up the door. "We used to have something to work with, you know? The bad guys made sense, the world made sense. There were motives and demands. But now . . ." He shook his head.

"Cool, cool, cool," Rick Ryan said, ending the moment. "It's done. I'd say wait a couple minutes, then you're on."

Jo took out her phone and opened the message thread with her nephew.

Theo's pocket vibrated and he strained against the seat belt to fish out his phone. Opening the message, he felt his brow furrow.

"What?" Liu asked.

"She says: 'Watch the news.'"

Liu pulled up CNB's website on her tablet. Waiting for it to load, she leaned over the partition. "How far out are we?"

"Approximately six minutes, ma'am," the driver replied.

A sea of red covered the device. "What the . . ." Liu muttered to herself.

The network was in full breaking-news mode, massive fonts and capital letters demanding the world's attention. The news anchor's eyes darted up and down from his notes to the camera, the pace of what was occurring too fast for a teleprompter. Liu turned up the volume.

". . . information is coming in as we speak. So far, all we know for sure is that some form of hijacking or terrorist incident is currently unfolding on board a midair Coastal Airways flight from Los Angeles to New York. Celebrity personality Rick Ryan is one of the passengers on board, and he has alerted the media to some sort of upcoming announcement. We are standing by, waiting for that . . ."

A box graphic of a tweet appeared on-screen:

> **@RickRyanyaboi**
> FLIGHT 416 HAS BEEN HIJACKED.
> LIVE VIDEO FROM CREW COMING. PRAY FOR US!!!

Tagged to all the major news networks, the FBI, Homeland Security—even the White House—the tweet had already been shared twelve thousand times in less than three minutes.

". . . the plane is an Airbus A320, which can carry up to one hundred and fifty passengers, plus a crew component of three flight att—"

The news anchor pressed his earpiece.

"Okay, I'm being told we have live streaming video from the plane. Let's watch."

The studio disappeared, replaced by a stuttering feed from the interior of a plane. The screen was filled with the face of a middle-aged woman in a flight attendant's uniform.

Theo almost gasped. *Aunt Jo.*

"Ladies and gentlemen," she said, her voice choppy as the video buffered. "By now you're aware that we have a situation on our hands."

Liu looked up at Theo with complete sincerity.

"Is your aunt fucking insane?"

Jo stared into the little camera on the back of Kellie's phone. The young flight attendant stood across from her, focusing intensely on the screen, occasionally raising or lowering the device to keep Jo centered in the frame.

"I know the whole world is watching right now, but they're not who I'm speaking to," Jo said into the camera. "I'm talking to you—the passengers of Flight four-one-six. I know you're confused and angry. I would be too if I were you. But from where I stand, things looks a little different. Ladies and gentlemen, you need to know what's going on. You deserve to know what the crew knows."

The engines hummed. It was the only noise in the cabin. Every passenger on board wore either their own headphones, or the airline's complimentary pair passed out by the flight attendants. They all watched the news intently.

"I'm not gonna sugarcoat this," Jo continued. "Our captain's family has been kidnapped. His wife, their ten-year-old son, and ten-month-old daughter are being held hostage on the ground back in LA as we speak. The individual who took them has said he will kill them—unless the captain crashes the plane."

A woman in first class gasped loud enough to startle Kellie. Daddy stood with his arms crossed against his chest, watching the passengers, taking the cabin's pulse as Jo spoke. He was to monitor for any signs of an accomplice among them; anyone becoming fidgety or looking around suspiciously. Glancing at Jo, he gave her an encouraging nod.

"Now I've flown with Captain Hoffman coming up on twenty years," Jo continued. "I know that man. I *know* that man. There is not a chance, not a single possibility, that he would crash this plane. None. And that's all I'm going to say about that because there is nothing else to say.

"But before I go on, I wanna talk to *you*," Jo snarled, eyes narrowing, weight shifting. "You, you sick son of a bitch, wherever you are. You think you'll get away with this? You have no idea the forces that hunt you right now. They *will* find you, I guarantee you that. And I promise you something else too."

She adjusted her scarf.

"That family you've got? They will live. And this plane? Is *not* going to crash."

Kellie stood a little straighter. Daddy clenched his jaw, widening his stance.

"So let's talk about those masks now. Why did we drop them? So that we can protect ourselves. Yes, ladies and gentlemen. This maniac has involved *us* in his sick plan as well."

Jo could feel her heart rate spiking the way it does in the moment before a confession. When you're scared and want to run or back down, but know you can't.

"Before we land, he's going to make the captain release a gas into the cabin from the cockpit. What is the gas? Well, we don't know. But we're going to assume it's pretty bad, and we're going to *plan* on it being pretty bad.

"Look," she continued. "Whatever it is, we sure as hell don't want to breathe it. That's what the masks are for. The flight attendants will brief you and prepare you for what's going to happen. But here is what you need to know most of all, what you must remember from this very moment up until those wheels touch down in New York."

She stepped forward.

"We are going to get through this. We will work together. We will protect each other. And together—as passengers and flight attendants and pilots of this flight—we will show this monster that we cannot be bullied, blackmailed, or taken down."

Jo paused. She had no idea where any of those words had come from. She had set an intention, opened her mouth, and the words simply flowed out. Her mind raced. What had she missed? She wasn't even sure what she just said.

"When I was a little girl, Daddy used to say to me: 'Sit deep and put your spurs on, girl.' Ladies and gentlemen, we have one choice. That choice is to trust and to be united. It's an honor to be here with you, and a privilege to serve you. Sit deep and put your spurs on—here we go."

Kellie pressed the red button. With a soft ping, the video stopped recording.

Theo watched Liu lay the tablet in her lap. Outside the van's window, the scenery passed by in a blur.

"Dehumanize the bad guy," she said. "Paint the captain as victim *and* hero. Unite the mob against a common enemy, which distracts them from their potential demise. Rally their warrior spirit into action." Liu turned to Theo. "This urge you have to disregard authority and piss on protocol? It's a family trait?"

Theo inhaled through an upsurge of pride that made his cheeks tingle.

"Yes, ma'am," he said, unable to hide a small smile.

"She didn't— Wait, did she talk about DC?"

"No, ma'am," another agent said.

Liu shook her head.

Aunt Jo was a thousand miles away and she was able to get under Liu's skin too. Theo loved it.

"Ma'am? We're here," the driver said, pulling into a run-down strip mall. Vacant storefronts with faded outlines of former signage filled the plaza. Small planters with overgrown grass and dry trees dotted the parking lot. A maroon sedan with two flat tires and a windshield thick with dust sat abandoned.

The only other sign of life was at the far end of the lot. Under a burned-out streetlight, shrouded in darkness, a large silver SUV straddled two spots, conspicuous in its newness. In the shortness of a late-fall day, nighttime had already fallen—but the car's sunshield was up, blocking a view of the inside from Alpha unit's vantage.

"Park behind that," Liu said, and motioned toward a planter with a sizable tree.

The vehicle slowed to a stop, rocking back as it set in park.

"All right, you sicko," Liu said. "Let's try this again."

CHAPTER SEVENTEEN

CARRIE WATCHED A BEAD OF SWEAT SLIDE DOWN SAM'S CHEEK. IT clung to the bottom of his chin before dropping onto his sleeve, leaving a dark circle on the gray CalCom uniform.

It was hot in the cramped quarters. Carrie's T-shirt clung to her where Elise pressed against her. Scott's hair stuck to his forehead with a sheen of moisture.

Sam set the phone down and started to work at the button on his sleeve. Holding the detonator made the simple task awkward and Carrie could feel his frustration rising with the heat as his fingers slipped around the small plastic button without success.

Carrie reached for his hand. He pulled back. The phone camera, angled up at the ceiling, would show the cockpit nothing and for that moment it felt like it was just the two of them. Him: alarmed, defensive. Her: calm, offering. His eyes narrowed in skepticism but she didn't budge. She didn't smile or speak; she did nothing to try and prove this wasn't a trick. She simply laid out her hands.

Slowly, he extended his arm and she took it in her bound hands, working awkwardly herself, but managing better. The button popped free and the cuff loosened in relief.

She rolled the sleeve up his arm, folding the fabric and pulling it taut as she went. It felt as natural and automatic to her as wrapping up a dirty diaper or straightening a tie. The van was dark, but she thought she could make out a thin, vertical scar that ran up the inside of his forearm. He quickly rotated his arm away from her, all but confirming it.

"My father died when I was young too," she said. "Car crash. Drunk driver. He was the drunk." Pausing her fingers, she added, "He was always the drunk."

She returned to working with the fabric as if that was that. Which it was.

Among Carrie's girlfriends, she was the go-to for advice. Yes, she was perceptive and nurturing—but she also had this innate ability to dig under the surface and pinpoint what the *real* problem was, not just what they were upset about. They called it her "Spock mode." Carrie could examine a difficult situation dispassionately, like she had laid it out in front of her on a table under bright lights, surgically cutting away the emotion that clouded logic and reason. She didn't think much of it. It was just how her brain and heart communicated. But if Carrie had to guess at how she became this way, she'd assume her father's unreliable and beer-soaked presence in an otherwise safe and happy childhood would be the starting point.

"I thank God he hit a tree," Carrie said. "He was driving the wrong way. It was a miracle that he didn't hurt anyone else."

Sam cocked his head at the word *God*.

"Was your father religious?" he asked.

"No," Carrie said. "Our family wasn't religious at all. Christmas, Easter-type Christians. He stopped going to even those." She frowned and looked at Sam but her eyes went farther away. "But honestly, we never talked about it. God, I mean. I don't know what he thought."

"You should be helping me with this, you know," Carrie said.

Bill smiled without looking away from the TV as he surfed through channels.

"God's not my thing," he said. "Wouldn't even know where to start."

"You think I do?" Carrie said, cross-legged on the couch, flipping pages in the Bible that lay in her lap. Their wedding was in a week and the pastor had said they needed to choose at least two passages for the ceremony.

"Don't they have a standard set of verses they use for weddings?"

"Sure," Carrie said. "But he wants it to have meaning to us."

"Two people who never go to church," Bill said, watching a basketball replay. Indicating the Bible in her lap, he said, "Where'd you even find that?"

Carrie smiled. "In a box at the back of my closet. It's from when I was a kid. I never got an adult version. I like the dumbed-down language."

She turned to the index in the back to see if the passages were organized by subject. Finding a long list under the heading "Love," she chose one and flipped back to the Book of Ecclesiastes, turning the thin pages until a handwritten note stopped her. Her pulse raced as she stared at the deep indentations and block letters of her father's distinctive scrawl. Bill said something, but she ignored it. He poked her leg with the remote and she looked up. His smile dropped at the sight of her face. She told him what she'd found.

"Your dad?" Bill said, sitting up and muting the TV. "You never told me he was religious."

"He wasn't," Carrie said, staring at the book. "So why did he find my Bible and write in it? And when?"

Bill didn't have a reply. "How do you know it was him?" he said.

"I'm positive. His handwriting was unmistakable."

"Well, what did he write?"

Carrie frowned, trying to interpret, not understanding. Her father had circled Ecclesiastes 9:3—"One fate comes to all alike, and this is as wrong as anything that happens in this world"—and beside it, he'd written one word. Underlined. In all capital letters. <u>YES</u>. She turned the Bible so Bill could see.

Taking the book in his hands, Bill stared at the page for a long while before handing it back. He looked as confused as she felt.

"So . . . everyone dies. And that isn't fair?"

Carrie looked down at the ghost of her father.

"Yes."

Carrie unbuttoned Sam's other sleeve. "I don't have many regrets when it comes to my father. But I do regret never asking what he thought about God. I always assumed he never talked about it because he didn't care. But the older I get and the more I look at his life choices—I wonder if he actually didn't have quite a bit to say about it."

"How old were you when he died?"

"Nineteen. Freshman year of college. Last time I saw him was in my parents' kitchen. I'd come over for dinner and was about to leave. I already had my purse in hand and my mom and I were finishing up our conversation when he came into the kitchen to grab another beer and asked what we were talking about. I told him I was trying to pick a major. He shrugged and told me that, whatever I chose, just make sure I chose to live."

Sam furrowed his brows, confused.

"Exactly," said Carrie. "He was always giving that kind of fortune cookie nonsense. Drove me nuts. So when he said that, I rolled my eyes like I always did. But I'll never forget—and I'll never forget it because it's the last thing he ever said to me—he looked at me and seemed . . . offended? No, not offended. Hurt. He seemed hurt and he said, 'You don't think everyone actually lives, do you? Most people just exist and roam around. It's a choice, to actually live.'"

Carrie finished with his sleeve, her words falling flat in the silence. Her gaze landed on the detonator and an ancient wave of understanding washed through her body.

Sam picked up the phone, returning the two of them to the situation at hand. "I actually think I understand what your father meant."

Carrie stared into the dark. She nodded her head.

A noise came from outside.

Sam looked at Carrie, wide-eyed.

He put a finger to his mouth. Silence.

His thumb moved on top of the detonator's red button. A reminder of what would happen if she didn't obey.

CHAPTER EIGHTEEN

JO STOOD NEXT TO KELLIE ON THE OTHER SIDE OF THE GALLEY curtain, listening to the sounds in the cabin. Right after they stopped the video, all three had held their breath. Would there be screaming? Pandemonium? About a minute had passed and there hadn't been much of a reaction at all.

"So far, so good," Daddy said without taking his eyes off the cabin. "Nobody's released their own poison. No one's saying they're a bad guy too. No one's even pressed a call button. I'm surprised. I thought that may—"

He cut himself off and broke away from the galley.

Jo ripped the curtain open, following Big Daddy as he hustled up the aisle toward a man who was charging forward. The two men met just beyond the bulkhead.

"I want to know," the man said, loud enough that half the plane could hear, "when we're getting on the other side of that damn door."

Big Daddy raised an eyebrow at the finger pointed in his face. "What door?" he asked.

"That one." The man's chin jerked toward the cockpit.

"Ah," said Daddy. "Unfortunately that won't be happening, sir."

The man exhaled a harrumph, his cheeks flushing even hotter. His was the type of face that had a natural pink to it, but his barrel chest and paunchy beer gut made it clear that it wasn't the result of running a quick half mile. If Jo was being honest, he made her nervous. She knew men like him. Big on ego, small on tolerance.

"Sir," Daddy said, "that door has multiple locks, all of which are controlled from the inside. There's no key. And even if we were able to unlock it—which we can't—there's a manual override inside the cockpit."

The man blinked, as though the thought of unlocking the door had never occurred to him. Jo put her hand on Big Daddy's shoulder to let him know she had his back and to remind him to stay cool.

"Then we'll bust it down!" the man hollered, spittle flying out of his mouth.

Someone a few rows back grunted in agreement. A few heads nodded.

"That door," Jo said, her voice low and firm, "is bulletproof. Kevlar reinforced. Impossible to break down by design."

"Didn't stop them on September 11th."

"That door is *because* of September 11th," Jo said. "You think it's luck no one's breached a cockpit since then?"

The man didn't answer, merely shook his head, nostrils flared. The crowd was starting to turn with him, their fear finding comfort in his overconfidence.

"We've gotta get in there!" a female voice shouted from somewhere. Jo couldn't even tell who had said it.

"Okay," Jo said. "Let's say we could break the door

down. Which we can't. But let's just say we could. What are you going to do once you're in there?"

The man blinked again. This too he hadn't yet worked out.

"We'll take 'em down!"

"Who?" Big Daddy asked.

"The terrorists!"

A couple people cheered.

"The only people in that cockpit," Jo said calmly, "are the two pilots flying this plane. Who we very much need alive and well. The terrorist you want is on the ground back in LA. Breaking into the flight deck would accomplish absolutely nothing and only put us at greater risk."

No one replied.

"Honey, if the bad guys were up there I'd be with you in a heartbeat. But the only thing you'll find up there are the good guys," she stressed. Jo didn't dare let on that there might actually be an accomplice among them in the cabin.

A man sitting on the aisle spoke up. "But you said a gas attack was coming from them?"

"That's right," Jo said with a sigh. "Our pilots have a problem. One they need our help with. There *will* be a gas attack, because if there isn't, an innocent family will die."

Jo let the statement hang in the air for a moment.

"Authorities on the ground are looking for the family but the pilots need to buy them time. Bill, our captain, is trusting us to be ready. Ready to protect ourselves. Which is something we can do. *That* is the way we fight, *that* is the way we beat the terrorist. We work together. We trust each other. We survive."

She looked around at the passengers. They all seemed to be considering.

"We do need to fight. But we do that by being strong enough to *take* the hit, not give it."

No one responded, which she took as a good sign. The main aggressor didn't seem sure where to turn now, either in his argument or on the plane. So he stared at her, breathing heavily, but silent. She thought of her sons when they were little. They used to square off against her with the same look that was in his eyes. Jo had gotten the picture real fast: a power struggle never ended well. Instead, she learned how to finesse the boys' frustrations. Redirect their energy. She empowered them, filled them with importance and duty. Really, she just needed them to pick up their toys. But her tactics got it done.

Stepping in front of Big Daddy, she faced the man straight on.

"What's your name, sir?" Jo said.

"Dave."

"The crew will need help, Dave. Can we count on you?"

His chest puffed up.

"We need to reseat people," Jo continued before he could think about it too much, and frankly, before *she* could think about it too much. They had no idea who was with them or against them. She was recruiting assistance blind. "There are eight seats in first class. I want two empty and the other six filled with people willing to help me fight. There are two young men, already seated in first class, who I believe will want to help. And you, sir"—she smiled at Dave—"make three. So let's get three more, then we'll reseat the passengers in first class. The attack will come from the front, so we'll want—"

"Women and children in the back," Dave interrupted.

A woman in a nearby window seat laughed. "Jesus Christ," she said, "we're not on the *Titanic*." Standing, she placed her knee on the chair, arm resting on the seat in front of her. "Ma'am, my wife and I volunteer." From the middle seat, her wife nodded solemnly.

Dave scoffed. "Ladies, I think it would be better for the women—"

"Let me rephrase," the woman said. In a calm voice she went on to explain that she was a six-tour Marine Corps veteran turned LAFD firefighter, and her spouse was a paramedic with a black belt in jiu jitsu. Dave didn't have much to say after that.

"Excellent," Jo said quickly. "That makes five. We need one more."

The hum of the engines went from background noise to prominence. No one moved, no one said a word. It was grade-school tactics. If you stayed still enough, the teacher wouldn't call on you for the answer.

A metal click; a seat belt unbuckled. Focus shifted forward toward the noise. Three rows ahead, on the aisle seat, aircraft right, a man stood.

Eyes followed him up. And up.

"Are we allowed to say 'No thanks'?" Big Daddy said under his breath to Kellie.

The man was enormous. At least six-foot-eight. Probably more. He turned to face them and heads pulled back to take him in, uncertainty passing through the collective. Black hair buzzed close to the scalp. Dark eyes, shadowed in the dim lighting, peered out from a pale face that was more bones than anything. Jo immediately understood why Big Daddy had failed to put a finger on the man's essence. He had an intangible mysteriousness, a mercurial quality of shadow.

The crew shared a look.

"I will help," he said with a voice that scraped the lowest registers. The faint accent was foreign but unplaceable. The tone, void of emotion.

Jo forced a confident smile. "Thank you, sir. That makes six."

CHAPTER NINETEEN

THEO WATCHED BRAVO UNIT PULL INTO A PARKING SPOT AT THE twenty-four-hour burrito joint across the street from the strip mall. They were far enough away from the Hoffmans' vehicle, but had direct line of sight. Everyone waited for their assessment.

"Nothing," a voice finally reported through their earpieces. The lights in the vehicle were off and no one was visible. But the windows were tinted so dark, it was hard to be sure.

Liu chewed on a fingernail while Theo watched the only storefront in the plaza with lights on. A minute later, a plainclothes agent walked out the door. Her voice filled their ears a moment later.

"This store and one other are the only open properties in this entire lot," she said. "Only one has a surveillance system, and it hasn't worked in months."

Theo hung his head.

If the family wasn't in the SUV, they needed to move on. They were running out of time and wasting what little they had by just sitting there.

The suspect set the stakes with the explosion at the first site. Following FBI protocol in situations like this was vital to ensuring the second location didn't hold any more surprises. The bomb squad needed to perform a complete sweep before they could even approach the vehicle.

But FBI protocol didn't take into account the aircraft's ETA. Every second the plane got closer to its destination. Every minute counted. Theo checked his watch at the same time Liu did.

They locked eyes. He knew they were thinking the same thing.

"Comms, how long until the bomb squad's here?" Liu asked into her radio.

"Seven minutes, ma'am," said a voice.

"And once they're here, how long to set up, sweep, and clear the car?"

"Probably half an hour."

The agents looked at each other.

"How long?" Liu asked Theo, meaning until the flight was scheduled to land.

He glanced at his watch again. "About an hour twenty. But the captain will have to gas the cabin before that."

Liu seemed to measure his words as she stared at the Hoffmans' SUV. She spit a piece of fingernail out and moved on to another.

"If we wait for clearance and then find out they're not in the car?" Theo said. "We'll still have to find them." Left unsaid was that they'd have no time to do so.

Theo knew he was right. He knew the agents knew he was right. And he knew Liu knew he was right.

She grabbed a helmet.

"No one's to follow until I say, is that clear?" Liu

buckled the chin strap. "I want it on record that I made this decision on my own and I accept full responsibility for whatever happens."

Theo warmed with fear. It was one thing to be reckless with *his* life. This was someone else's life. Theo thought of the politician nodding his head, trusting him.

Since the explosion, excruciating pain had radiated out of his injured left arm, up and down his body, nearly nonstop. He'd blocked it out, a well-honed mental toughness he'd developed over many years of his coaches preaching mind-over-body. But as he watched Liu suit up, the pain seemed to pulse more intensely, as though it were a warning. Doubt crept into Theo's mind in places it didn't usually have access to.

"I thought you told me acting like this was a bad idea," he said, lifting his slung arm.

"It is," she said, taking her gun from its holster.

Cocking the weapon, she opened the car door and hopped out.

Stunned, they all watched Liu dart across the parking lot, gun drawn, open and exposed, nothing but asphalt between her and the Hoffmans' vehicle. The sunshade in the windshield would have blocked anyone inside from seeing her head-on advance.

Nearing the vehicle, her gait slowed before she ducked into a squat by the hood of the car, which remained motionless and dark. As she tilted her ear slightly toward the vehicle, Theo became aware of the distant sound of traffic as though his body were taking commands from hers.

Dropping to her hands and knees, Liu peered under the vehicle. Moments later, she popped up, apparently satisfied that the car's undercarriage was clear.

Brushing off her palms, she crouched and slowly

made her way around the driver's side of the vehicle, keeping the top of her head below the window line. At each door, she inspected the handle for trip wires. She didn't stop, so Theo assumed the handles were clear as well. Rounding the back bumper, she dropped out of sight.

"Alpha unit lost visual," the agent in the driver's seat said.

"We got her," a voice in Theo's ear replied. He knew there were snipers locked onto the situation from three different vantage points, triggers ready.

The anticipation in the car was palpable, the enclosed air becoming thick and warm. Theo bit his lip until he thought it might bleed.

"Standby . . ." one of the agents with a visual on Liu said in their ears. Then there was a scratching sound followed by a string of very loud, very angry, expletives.

"Clear," Liu's voice said. "No one touches the car until the bomb squad sweeps. But the family's not here." Reappearing around the back of the car, Liu jammed her gun into its holster and checked her watch.

Theo checked his watch too. They'd have to wait for the techs to clear the car before they could search for evidence, but the chances that the suspect left anything useful behind were slim. Fingerprints, DNA; he wouldn't be that careless. There wasn't time to run it anyway.

Theo climbed out of the car wondering where the terrorist would have taken the family. And in what? Liu was looking up at the night sky beyond the gnats that swarmed in the plaza's streetlights. Theo looked up and saw a plane, miles above, its lights flashing on and off as it flew by.

Liu pressed the palms of her hands into her eyes for

a moment before sighing loud enough for Theo to hear. Reaching into her pocket, she took out her phone.

Theo strode over the dirty parking lot asphalt, and with each step he reminded himself to focus. Lay out the evidence for review. Assemble the clues.

But the realization hit hard.

There was no evidence. They didn't have any clues.

"Yeah, Liu here," the assistant director said into the phone just as Theo reached her. She cleared her throat. "Second location is a negative. Begin phase one of asset evacuations in Washington, DC."

CHAPTER TWENTY

PERCHED IN HIS TOWER, HIGH ABOVE THE RUNWAYS OF JFK INTERNA-tional Airport, George Patterson was used to adapting to circumstances that were outside of his control.

This was different.

Fingers interlocked, he rested his forehead against his knuckles, his elbows sitting on the pile of papers that littered his desk: flight routes, weather reports, emergency protocols. Pages full of symbols, codes, and acronyms that would be clear as chicken scratch to most people.

I'm a birdwatcher, George would tell people with a smile when asked what he did for a living. He meant it tongue in cheek, but for twenty-seven years he had done just that, metal wings reflecting the sun and moon as he watched them soar. Birdwatcher was easier for most to understand than chief operating manager of JFK Air Traffic Control.

Weather. Mechanical failures. Time. The laws of physics. He was at peace with where he stood with those factors. He had no control. They were what they were. Accept the given circumstances and deal with what you *can* control. Don't waste time on what you *can't*. That's how he ran the tower. That's why he was the boss.

But for the second time in his career, frustration simmered under his usually steady demeanor. *It didn't have to be this way,* he thought. He'd had the same thought at the end of the day on September 11th as he sat on the side of his bathtub weeping, hiding from his wife and kids. His entire job was to maintain balance in an environment fraught with uncontrollable factors. And standing in front of the TV watching the flight attendant's video, he found himself frustrated, again, that the problem they faced today was not one of chance. Someone had created it.

Walking to his office window, he watched his staff at work. Every station occupied, controllers leaning forward in their chairs, speaking rapidly into their headsets, turning dials and changing displays on their monitors. He knew countless other towers and centers across the nation had received the same emergency NOTAM directive JFK had.

```
It is believed CA416's first officer does
not know about the captain's predicament.
Do not discuss the situation over open
air. Direct all cockpits to alternate
frequencies for briefing.
All incoming JFK area traffic will be
diverted to alternates, a no-fly zone
will be enforced as CA416 approaches.
All communication with CA416 needs to
remain standard. Diversion and discretion
is our aim and their best hope.
```

In planes all over the country, captains and first officers were looking at one another, curious as to why they were being directed to new channels of communication. But the intrigue would disappear as emotionless protocols were enacted by aircraft after aircraft as they were brought into the loop. It was miraculous almost, the speed at which the web of communications spun itself across the sky, every pilot at work that day made aware of the situation at hand, responding as they had been trained.

Only those on a need-to-know basis knew that the airports in DC—Dulles International Airport, Reagan National Airport, and Baltimore/Washington International Airport—were also preparing as JFK was. For what, they had no idea. They weren't supposed to deal with this flight; this wasn't their bird. And if the captain ended up crashing the aircraft into the terrorist's target, they wouldn't handle 416's path at all. But they still had to be ready. For anything.

But in New York, as soon as the controllers saw the video on the news, as soon as they knew the plane's destination was JFK, they came into work without needing to be asked. George could see one of his controllers wearing what were clearly his pajamas. Another had taken her high heels off and slid them under her desk. The first date wasn't going well anyway. Sweat soaked the T-shirt of one of his guys who had come straight from the gym.

My god, he loved these people. How proud he was of their dedication to their duty. Like a lighthouse, they served as a steady reassurance of hope. Through the chaos of the storm, they would be the predictable in the unpredictable. They would be the beacon home. Not just his tower. Every controller and every center that 416 would encounter had a unified purpose: guide them in.

In a twenty-four seven, three hundred sixty-five industry, this wasn't an office or a workplace. This was their tower. Where they spent holidays, weekends, late nights, and early mornings. Together. It was their second home.

But George knew, any minute now, military officials would arrive and it would be turned into a crowded war room.

"Hey, boss?"

George looked to the man standing in the doorway. Blond hair flowed to his shoulders from under a faded Mets cap while a wrinkled and untucked Hawaiian shirt rode up to betray a sliver of potbelly. The slop of manhood was George's smartest and most senior controller. *It was this or storm chasing*, Dusty Nichols had said of his decision to become an air traffic controller. Those were the only two jobs he could think of that didn't require a tie or regular bathing.

"What's up?" George said.

"I've got Chicago center on the line. They're telling me they're communicating with four-one-six's captain—but not in vocal transmissions."

George tilted his head. "Okay . . ."

Dusty adjusted his hat, shifting his weight foot to foot. "It's wild, man. The captain's using his hand mic to tap out Morse code."

CHAPTER TWENTY-ONE

BILL WAS AS RUSTY AT LISTENING AND TRANSCRIBING MORSE AS HE
had been transmitting it earlier in the flight when no
one seemed to be listening. His old knowledge was
coming back quickly, but he could feel sweat lining his
palms in the intense focus. Morse was hard enough to
do on its own—never mind having to do it in secret
while juggling another conversation.

The average pilot doesn't know Morse code. Some of
the military old-timers might. But for the most part, the
language was dead. That was true now, and it was true
thirty years ago when Bill had made the same argument
to his first flight instructor. But the World War II vet
wouldn't hear it. He didn't care that Bill found Morse
to be difficult, tedious, and a complete waste of time. It
was one more tool for the toolbox. He said Bill would
learn real quick that things could get real ugly, real fast.
And when they did—which they would—Bill would
want his toolbox to be as full as it could get.

Bill had never been so glad to be so wrong.

From the other side of the screen, Carrie watched

him intently. This deep into their lives, Bill honestly believed she knew him better than he knew himself. By the look on her face, she knew his mind was elsewhere. He wished he could tell her where.

Hold on, baby. I'm going to figure this out.

Sam checked his phone. "We're getting awfully close to decision time. I'm going to need your choice, Bill."

Bill's heart leapt into his throat. He shifted in his seat, stammering in his attempt to stall.

Sam cut him off. "C'mon, Bill. What'll it be?" His tone was mocking. Out of the corner of his eye, Bill saw the gun extend closer to his head.

"Please," a voice said. "Take me. Just me."

The boy's quiet voice had a purity that shattered Bill's heart.

Scott's bottom lip trembled. His plea was not the bargain of a mature man knowingly accepting the burden of his fate. It was the cry of a little boy forced from innocence, but left without the tools for understanding. A child merely mimicking what he saw the hero in the movies do. What he figured his dad would do.

The toy train looped around again, Scott's eyes widening with delight as its tiny engine, chugging and puffing, passed them. Disappearing into the papier-mâché tunnel, it popped out a few feet away near the area where the plastic horses grazed. The boy's hands pressed against the barrier, his breath fogging the glass.

Bill looked at his watch. Forty-five minutes and not a word. He turned at the sight of a group of nurses walking by with their paper coffee cups.

The unplanned pregnancy had brought Bill and Carrie a world of shock. Their stunned reaction gave way to excitement—but the medical and statistical realities of a

woman pregnant at forty-two years old had hung omi-
nously over the last nine months. Bill checked his phone
again for word from the doctor. Still nothing.

"Do you think she'll like trains?" Scott asked.

Bill smiled. "I bet she will. You can teach her all about
them."

Scott's eyes never left the circling toy. "Where's she going
to sleep?"

Bill considered. "Well, she'll sleep in the nursery. That's
her room." Bill had painted the room light yellow just the
weekend before. He had asked Scott if he wanted to help, but
Scott declined without much of an explanation. Bill didn't
push it.

"You mean my old play room."

Bill hesitated. "Yes . . . your old play room. But now you
can play in the living room. And when she's old enough, you
can play together."

Scott muttered something under his breath. Bill was
going to let it slide, but then he noticed the young boy was
trying not to cry. He knelt down, eye level.

"Do you think she'll like baseball?" Scott whispered. A
tear slid down his cheek.

"I don't know, bud," Bill said. "We'll have to wait and
find out. Do you think she'll like baseball?"

Scott shook his head.

"Okay," Bill said. He was barely able to discern Scott's
whisper.

"We like baseball."

Ah. There it was. Now Bill understood.

A decade ago, Carrie had handed him a positive pregnancy test. In that moment he felt what he knew Scott was
now experiencing. Bill wasn't ready to become a dad. They
had only been married a year. They were going to travel,
stay up late, sleep in without setting an alarm. Drink wine

whenever they wanted. Carrie was finishing grad school. They lived in a crappy one-bedroom in a crappy part of LA. He wasn't anywhere close to paying off his flight school loans.

But most of all—selfishly—he wasn't done being the center of Carrie's world. He had found the love of his life and he wanted her to himself. He wanted to be the only one she loved. He hated himself in that moment as he stared at the pregnancy test because his first thought was one of resentment. And now, all those years later, Bill knew Scott was feeling that resentment. Scott wanted to be the center of his parents' world, he wanted Mom and Dad all to himself. He wanted to be the only one they loved.

Bill's phone buzzed with a text.

"C'mon, bud. We gotta go," Bill said. "She's here."

Three floors later, Bill knocked softly on the door, opening it to let Scott walk in first. Carrie lay in the bed cradling a wriggling pink blanket. Her swollen face lit up when they entered, her eyes nearly disappearing in a joyous smile.

"There's my men," she said, her voice weak and raw. "Now I'm okay."

It took everything Bill had to not run to his girl and take her safe in his arms. The labor had been long and hard and when the baby's blood pressure dropped, Bill was kicked out of the room as they rolled Carrie into surgery. He watched, helpless, open-handed, as the doctors flanked her bed, running along the corridor with her, disappearing down another hallway. Bill was left alone with nothing to do but wait and console Scott.

"You are so incredible," he whispered to her. "You did this, Carrie. Look."

Baby Elise, pink-faced and perfect, stretched her arms out. Her mouth opened in a yawn with a tiny noise, almost a kitten's mew, escaping her puckered lips.

Scott stared at the newborn, wide-eyed, and the stuffed animal he and Bill had bought in the gift shop dropped to the floor. Sticking out one little-boy finger, he touched her cheek.

"She's so small," he whispered.

Bill helped him into the bed beside his mom and Carrie gently passed Elise to him; two hands, support her head. Scott stared into his sister's eyes and she into his, and somehow, an understanding was met between them. Bill didn't know the message, but he understood the messenger as the same that visited him the first time Scott was placed in his arms.

There was everything before that moment, and then everything after. The paradigm shift was supernatural.

"I'm going to teach you all about trains," Scott whispered to his baby sister. "And baseball too."

"Buddy," said Bill, his cheeks quivering. "That's the bravest thing I've ever heard anyone say in my whole life." He desperately tried not to cry, to be half as brave as his son was being. "You just stay with Elise, okay? She needs her big brother right now. Just take care of our baby girl, okay?"

Bill watched Carrie lean over and kiss the top of their son's head, tears falling onto his mop of hair, that cowlick stubborn, even now. Carrie and Scott glanced up in tandem again, watching something out in front of them, just like they had before.

Bill's jaw dropped. He recovered quickly.

Placing his elbows in front of the computer, Bill buried his head in his hands. He looked like a defeated man in a pose of frustration—but the new position situated his ear closer to the speaker, where, with eyes closed, he homed in on the silence coming from the machine, listening for confirmation of what he suspected.

There! There it was. The background noise changed, ever so slightly, the far-off rumble of a jet engine growing fainter with each moment.

They were watching planes take off. They were near the airport.

Ben tapped the gun impatiently on the dash, the noise making Bill jump. He dropped his hand out of sight and began tapping Morse with the button on his hand mic as fast as he could.

Ben interrupted Bill's concentration. "It's just about time to throw the canister," he said.

"I'm not throwing anyth—"

Sam held up the detonator. "So that's your choice? The plane lives?"

"No," Bill said quickly, reaching for his laptop as though he could touch his family. "No. That's not my choice."

"If you don't throw the canister, that *is* your choice," Sam said.

Bill's jaw hung open, trying to find words besides the ones he knew he had to say.

Ben extended the gun. Sam adjusted his grip on the detonator.

"Okay," Bill said. "I'll do it."

CHAPTER TWENTY-TWO

JO STOOD AT THE FRONT OF THE PLANE, LOOKING OVER HER SQUAD of volunteers. The tall man reclined with his eyes closed, head back against the seat. Jo wondered how he could possibly sleep at a time like this. Everything about him seemed odd. According to the manifest, his name was Josip Guruli, and Kellie's online search of the name had come up empty. They had no reason to distrust him besides a gut feeling. But today, that carried weight.

She watched Daddy briefing the over-wing emergency exit row passengers, making sure they understood how the doors worked and where they should position themselves during the evacuation. His firm hand assigned roles with a confident authority: you and you—stay at the bottom of the slide and help people off. You—run away from the plane and call people to you. Heads nodded up and down.

Pulling a tray of small water bottles out of her galley, Jo passed them to her six new recruits while watching a younger female passenger squeeze past Big Daddy on her way to the back. *Now where was she going?* Jo shook her head, frustrated that everyone was suddenly guilty until proven innocent. It went against her typical view of humanity.

"Take off your ties," she said in passing to the two young businessmen who were now in the aisle seats of row one. "Choking hazard." The young men complied.

Water distributed, she resecured the empty carrier before ducking behind the galley curtain to check her phone. Nothing new from Theo. She pocketed her phone and grabbed her supplies before stepping out of the galley and addressing her volunteers.

"All right, ladies and gentlemen," Jo said. "Let's get to it."

The ABPs came together with Jo at the head of the huddle. Arms crossed, focus aligned, they were preparing for battle and Jo was the commanding officer. No one interrupted her, not even Dave.

"Our tools are limited," she said, "so we gotta work with what we've got. Our advantage is that we'll be prepared and we'll be coordinated. Okay?"

All six heads nodded up and down.

"Our number one objective is containment. We want as little of this poison in the air as possible."

Jo felt a twinge of guilt as she spoke. She didn't need to explain why containing the gas was important, but she was omitting the fact that the passengers' oxygen supply would run out twelve minutes after being activated. So they really did need as few toxins as possible floating around, but a ticking clock they could do nothing about was an added stress they didn't need.

She extended her arms. Sturdy gray trash bags hung from her hands.

"This is the best we got," Jo said as she handed one to each of the ABPs, explaining how it was going to go.

All six of them would be seated with their oxygen masks on. Jo would be wearing a portable oxygen bottle. She would stand in front of them at the bulkhead, directly in front of the cockpit door, waiting for it to open. When the canister was thrown, she would go after it, because her portable oxygen would allow her to move. After she got ahold of the canister, she would throw it into whichever bag was closest to her at that point. That person would tie the bag shut as quickly as possible and then throw it into the bag closest to them. Then Jo would take the double bag, put it in the toilet, close the lid, and shut the door.

Heads nodded.

"Keep your mask on, understood? If you have to take it off for some reason, hold your breath. Then get it back on, quick. We work as a team. No one can be left exposed for long."

The ABPs murmured their agreement and leaned forward, ready for the next part of the plan. They seemed eager and determined to help—but what if the backup was one of them? What if she had just shown her hand to the very person they were worried about? Jo looked at her team and realized: she had no plan for that dark possibility.

"Any questions?"

CHAPTER TWENTY-THREE

THERE WAS A CRACKLING IN THEO'S EARPIECE.

"You guys aren't going to believe this," said a voice from the communications van. "We just got word that Captain Hoffman's communicating with ATC. Secretly. Using Morse code."

Bill had told them his family was in a parked vehicle. Something big enough for them to sit in the back of. He didn't know the exact location, but he knew they were somewhere near LAX.

"He said they're looking out the vehicle's back window—watching the planes take off."

After Jo finished briefing her volunteers, she collected the last of the first-class glasses that were still out before ducking into the galley with a look back at the main cabin. Kellie and Big Daddy were almost done with their first round of compliance. Jo had watched them out of the corner of her eye while she addressed her own team, and she'd been surprised at how little time it had taken them.

Most days, cabin compliance was a struggle. Passengers don't like to be told what to do. But today it looked like Kellie and Big Daddy didn't need to correct a single person. Decades into her career, Jo finally understood why passengers often resisted little requests like putting a bag away or raising their seatback, or why they ignored the safety demo. It was the same impulse that stopped them from saying the things they wanted to say, doing the things they wanted to do, being who they wanted to be. They'd do it tomorrow. Next time. Later. And now, too late, they realized that tomorrow had never been a guarantee. Now they willingly, even desperately, did everything they could to buy themselves a little more time.

Jo dropped the glassware into a divided carrier in the beverage cart. The masks were out, her ABPs were briefed, the cabin was compliant, and her galley was secure. They were nearing the end of their prep and she peeked out at the passengers, at these strangers turned kin, wondering if she'd missed anything, when out of nowhere Jo felt the urge to cry.

Perhaps it was because time was running out. Or perhaps it was because Jo had watched a man, unprompted, tell the elderly woman next to him that when the time came to evacuate, he wouldn't leave her. Perhaps it was because she had seen a teenage boy—too old to be considered an unaccompanied minor, but nonetheless traveling by himself for the first time—being reassured and comforted by the family across the aisle. Jo could see his adolescent pride melt away as he allowed himself to feel safer in the confidence only a parent can provide.

Perhaps it was because she saw strangers holding hands, praying together.

The souls on board had become a family—as perfect as imperfection is. The short life of this family was about to reach its end, and as a group, they faced their mortality together.

Jo wanted to take the plane in her hands like a toy, kiss it gently, and place it up high on a shelf. Safe. She was so proud to be with these people, so proud to have added her own voice to the chorus. She and the other two flight attendants might have played different roles than the rest, but they were all in this together.

A green light appeared overhead with a high-low chime. Jo grabbed the interphone.

"You guys done with compliance?" Jo asked.

"Yes, ma'am," Daddy said on the other end of the line.

"And you're all briefed?"

Daddy confirmed that they were. "And you owe me five dollars."

"You've got to be kidding me. Who?"

"The couple in row thirteen. Look in the aisle."

Jo turned around and stifled a laugh. Sure enough, a middle-aged couple stood in the aisle, struggling to remove their inflated life vests.

"Oh, bless their hearts," Jo said, and laughed, not actually that surprised.

The plane dipped slightly. It made the threat feel imminent.

"Okay," Jo said. "Put your masks on first, then direct the passengers to. Then I want you and Kellie in the back, in your jump seats, ready for landing. Got it?"

"But—"

"This landing could be rough," she said, cutting him off. "Last thing we need is you two flailing about. And we don't need you up here. I've got my ABPs and we'll handle it. But you two know this plane and you know what to do in an emergency. The passengers are going to need you alive for this. Understood?"

Daddy sighed. "Understood. But for the record, I don't like you up there alone with that guy."

Jo looked over to Josip. She didn't like it either. He had nearly two feet on her.

"I won't be alone," Jo said, trying to sound more convinced than she was. "If he tries something I got a whole plane full of backup. The mob is with us, remember?"

Daddy mumbled his agreement. He was clearly not convinced, and neither was she. But they both knew they didn't have another option.

After hanging up, Jo opened the first overhead bin, aircraft left, and unbracketed her portable oxygen bottle. She pulled the strap over her head, the bottle crossing her body at a diagonal. Taking the yellow mask out of the pouch, she twisted the valve counterclockwise until the number "4" appeared in the little window at the bottle's neck. Placing a finger inside the cup, she felt for a flow of air before sniffing it. It was odorless. Donning the mask, she pulled the loose straps tight, the plastic cup cutting into the bridge of her nose. Then she swung the bottle around until it came to rest awkwardly across her back. With a glance aft, she saw Kellie and Daddy finishing the same maneuvers.

Walking through first class, she helped her volunteers into their masks and pulled down the tubes to start the flow of oxygen. It was a calm and even intimate exercise. But when she resumed her place at the front of the plane and turned back to look at them, the mood shifted.

It was the eyes.

The masks covered the passengers' faces. Jo couldn't tell if someone was smiling or frowning. If they were wrinkling their nose or sticking out their tongue. Asking a question or yelling at her to watch out. Every action, every intention, every emotion was channeled through the eyes.

Jo started a final compliance check. A nod here, a thumbs-up there. Her cabin was ready to go and Kellie and Big Daddy were almost finished in the main cabin. Jo nodded to Big Daddy halfway across the cabin. He tipped his head in response, retreating to the aft galley to assume his post. Jo turned around at the bulkhead. Something caught her attention.

It was light, reflecting off a pair of shiny plastic pilot wings. The little boy who had visited Bill and Ben in the cockpit before the flight sat in the first row of the main cabin.

His father grasped the child's hand in a protective gesture. The boy's feet dangled off the edge of his seat, small shoes punctuating the ends of short legs; it would be many years before they'd be long enough to reach the floor. His intense green eyes were positively glowing, overpowering the mask that dwarfed and marred his cherub face.

The boy's father checked his seat belt, probably for the tenth time. She could see the man mentally preparing their evacuation. Unbuckling their seat belts and grabbing the boy in his arms as they moved toward the exit, clutching him to his body as they slid to safety. The man was living in the future but the boy was not with him.

The boy was still in the plane, still in the here and now. He looked around at the swaying masks and the sparkling lights. Jo could imagine his angelic mouth under the mask, parted in awe. The boy wasn't full of fear. He was overcome with wonder.

Witnessing that, Jo found that the weight of the moment was still painfully heavy, but she didn't need to suffer while carrying it.

A high-low chime rang through the cabin with a green light. Jo glanced to the back of the plane as she walked to the phone, wondering why Big Daddy was calling again.

"Everything okay?"

"Yes, ma'am," Big Daddy answered.

She waited for him to say something else.

"Y'all good on your oxygen?" she said after he didn't speak. She adjusted her tank, the awkward bulk shifting across her back.

"Yes, ma'am. We strapped them over one shoulder, diagonal across our backs. You?"

"Same," Jo said, watching Kellie in the back of the plane tightening the strap on her tank, Big Daddy beside her on the phone. "Anyway," Jo said, turning the cabin lights one shade brighter, "I think we're ready." Glancing at Josip, she dropped her voice. "Nothing new to report from up here."

Again, she waited for Big Daddy to say something. But he didn't say anything else. Jo needed to focus.

"All right, I gotta go. I'll see you down there, baby."

"Jo!" he choked out before she could hang up the phone.

She'd known Big Daddy for many years. But as she listened to him struggling for words, she realized this was the first time she'd heard him tongue-tied. Looking to the back, she watched him wipe his cheek.

"Jo," he whispered. "I don't have anyone to call right now." He covered his face with his free hand, and repeated himself, breaking into tears.

Jo's voice shook as she said, "Well, you just called me. And I answered."

A stifled sob filled her ear, though she could feel him try to catch it as it slipped out. Her own eyes misted in spite of her best efforts. Jo watched Kellie grab a tissue from the bathroom and pass it to Big Daddy. He accepted, pointing a finger at her.

"If you tell anyone about this, young lady, I'll tell the FBI you were working with the terrorist."

Jo heard Kellie laugh and she smiled. "Don't worry, Daddy," Jo said. "Your secret's safe with us."

Hanging up the interphone, Jo pulled out her cell phone, opened the text thread with Theo, and began typing.

Bill pulled the canister of poison out of his messenger bag, setting it carefully on the dash. The smaller vial lay at the bottom of his bag.

"What about the powder I was supposed to use to kill you?" he asked Ben.

Sam and Ben both laughed.

"Put it on French toast?" Ben said. "It's powdered sugar."

Bill felt the crown on his back tooth crack under the pressure of his clenched jaw.

"But that," Ben said as he indicated the silver canister in front of the captain, "is definitely not sugar. Look, I couldn't die. Someone had to be here to make sure you made your choice. If you hadn't broken the rules, I never would have revealed myself. You'd have poisoned me and I'd have faked my own death. But I had to be alive to make sure you went through with the crash."

Bill shook his head, trying to understand. "But what if I chose the plane? And I didn't poison you, and we landed just fine and my family . . ." He couldn't finish the thought.

"Then that would have been your choice," Ben said. "We'd have landed without incident and I'd have shot myself in the head later tonight."

Ben bowed to Sam, saying something that wasn't in English. Sam bowed his head as well, repeating the phrase.

"You see, we will die today. Sam and I both. It's been decided. But now, in our deaths, our lives will have purpose."

Bill shook his head in disgust. "Martyrdom is a coward's death."

Sam brought the phone right up to his face, his cheeks quivering as he tried to maintain composure.

"This has nothing to do with religion," he said. "The only cowards are people like you who are too scared to face the truth of how you keep your peace and privilege and at what cost."

Bill didn't hear a word he said.

Eyes narrowed at the computer, Bill focused on what was over Sam's shoulder. The new camera angle had brought the light closer behind them, illuminating . . . wood beams?

It clicked. Bill almost gasped.

Years ago, when Carrie moved from Chicago to Los Angeles, they rented a U-Haul for the drive. She didn't need anything huge since she'd sold most of her stuff, so the seatless sixteen-seater the moving company offered

was perfect. Bill had had to get in and out of it probably a hundred times. He had a splinter in his hand
for a week from the wooden beams he used to hoist
himself up.

The family was in a moving van.

CHAPTER TWENTY-FOUR

THEO LOOKED UP AT THE SOUND OF A HELICOPTER'S PROPELLORS droning above the strip mall as its searchlight illuminated the streets of southwest LA. Back and forth, it searched for a needle in a haystack.

"Three-mile radius?"

The agent pulled up a map, the screens inside the comms van brightening. Aerial and street views of the area surrounding Los Angeles International Airport popped up.

"No, let's start with two," Liu said.

Theo stood with his arms crossed next to Liu outside the van as they looked over the other agent's shoulder, images on the map narrowing and refocusing in response to the buttons he pushed. Even with only a two-mile radius, the vantage points for spotting LAX traffic could take days to search. Neighborhoods, hotels, shopping centers, parking garages. The range of possibilities for where the family could be was overwhelming. The one bright spot was the fact that they only had to search three sides. The entire west end of the airport butted up against the ocean.

"I want our units north, east, and south of LAX," said Liu. "Start as close to the perimeter as possible. Sweep every street and continue out. Have airport police search the garages and review their tapes."

Theo and the other agents nodded and began talking into radios, tapping on their phones.

Liu glanced up at the helicopter. "Air cav will get the bird's-eye view," she said. "And we're going to hang back and try to put the puzzle together."

Across the lot the bomb squad was still working over the Hoffmans' SUV.

"You guys got anything for me?" Liu said into her radio.

Theo looked across the parking lot. One of the agents near the car turned and flashed Liu a clear thumbs-down.

Liu's phone beeped. She read the message before sharing it with the group. "Phase one evacuations are almost complete in Washington." Theo knew that meant the top-ranking government officials had been evacuated, the line of succession secured, and that the Secret Service was ready to move the president to the White House bunker at a moment's notice.

No one said anything. Theo thought about the logistics of that operation. The whole situation was expanding, the web of people affected growing at a wild pace.

"What about . . . regular people?" Theo asked. "Does the public know? Is there an official statement?"

Liu shook her head. "And there won't be—if we can find the family."

A noise suddenly came through their earpieces.

"A moving van! Another Morse message—he says they're in a moving van!"

The fingers on Theo's bad arm tingled as a hope-

ful shot of adrenaline pulsed through the injured nerve
endings. Liu turned to him. "Get on the phone with
every moving company in the area and see what you
can find."

Stepping away from the group, Theo took note of
the time and made a quick calculation. He figured the
plane was less than an hour out from its final destination.

The gas attack would be happening soon.

Bill's heart thumped with a newfound hope. He couldn't
zero in on his family's exact location, but he was narrowing it down. If the FBI hurried, if they found the
moving van soon, maybe Bill wouldn't have to throw
the poison into the cabin. Yes, there would still be a
gun pointed at his head—but one thing at a time. He
needed his family safe first. He could figure out the rest
after that.

He looked to his family, but had to shut his eyes.
It was unbearable to watch his wife, her hands bound,
struggle against a ten-month-old in the throes of a
temper tantrum. With his eyes closed, Elise's incessant
screams only intensified; his child, his defenseless little
girl. The fact that she had no idea what was happening
was unfair, her ignorance anything but bliss. Bill wondered if her diaper needed to be changed.

Hearing Carrie's shushing intensify, he opened his
eyes. Her forehead wrinkled with anxiety as she rocked
the baby, but it made no difference. Scott put his hands
on his sister's feet and tickled lightly, sticking his tongue
out at her. The baby's eyes were screwed shut. Wide
tracks of tears ran down her cheeks.

"It's okay, Leesee," Scott said, using the nickname

he'd given her, the timbre of his voice rising with the baby talk. "Shhhh, it's okay. Do you smell that? That campfire? Let's pretend we're camping. With Dad. In the woods."

Bill caught his breath.

"We'll make s'mores and look at the stars," Scott said. "Pretend, Leesee. Pretend."

Bill slowly dropped his left arm. Taking hold of his hand mic, he made sure it was below the chair where Ben couldn't see. Methodically, he began tapping.

Elise screamed louder.

Sam took hold of the baby. Carrie gasped, pulling the child closer to her body. But Sam's hands were laid gently; not as a threat, but as relief. The child, in a stabbing betrayal, pushed away from her mother, toward the man. Reluctantly, Carrie let go.

Bill's skin chilled watching his daughter lay against the man's chest, her cheek pressed against the suicide vest. Swaying from side to side, Sam became a metronome while Elise's body throbbed in time with her gasping screams. Making small circles, he rubbed her back, the detonator intertwined in his fingers.

Sam began to sing. A soft melody, melancholy but sweet. The words were foreign, but to the baby, no words held meaning anyway.

Ben began to sing along, just loud enough for Bill to hear, but even then, barely.

Elise's screams slowly turned into cries, surrendering shortly thereafter into whimpers. Her tiny body gradually stopped shuddering as she eased into relaxation. As he sang the final note of his song, the only movement was Sam's gentle swaying.

No one said a thing in the peculiar moment of peace.

Bill wondered if the men regretted their choices. Regretted putting this baby, this little boy, this woman in the position they had. Perhaps it wasn't too late. Even with everything that had already happened, maybe Bill could find a way to talk them out of it. He went to capitalize on the moment but Ben got there first.

"Bill. It's time."

Theo pressed the red button ending the call. It was the seventh moving company he'd contacted. Seven dead ends.

Looking across the lot, he saw Liu and the agents moving with purpose but no urgency.

The bomb squad was packing up and all the doors of the Hoffman car were wide open as agents went over it. Watching both teams at work, he knew their actions had been as fruitless as his.

Clenched in his hand, his phone vibrated.

The attack up here is about to start. But I wanted to tell you how proud of you I am. It's all going to be ok, Theo. I love you so much.

Theo didn't want to be in control. He didn't want to be a part of this mission. He didn't want to be the little boy who declared himself a man anymore. Adults handle situations; they fix things. Theo had been trying to do that ever since his mother drove them away from their home in the middle of the night. But he didn't want to do it anymore.

You've got this, Aunt Jo. We've got it down here. Now you handle it up there. I love you too.

A thought floated up: *I hope the captain chooses to sacrifice his family.* Theo's head drooped with shame and guilt.

Across the lot, Liu and the agents burst into movement. Something was happening. Theo broke into a run. By the time he reached them, the team was almost done packing up.

". . . look up any public area in a two-mile radius that allows campfires. Think parks and . . ."

"What's up?" Theo asked Rousseau.

There had been another Morse message. The pilot said the family could smell smoke. Campfire-type smoke.

Theo tried to picture the airport's surrounding areas from above. To the east, the line of hotels on Century Boulevard. Maybe one had a courtyard fire pit? South was pretty much all residential. And too far from the runways. North, also residential and—

"Dockweiler!" Theo yelled as it came to him. He took off running toward the nearest vehicle but seeing no one follow, he stopped.

"What's Dockweiler?" Liu said, without turning away from the screens in the comms van.

"It's a beach," Theo said, speaking quickly. "It's at the end of the runways—look, I'll explain on the way. But we gotta go."

The agents went to finish packing up but Liu stopped them with her hand. After directing the agent working the screens to pull up all of the information they could find about the beach, she turned back to Theo.

"We'll see. Look," she said, indicating the information beginning to pop up on the displays, "we *are* seeing. But we don't have the resources to send agents to every location you have a hunch about."

"But, we don't have time—"

"What we don't have time for are mistakes. Got it?" Liu's tone was final. She turned back to the van.

Theo gaped in disbelief. He was absolutely certain he knew where the family was. Dockweiler was a public beach located at the west end of LAX's runways. The planes took off directly overhead and there were fire pits on the beach. He knew Liu would discover all that through her research and he knew she'd come to the same conclusion he already had. Eventually they would head in that direction—but once they got there, Liu would *still* want to do reconnaissance before they could surround the area and establish a perimeter.

There was not a doubt in Theo's mind that by then it would be too late.

He tried to sound calm. "Ma'am, I really think—"

One of the other agents stepped in front of him. "Dude," he said to Theo, his voice low, "I know. But you gotta chill. Just let her do her thing."

Theo stared, momentarily confused, before he glanced around him. The other agents stared back at him. He knew they didn't have the responsibility Liu did or the personal connection to the case that he did. They had no reason to stick out their necks, which made it easy to go along with the boss. Taking orders was safe.

"Theo."

He turned to the sound of his name. It was Rousseau. The agent glanced down at Theo's shaking hand, which was still clutching the cell phone.

"Sorry," Theo said. "It's just, my aunt, you know?"

The agents murmured their understanding and Theo stepped away from the group. After a few moments, he glanced back over his shoulder. No one watched him. They'd all returned to their own business.

Theo set his jaw and walked to the nearby SUV. No

one tried to stop him because they'd never imagined an agent would do what he was about to do. As he sat in the driver's seat and started the engine, he felt no hesitation. His desire to be elsewhere and not in control was gone entirely. He knew this meant the end of his career. But inaction and cowardice weren't what he signed up for anyway.

As Theo sped out of the parking lot, he didn't look back.

CHAPTER TWENTY-FIVE

JO SMILED AT THEO'S TEXT.

Pocketing her phone, she stood alone, her back to everyone else who sat. She braced herself, directly in front of the cockpit. She whispered a prayer for her nephew, the family, and the ground rescue.

This close to the flight deck, she could hear the pneumatic hiss of a pilot's oxygen mask being released from its case.

She knew Bill was protecting himself from the poison, just as they were in the cabin. His mask would be military grade, though. It could create suction with an airtight seal, cover his whole face, and effortlessly pump an endless stream of oxygen into his lungs. A far cry from the cheap, mass-produced plastic cups the passengers had secured to their heads with an elastic strap. The disadvantage felt unjust.

She heard the hiss again, and assumed his mask was now secure.

It was time. The attack would begin at any moment.

• • •

Bill adjusted the mask on his face, turning to watch Ben slide the straps of his own oxygen mask over his head, releasing his pinch on the sides of the mouthpiece. The mask sealed itself to his face with precision, protecting his eyes, nose, and mouth.

Bill shook the canister in his hand, an agitator ball clanking up and down inside. As the pressure mounted, he could feel the beast within begging to be released.

Waiting until Ben had finished adjusting his mask, Bill paused the shaking as a cue.

The first officer flashed a thumbs-up.

What was that clanking noise? Jo's eyes scanned the door, which gave no clues. What if their assumptions were wrong and the trash bags wouldn't work? What if she couldn't manage it? What if the gas incapacitated her instantly? What if she succumbed and couldn't even fight? What if there was an accomplice among the passengers to make sure the gas attack was successful?

She glanced over her shoulder at her six volunteers. Giving them a thumbs-up, she smiled as each of them responded in kind. She was not alone.

Josip, tucked in the back corner of first class, watched her intently. He lifted his chin slowly. It was a sign of solidarity. Or it was a threat. Jo didn't know which. She lifted her chin in return, intending it as both.

This was her cabin, she reminded herself. She was in control.

Turning back to the door, she exhaled. The smell of her own stale breath, warm and wet against the plastic cup, pissed her off. It reminded her she was only human. She needed to be more.

So in that last moment before battle, she decided she would be.

Jo stood a little straighter, closing her eyes. Her focus narrowed to a pinpoint of black; stillness before action. She made a mental bow to the generations of goddesses, warriors, and survivors who coursed through her DNA, recognizing now that she did indeed belong among them.

There was a sound of metal retracting.

Her eyes slid open.

The door unlocked and swung inward. A cascade of illuminated buttons flowed from ceiling to floor, the cockpit's windows a horizontal gash of darkness. Captain Hoffman twisted backward in his seat, purple cabin lights reflecting off the plastic shield of his mask. There was a movement from inside. Something flew through the air.

Jo could see the canister's details as it left Bill's hand. Silver, small enough to handle, it spewed a stream of white residue that dissipated the further it went from the source.

Jo extended her hands, eager to grab it. Eyes never leaving the proverbial ball, she watched it float toward her grasp. Just as it hit her hands, something slammed into her from behind and threw her hard to the ground. She screamed as she watched the canister topple out of her reach. Crashing against the bulkhead, it rolled to the other side of the galley, lodging itself under a cart.

Bill's hands flew to his mouth, smacking against the mask he forgot he was wearing.

Jo!

Her scream echoed in his head even after it stopped. That sound—a noise of pure human terror, human pain, human fury—ripped through his conscience.

You did this, Bill. You brought this on her, on them.

The image burned in his mind. Jo, ready, as she promised she would be. Anticipating, prepared, armed— blindsided.

She never saw the man coming and Bill couldn't scream a warning, the door already shutting with a slam, the sounds of madness and chaos erupting on the other side.

He looked over to Ben, who leaned forward, staring out the window. The first officer panted as heavily as he did.

"Tell me who that was!" Bill screamed.

The first officer said nothing, and neither did Sam.

Everything happened at once, though it played out in slow motion.

Jo whipped her head toward the door as her attacker lunged at it.

He kicked and clawed at the door, screaming as he rammed his shoulder repeatedly into the impenetrable surface. His efforts were pointless. The door was shut. The cockpit had not been breached. A flash of relief coursed through Jo. The man at the door turned on her, grabbing her by the uniform. Pulling her up, she came level to his face.

"No! The gas!" Jo screamed over her shoulder to her first ABP, the businessman in row one, who was coming to her aid. He ran into the galley to find the canister.

Dave wrapped his hands around Jo's throat, squeezing tightly. She'd misjudged him. She thought she'd won him over, that he was part of the team. She was wrong.

Jo's eyes bulged as she watched the businessman frantically search for the canister, turning around and around in the galley. She tried to point, to direct him, but Dave thrashed her body too violently. Jo could feel herself starting to tremble due to the lack of oxygen. Watching the businessman start to shake, though, she wondered if it was actually the poison.

"I have to get up there!"

White foam trickled out of Dave's mouth as he screamed in Jo's face. It dripped down his sweat-covered chin. His bloodshot eyes watered as he blinked against the burning. Jo watched him slowly succumbing to the gas, tiny blisters popping up across his neck next to veins that protruded and pulsed.

"Not on my watch!" he screamed at her. "Not on my watch!"

The businessman, unsuccessful, ducked back to his oxygen mask as the second ABP, the other young businessman, leapt forward to relieve him. He dropped to a knee and started searching under the wrong cart.

Jo tried to point to the right one, but stars began to dance across her vision. Her brain seemed unable to send a message to her hand. Her vision went in and out, melting into darkness and back again. It couldn't have been ten seconds since the door had shut, but it could have been ten lifetimes.

Dave screamed as his grip loosened. The poison was taking him. Out of nowhere, a blunt object struck him across the face. Jo slipped out of his grip, caught before her body hit the floor. Dave fell at her feet.

Looking up, Jo found herself in the arms of Josip.

His hand clutched a rolled-up magazine. He used it a second time, like a billy club, and the blow rendered Dave unconscious.

Jo pushed herself from his grip with a strength he probably didn't expect, passing the second businessman as he went back for air. She stumbled to the last cart. Releasing the foot brake, she pulled it forward, slamming it against the secondary lock. Knocked off balance, she fell backward against the bulkhead. The cart slid back into place, the canister still stuck underneath. White poison streamed out like a ghost.

Josip understood and he unlatched the secondary lock. His massive hand placed on top of hers, they pulled the cart free, the canister rolling out in a cloud of poison.

Josip kicked the canister away from them. At the top of the aisle in the center of the galley, the former Marine kneeled in wait. Scooping the canister into her trash bag, she tied it shut with such force that Jo hoped the bag didn't rip. Turning, she dropped the bundle into the arms of her wife, who waited with the next bag. Tying it just as forcefully, she double-knotted for good measure.

Josip dragged Dave's body across the galley, freeing the way to the bathroom. Jo staggered forward, taking the bags from the paramedic while simultaneously pointing toward her seat. The woman nodded, stumbling backward, her wife extending an oxygen mask to her. Helping her put it on, she pressed the mask to her wife's face as they both gasped labored breaths of clean air.

Josip ripped open the door to the lav and Jo tossed him the bag. He dropped it into the toilet and closed the lid with a slam before shutting the door. Jo pushed him out of the way, dropping to her knees in front of the lav. She shoved a soaking-wet first-class blanket into the crack at the bottom of the door. It was their last line of defense.

On her hands and knees she worked, not noticing her oxygen tank had slid around her torso and dangled from her body. Her mask was now covering her left ear. The elastic strap cut across her face. She worked as fast as she could but her hands felt stapled to the floor. Was she even moving? She honestly couldn't tell. Something in her knew the poison was wrapping its bony fingers around her mind. She fell against the cockpit door with a thud.

Josip grabbed her, hoisting her upright. Sliding the mask around, he placed it firmly onto her mouth and nose. He pantomimed deep breaths. Jo mirrored him, the cool air acting like a slap across the face.

Josip had turned an unnatural shade of red, his eyes bloodshot. Jo took a massive inhale before she ripped off her mask, pressing it firmly against his face. Josip gasped inside the plastic, sucking in as much air as possible. Tears leaked out of the corners of his eyes. He gave Jo a nod.

He got to his feet and pulled her up when she grabbed his arm and pointed toward the seats. Josip nodded, taking another deep breath before handing the mask back to Jo. Picking Dave up off the floor like a rag doll, he tossed him into his old vacant seat.

Jo watched Josip as she resecured her own mask. She wanted to cry at how good it felt to be so wrong about someone.

Looking around, Jo took stock. The first business-man was throwing up into one of the trash bags, vomit already covering the front of his shirt. The second businessman looked like he too might be sick, his whole body red and slick with sweat. He convulsed and shook, clutching the armrests, just as the Marine in the row behind him did. Her paramedic wife looked into her constricted pupils. She took her pulse. Josip sat across the aisle, breathing with apparent difficulty, examining the blisters and rashes that were forming on his hands and arms. Next to him, Dave slouched forward, still unconscious, but wearing the mask Josip had put on him.

Beyond the cabin divider, the rest of the passengers sat in their seats pressing the masks to their faces. Most craned their necks, trying to see what was going on. Many leaned forward, hands clasped, eyes shut. They clutched each other, tears streaming down their faces and someone, somewhere back there, let out a moan.

Jo could see Kellie and Big Daddy in the back obediently strapped to their jump seats. They leaned forward from opposite sides of the plane looking down the center aisle at her. They were desperate to help.

Jo raised her shaking arm and gave a thumbs-up.

Twinkling stars crisscrossed her vision. A numbness spread over her face. She wiggled her nose and lips in an attempt to increase circulation. Sweat dripped out of the mask, down her chin. It was sweat, right? What if it was drool? Or was she foaming at the mouth? Unable to touch her face, she couldn't gauge the extent of what felt like a slowly developing paralysis.

Jo registered a nagging hesitation that a potential Plan B remained onboard. But she allowed herself a small relief in knowing that she was alive, they were all still alive.

The poison gas attack was over.

Time was a slippery concept at the moment so she had no idea how much of the twelve minutes of oxygen the attack had eaten up. She was confident it wasn't the full twelve, but it was close. Any remaining poison they hadn't captured should dissipate harmlessly enough before the masks were useless. And not long after that, they would land, and hazmat would meet the plane and medical professionals would be ready and waiting to take over.

It was going to be okay.

Jo nodded.

It was over.

CHAPTER TWENTY-SIX

CARRIE'S WHOLE BODY SHOOK.

It started as a tremble, but after Bill threw the canister, it grew into something more animal, something more compulsive.

Elise began to cry again as Carrie's tears dropped onto the baby's face. Scott was buried in her lap, but now that the attack was over, he started to sit up. Carrie pressed him back down. His body shuddered under her weight and he began to cry along with his sister. Carrie gasped for air.

Sam tried to shush the children but it only amplified their noise and increased the feel of chaos in the enclosed space. They had been pushed too far.

Resisting Carrie's halfhearted attempts to stop him, Scott sat upright. There was a break in the noise just long enough for everyone to hear, "Mom?"

Scott stared at his mother's lap, which was dark with wetness. He looked up, confused. Moms aren't supposed to pee their pants.

Carrie felt his pity and saw his embarrassment. It

was unbearable to witness so she turned away—directly into Sam's stare.

"I need to go to the bathroom," she said, without the energy to beg. "Let me have that dignity." Her voice dropped. "Not in front of my children. Please . . ."

The children's sobbing cut off anything else she tried to say. Sam looked from her wet lap to the snot that dripped from her nose. She laid her hand on his shirt sleeve, the one she had rolled, and he did not pull back. Her voice was barely a whisper.

"Sam. Please."

His eyes rose and met hers, but only for a moment before she looked down in deference.

"Fine. Hold your sister," Sam said to Scott. The boy took the baby awkwardly. Sam looked around the van and found a rope lying in the corner. "Move down. Here, hold this."

He passed the phone to Carrie while Scott scooted down the metal floor with his sister in his lap. Together, the children moved to the far side of the van, away from the back door. Sam tied the rope around a column of the van's internal metal siding and then tied the other end of the rope around Scott's slender waist. The boy struggled to lift Elise up out of the way.

Sam tugged on the rope a few times. The knots only tightened.

"The van will be locked, so don't try anything heroic," he said quietly to Scott with a finger in his face. "If you do—I'll shoot your mom in the head."

The blood drained from the child's face.

All this happened behind her while Carrie stared into the camera trying to figure out how to tell her husband what she couldn't say out loud. On the other side,

Bill paid her no attention, looking over her shoulder at the man who was tying up their children.

A memory tapped her on the shoulder.

Before their wedding. The couch, her old Bible. Her father's handwriting.

So . . . everyone dies. And that isn't fair?

Yes.

"Bill," she said, as Sam was finishing with the children. Her voice tripped over the lump in her throat but her eyes were dry. "If you asked me to marry you? Right now? Even with all of this? I would say yes. Yes. Underlined deeply. In all capital, block letters."

Bill frowned, turning his head slightly to the side.

As she watched him trying to piece the message together, memories surfaced. Sitting side by side at a movie, her hand accidentally brushing his. Catching him staring at her from across the party. Hearing him call her his girlfriend for the first time. She smiled to herself, feeling at peace with her decision, when on the other side of the screen, Bill blanched. She knew he understood.

The camera shook as he clutched at the sides of the laptop.

"Carrie, I can't . . . I . . . dammit . . . ." he stammered, also clearly trying to figure out how to say what he needed to say without saying it. He ran his hands through his hair, looking around the cockpit before he stopped and stared dead into the camera. He sat up straight, chin thrust forward, and spoke in a firm, steady tone.

"Marry me again, Carrie. I'm asking you now just like I did then—will you marry me? But don't just say yes. Underlined. All caps. Not yet. *Wait.* Be patient. See if I prove myself worthy of you. I promise you I will. Carrie, I promise you. Don't say yes until you believe I deserve you."

Carrie smiled sadly. "You have alw—"

"All right, let's go," Sam said.

Taking the phone from her hands, he set it on the floor of the van. The camera lay stationary, angled up at the ceiling, showing nothing.

Bill stared unblinking at the screen, which was nothing but a fuzzy, dark gray, Scott's heavy breathing the only indication the call was still connected. There was a sound of a key being inserted and turned.

The children were locked inside, tied up and alone, and Carrie was out of sight in the clutches of a lunatic. And he—their father, her husband—was thousands of miles away and moving farther away with each minute.

She's going to do something, Bill thought.

Carrie is going to do something.

CHAPTER TWENTY-SEVEN

THEO DROVE WITH THE LIGHTS FLASHING AND SIRENS BLARING AS HE made his way down Sepulveda Boulevard toward the airport. Cars parted to let him through, but the congestion around LAX made maneuvering nearly impossible. There wasn't a moment of any given day that cars weren't bottlenecked; the airport's terrible positioning and layout were maddening under the best of circumstances. Theo tried to keep his road rage in check by tapping anxiously on the steering wheel. Today, the stakes were a lot higher than missing a flight.

His phone began to ring. DIRECTOR LIU. Theo declined the call and the screen went black.

Minutes ticked by. He tried to distract himself by calculating how far there was to go, but after realizing he hadn't even reached Century Boulevard, he swore in frustration. This route would send him through the tunnel that went under the east end of the runways to connect to Imperial Highway before he would then have to make his way down the whole length of the far side of the airport, toward the main entrance to—

You idiot, he cursed himself as he made the connection.

Without checking for traffic, Theo sent the vehicle into a screeching U-turn. An oncoming car swerved out of his way, bleating its horn as another car swerved to miss it.

Theo pressed his foot on the gas and the tires squealed in response as the SUV shot forward and away from the airport.

He barreled down the road as cars moved to the right, out of his way, when up ahead, he spotted a black SUV with flashing lights stuck in traffic going the opposite direction.

"You've gotta be kidding me, Liu," Theo said to himself as he slowed to the speed limit and flicked off his own lights and sirens.

As he passed the vehicle, he glanced over quickly, not wanting to attract attention—and saw two of his colleagues craning their necks, trying to figure out a way to circumnavigate the cars. They never noticed him.

Were they backup? Or, in the middle of an operation, with lives on the line, was Liu willing to waste two of her agents by sending them to find Theo and drag his ass back in? He didn't trust her enough to wait and find out. Accelerating the SUV, he left them behind.

Cool, fresh air blew in off the open sea, a startling contrast to the hot stuffiness of the van. Carrie gazed out at the inky water of the Pacific. Waves crashed on the shore in a ceaseless cadence of indifference. Tomorrow the tide would go out and come in just the same as it did the day before and would do the day after. She found relief in knowing that the earth would keep turning and that, ultimately, it didn't care.

On the far end of the lot, out on the beach, a bonfire spat orange sparks up into the stars with a satisfying crackle. Behind the blaze, a couple reclined, their feet propped up on the gray concrete fire pit. Carrie inhaled deeply the smoky scent of nostalgia and immediately felt the cold barrel of a gun pressed to the back of her neck.

"I wasn't going to yell," she said. "I was just . . . savoring."

"Let's get this over with," Sam said, pulling her arm in the other direction.

Together they walked away from the van toward the other end of the parking lot. In that corner, the bulb in the streetlamp was out. A pile of sand and discarded construction equipment underneath took on eerie shadows in the moonlight. A seagull perched atop another lamp, his head cocking from side to side as he watched them go by. Carrie considered them from the bird's view: two people, shrouded in explosives, calmly moving into darkness. The salty wind blew her hair across her face and she shivered.

"Back at the house, you said you had plans," she said. "But then your father died."

Sam nodded. "Ben and I were all set. Our paperwork and visas were done. We'd been saving our money for ten years. Our flights were booked. And then four days before we were supposed to leave, he died."

"So you stayed and Ben left without you?"

Sam nodded. The sand crunched beneath their feet. He walked just enough ahead of her that she could see the handle of the gun sticking up over the waist of his pants against his back.

"Did you resent him?"

Sam turned his head. "Ben?"

"Yeah. When he left you behind."

They had almost reached the end of the lot and the pile of discarded rubble.

"No. Never. I made him go. He wanted to stay, didn't think it was fair. Which it wasn't," Sam said with a shrug. "I told him to go and I made him take my money too. It would make it easier for him. I said he should get a head start and I'd join him when I could. And seventeen years later I did. But at the time, I just couldn't leave."

"But your family. What happened? What happened to Ahmad?"

The name of the youngest sibling, the deepest wound, hung in the air after it left her lips. She knew instantly it would have the effect she thought. She braced herself.

His pulse beat visibly against the side of his neck as he turned on her, stopping himself just before he struck her. She flinched and tried to run but he grabbed her under the jaw and pulled her back toward him, his fingers wrapping around her neck. Bringing her close, he turned her head to the side, his lips lingering over her ear. His breath painted a warm dampness across her cheek and she squeaked involuntarily as his fingers dug into her skin.

"Do not bring his name here," Sam whispered into her ear.

Don't fight. Don't fight. Don't fight. Carrie desperately tried to override instinct. Closing her eyes, she focused on the sound of the crashing waves.

Slowly, his grip began to loosen until he released her completely. She stumbled backward, taking deep breaths. Bending over, her hands went to her knees. She averted her gaze.

Sam motioned toward the pile.

"Hurry up."

The stoplight turned yellow. Theo accelerated, checking both ways as an afterthought. The light was red before he even reached the intersection, but he barreled through anyway.

To his left, a plane tore down LAX's north runway in its takeoff roll. Theo checked his speed. Seventy-five miles per hour. The speed limit was thirty-five. With a glance over at the plane as its wheels left the ground, Theo pressed his foot into the pedal and the needle went over eighty.

Westchester Parkway ran parallel to the airport. Traffic was light and the few cars that were on the road obediently slowed and pulled to the right when they heard the siren and saw the flashing lights. Theo surveyed the area, desperate for visual cues that would fill in what his memory left out. It'd been years since he'd gone this way. The area looked different from how he remembered.

As a kid, when his family went to the beach, they went to Toes. Toes Beach had been a surfing mecca in the '60s, but after rock jetties were built to prevent beach erosion, the surf that had brought people in disappeared. It was now primarily a locals' beach with calm waves, a winding bike path, and very few tourists.

Theo pounded his fist on the dash in frustration and a shockwave of pain roiled through his injured arm. He was glad for the pain. He deserved it for being so stupid, for taking so long to put it together.

Toes connected to Dockweiler.

The end of the road approached, and Theo faced

another red light. He slowed, checking for oncoming traffic, and saw none coming. Speeding back up, he began to turn right-on-red with a glance up at the street name as he rounded the curve. Pershing. He thought that street might—

He heard the brakes before he saw the car.

The tires screeched, one second before the car slammed into him at full speed, hitting the SUV just behind the driver side door. The car spun out of control until it struck something else—something large, something metal—that sent the SUV spinning in the opposite direction. There was a loud pop and glass rained down on him, followed by a rush of cool air.

For a moment, everything around him was stationary. Cool, and still. Theo didn't move.

Theo unbuckled his seat belt with bloody fingers and went for the door handle. It wouldn't budge. The door was stuck. The car was pinned up against what he assumed was the undercarriage of another car. Theo coughed as smoke seeped into the interior through the smashed window.

Crawling into the back seat, Theo became aware that his whole body was in pain—but he kept going. He tried the back doors, but they were locked.

The rear window was a spiderweb of fractured glass. Theo climbed over the back seat. There, he was able to get to his feet, stooped over in the tight cargo space. Holding himself steady with his good arm, Theo pulled back his left leg and kicked at the glass. On the third blow, the window shattered around his leg with a tinkling crash. Theo scrambled out the back of the car, sucking in deep breaths of fresh air.

A stranger ran up to him. "Are you okay? You need to sit down. An ambulance is on its way."

Theo heard it all, but none of it registered as he surveyed the scene. Three cars. One on its side. A motorcycle. All mangled. Broken glass and twisted metal was strewn everywhere. A half dozen people lay on the ground, moaning. Bystanders stood by their own cars, helpless.

Helpless.

The Hoffmans.

He had to keep going.

Theo pulled away from the man who was trying to get him to sit down and headed for the overturned car. A young couple knelt on the ground speaking with the driver who was stuck inside the vehicle, still belted into her seat. She was conscious but covered in blood. They told her not to move.

"Is she alright?" Theo asked.

They nodded. "I think so," the husband said. A siren was heard in the distance. "Hang on," the man said to the driver. "Help's coming. They're going to get you out, okay?"

The sirens got louder. That could be an ambulance—or it could be the FBI. Theo needed to get out, too. Amidst the commotion, he walked over to the motorcycle that lay on its side on the ground. The key was still in the ignition.

Before anyone could stop him, Theo righted the bike and straddled it. Putting it in neutral, he pressed the kill switch to the on position before pulling the clutch and pressing the starter button. Miraculously, the engine stuttered into a throaty purr. Theo gave it a little gas as he eased out the clutch, and the bike took off.

Theo hadn't ridden since learning on his freshman year roommate's old dirt bike, but it came back quickly. Soon, he squinted into the wind as the motorcycle raced down the street, horns honking at him as he dodged and weaved through the cars. Theo ignored them.

His arm was harder to ignore. The way he needed to drive meant riding one-handed wasn't an option. The pain he felt as he extended his left arm out of the sling nearly made him lose control of the bike. As his right hand worked the throttle and front wheel brake, he was relieved the injury wasn't to that arm. His left hand trembled in its loose grip on the handlebar, struggling to keep things steady and on line. The front tire quivered precariously.

Theo scanned the upcoming streets and was certain the next intersection was the left he needed to make. There was one car ahead of him: a minivan waiting for a jogger to clear the intersection so it could turn in. Theo gave the bike a little gas and upshifted. The van was midway through its left when Theo pulled up on its inside. The van's tires squealed as it swerved to the right. The jogger leapt onto the curb, narrowly rolling out of the way. The motorcycle wobbled momentarily before regaining its balance as Theo sped up the street into the residential area.

The neighborhood was exactly as Theo remembered: winding and hilly. He navigated the bike through the maze of streets that led toward the coast knowing there would be one more left, then a right that would jag to connect to an access road. That access road would then run parallel to the beach, ending in a connection with Dockweiler's parking lots.

He just needed to find the right street.

Theo slowed, glanced both ways, and then blew through a stop sign to start up a steep hill. He had no time to ride carefully—but he had enough sense to recognize that there were no seat belts now and he wasn't wearing a helmet.

Driving down the other side of the hill, he focused on the second street ahead. He thought that was it, but as he passed the first street, something in his memory bank stirred.

The first street. That was it. The one he just passed.

Theo braked hard and torqued the handlebar. The rear tire left a black stain in the shape of a semicircle as the bike spun around. Revving the engine, Theo sped back up the street toward the correct turn, just as a car crested the hill in front of him.

Theo squinted into the oncoming headlights and banked right as the car braked and swerved the opposite direction, narrowly missing the motorcycle. Jumping the curb, the car plowed into a fire hydrant with an explosive bang. Theo brought his foot down in a desperate attempt to keep control as the bike tottered across the road. He looked over his shoulder at the geyser of water that shot into the air at the front of the wrecked car and the driver inside who wrestled with the airbag.

Theo kept going.

The bike tore past the multimillion dollar homes that lined the street. Theo knew the ocean lay just on the other side. Up ahead, sand had blown across the road near a light pole that displayed a reflective blue sign halfway up. BEACH, it read, with an arrow. Theo accelerated.

He was almost there. Once on the access road, it was a straightaway. He could reach the family in minutes.

If that's where they were.

Doubt rushed through him as he thought of all that

had happened since he'd left the FBI team. What if he was wrong? What if the family wasn't there? Theo shook his head. No. They had to be there. They *had* to be.

The street approached. Theo accelerated into the turn but immediately slammed on the brakes. His body nearly went over the handlebar as the motorcycle came to a stop, almost ramming into the security barricade that blocked vehicle entry to the access road. Waist-high metal columns were spaced just close enough that the bike couldn't fit through. It was a dead end.

"No!" Theo yelled, his voice smothered by the sound of the crashing waves out across the beach in front of him. He stood, straddling the bike, panting, ignoring the pain. A memory of the house exploding earlier in the day filled his mind, followed by the Hoffman family picture.

Theo sat down on the bike, twisted the handlebar straight, and kicked off.

Scanning the area as he drove through the neighborhood, Theo searched for a backup plan. Dockweiler was still too far to go on foot. He needed to get the bike around the line of houses to the access road.

Up ahead, an earth mover was parked in front of a dumpster at a construction site. Spurred by hope, Theo sped up. He narrowed his eyes as he approached the lot to get the lay of the land and found wood and steel supports rising up out of a concrete foundation. But more important was what he saw through and beyond all that: the beach and the access road.

Without thinking it through, Theo jumped the curb and rode the motorcycle up the plywood make-shift ramp that workers had laid against the foundation. He slowed as he drove carefully through the long, skinny house, steering left and right to avoid the metal pipes sticking up from the ground where the kitchen and bathrooms would soon be. At the back of the foundation, excess pipes laid atop metal scaffolding. Theo's eyes widened as he judged the clearance.

Ducking down as far as he could, Theo rode under the pipes. He cleared it, barely, but in the distraction, his foot clipped the edge of the scaffolding frame. The bike spun violently to the side and Theo was thrown off, landing in the sand a short distance away. The scaffolding and pipes began to collapse in a terrifying chorus of uncontrolled metal crashing against itself as Theo scrambled back to the bike, dragging it upright and away from the lot.

Theo's shoes dug into the sand as he pushed the motorcycle to the access road. "Don't you dare," Theo said as he heard the bike's engine begin to sputter. As he straddled the machine, it seemed to groan in protest and Theo noticed a nail sticking out of the front tire. Theo gave it a little gas and the bike trudged on.

Holding on to the handlebar, he noticed both arms had begun to shake, and his left arm had gone completely numb. He put it all out of his mind. The damage to his body. The end of his career. The path of destruction he'd left in his wake. The image of the politician nodding at him, trusting him, just before the house exploded. Theo forced himself to shut it all out. He needed to focus on the family and what he could do to help them. That, and only that.

The front tire was now completely flat and the metal rim scraped on the concrete. A thin whisp of smoke trailed from the engine as it hiccupped, the bike lurching irregularly in response. With a sad puff, the motor seemed to extinguish itself, and the bike coasted forward on momentum alone.

Theo looked up, defeated, when not far ahead in the distance, he saw a building. It was a kind of municipal maintenance site or something of that sort—and he knew that just beyond that was Dockweiler Beach.

Theo dropped the motorcycle into the sand and started running, unholstering his gun as he went. The building took a more definitive shape the closer he got: solid wall to the ocean, but on the back side, open space for city maintenance vehicles and other equipment. The access road wound around the back side. Just beyond the building: the far edge of Dockweiler's first parking lot.

Pulling up to the cover of the building, he drew his gun into a defensive position as he passed behind the building. It appeared vacant, save for a few trucks and a large tractor with a beach rake attached to the back. No lights on, no one around.

He slowed his stride, easing his way to the end of the building with his back pressed up against the wall. Cautiously peeking around the corner, he swept the area for a moving van but froze at what he saw. At the edge of the parking lot was a woman, bent over, hands on knees, and a man standing over her. Even from a distance, Theo could make out the explosive suicide vests they both wore.

Theo caught his breath as he scanned the lot, spotting the van at a distance. But what were Carrie and the suspect doing? As she stood up, the man motioned toward a pile of what looked like discarded construction barricades. She moved toward it.

Theo rounded the corner and ducked out of sight behind a truck.

•   •   •

Walking over to the pile, Carrie attempted to undo the button on her jeans but her bound hands made it impossible. Her shaking fingers failed to twist just right at the awkward angle. She turned back to Sam.

"Sorry, a little help?" she asked meekly.

Looking at her wet pants and the button above them, he seemed both agitated and embarrassed as he walked over to help. As he placed his hands near her waist, she looked away.

He fumbled with the button as well; it was stubborn and his hands were full. Placing the detonator in his pocket, he grabbed the little metal button and popped it through the opening just as Carrie's knee drove hard into his crotch. His eyes bulged and a grunt shot out of his mouth, his body doubling over in pain. Carrie lunged forward and grabbed the detonator from his pocket. Jumping back, she scrambled out of his reach.

They stared at each other, eyes wide, breathing heavily. Carrie's bound hands sandwiched the detonator between her palms, her fingers wrapping around the device like Sam's had around her throat. The look on his face told her that despite all his planning and scheming, despite all his redundancies and backup plans, *this* was not something he'd anticipated.

Once she pushed the button the children would be safe. The plane could land. She would be granting Bill absolution. This was how it had to be. This was the only way.

"What happened to Ahmad?" she asked.

His eyebrows lifted a little before sinking into a look of painful defeat. As though the act of letting someone in was more difficult than kidnapping her family, than crashing a plane.

"I got to LA in September of 2019," Sam said in a

dark, bitter tone. "It was heaven. The sun, the ocean. Everything so fucking clean. I was doing it. We were doing it together. Finally. All of it. Life was just . . . outstanding.

"A month later your president ordered a troop withdrawal from northern Syria. Our little pocket of Kurdistan. Which gave Turkey the green light to attack. They came after our people within days." He shook his head with a dark laugh. "Betrayed, again. Abandoned, again. And after we had sacrificed so much, fighting alongside you, destroying ISIS for you—we lost eleven thousand YPG fighters defeating ISIS for you. Eleven. Thousand. And you do *that*. You betray us like *that*.

"When Ben and I saw our town on the news it took three days before we were able to make contact with anyone on the ground. Do you know how many in our families died?"

She didn't respond.

"All of them, Carrie. Every single one. We were sent pictures so we could identify the bodies. The last image I have of my mother is her bloated, rotting corpse. Blisters on her lips. Burns across her skin. Ahmad. My baby brother. Laid across her. Foam around his mouth. Yellow pus from the chemicals. My brother's last act was trying to protect our mother."

His eyes had filled with tears and now they narrowed in on her. She tightened her grip on the detonator.

"Were you aware of the troop drawdown?" he asked. "And the attacks that came as a result?"

She felt the shame blossom across her cheeks. She shook her head.

Sam nodded a few times, crossing his arms. "Well, I'm sure you were busy. Probably had a deadline with work. Scott's baseball practice. I bet friends were coming over for dinner. Or maybe you saw it on the news but just couldn't be bothered to care. It was just some poor country. Some poor people. Attacks like that just happen there. That's just how it is."

His voice began to rise.

"I know it's how you reacted because I saw it happen. I was here. So was Ben. We were safe. We were in a country where attacks like that don't happen. And all around us we watched you get your green smoothies and go to the gym. We watched you take selfies and go on vacation. I watched a grown woman sob hysterically, I mean, rolling around in the grass hysterical, when she saw a dog get hit by a car. And all I could imagine was the look on her face when she clicked past the news of my village's annihilation. Bored. Distracted. I mean, the *privilege*."

He snarled against the word, and Carrie flinched against the truth. The detonator hung between them.

"Ahmad. My baby brother. He was the reason I never resented losing all those years. He was what I was most proud of in my life. And he was taken from me, taken from me because this country sees him, sees our people, as nothing. Expendable. Just poor people they can do whatever they want with."

A wave rolled in. And another.

"Sam," Carrie said in a voice that was grounded but full of tenderness, "I get why you're doing this, but it doesn't justify what you're doing."

He didn't have a response. He just blinked at her.

"You have every right to be angry, Sam. I would be too. But your guilt can't—"

"*My* guilt?" he screamed. "My guilt? What about *your* guilt? You and your ignorance and inaction. This country and the way you think—"

"But Sam! You were here with us!"

Carrie saw her mistake immediately. Every moment in which he'd blamed himself for leaving them, for not being able to protect them because he too had abandoned them, for living a life of ease while they suffered. It all played across his face, the sucker punch of survivor guilt breaking him open right in front of her.

All he could do was nod his head. Something in him had changed. "You're right," he said finally. "You are. But does it change my mind?" He laughed and looked around at his surroundings, shaking his head vigorously, a bit maniacally. He pointed to the detonator. "Your little trick was cute. And your little mind games are cute. But you're forgetting that I've still got a bird in the hand. I've still got the kids."

Carrie's body went cold.

"And that means—I don't need you."

Faster than she could react, Sam reached behind himself and produced the gun, leveling it at her head.

Without even thinking, she flipped up the plastic safety on the detonator and moved her thumb to the button.

A gun fired. Seagulls flew into the night sky.

Sam buckled, blood spurting from the gunshot wound in his left thigh. Screaming, he fell to his knees, the gun dropping at his side.

Carrie kicked at it, the weapon sliding across the sandy asphalt out of reach. Spinning, she saw a young man in a bulletproof vest scrambling down the hill toward them.

"FBI!" he screamed.

Squealing tires cut through the scene. Carrie whipped around to find two black SUVs speeding into the parking lot toward the moving van.

Sam took off, running awkwardly down the beach, sand flying, a trail of blood left in his footsteps.

"I'll get him," the FBI agent called out to her as he tore down the beach. "Go!"

Taking off at a dead sprint for the van, Carrie ripped at the vest's Velcro. Freeing herself, she stopped long enough to set it down carefully on the asphalt, laying the detonator beside it. She raised her arms to identify herself as a nonthreat for the armed agents who were pouring out of the vehicles around the van.

"He needs help!" Carrie screamed. "The other guy. They're down the beach. Hurry!"

CHAPTER TWENTY-EIGHT

THE SOUND OF A DISTANT GUNSHOT FROM THE OTHER SIDE OF THE screen hung in the air of the cockpit. Bill and Ben leaned forward, desperation seizing them both.

"Mommy!"

With a hiss, Bill ripped off his oxygen mask. The chances that enough gas had leaked under the door to hurt him was minimal—and in the moment he didn't care. Bill clutched the sides of the laptop. "Buddy. It's okay. I'm here," he said.

The boy's wet sniffles filled the cockpit. "Mommy. Mommy, please."

Something slammed against the van. The children screamed and the pilots jumped.

"Scott! Mommy's here," said Carrie's muffled voice. "Babies, Mommy's here."

Sounds of metal striking metal came from outside the van, the screen jiggling in response to each blow. Both Carrie and Scott were screaming until suddenly the van doors flew open and yellow light flooded in. A blurred figure jumped into the van, kicking the phone and obscuring the camera's view.

"It's okay," Carrie said over and over as she wept. "It's all going to be okay."

The suspect had a head start but he was wounded and Theo was the faster runner.

Theo holstered his gun. No matter what happened, Theo could not shoot while they were both moving. The man was covered in explosives. Chasing him down the beach, Theo closed in little by little until he was close enough to touch him. With a final burst of speed, he leapt onto the suspect's back, the man collapsing under the weight as they both tumbled to the ground. White sand flew into the air and stuck to their skin as the men grappled for control despite each of their physical limitations. Arms and legs thrashed in a blitz of blood and pain.

The suspect rolled into Theo to deliver a punch, leaving his own stomach exposed. Theo saw the opportunity and jabbed his elbow into the man's torso, the blow striking the suspect's gut right below the ribs. The man doubled over with a grunt.

Out of the corner of his eye, still far in the distance, Theo saw the backup agents running toward them, the headlamps on their helmets jostling light all over the beach.

Rolling onto his back, Theo pulled the man on top of him, wrapping his left leg over the suspect's waist. Slipping his left foot under his right knee, Theo locked the suspect's body into place before wrapping his arms in a figure-eight around the suspect's neck. The suspect was immobilized in a rear naked chokehold before he even knew what was happening. The suspect swatted at Theo's arms, but beyond that he couldn't move.

Theo's sling must have come off completely at some point in the fight, but he hadn't noticed. A cool numbness had replaced the incessant throb of pain he'd felt in his arm all day, and he assumed he was in an adrenaline-fueled state of shock.

The backup agents were getting closer, but as they approached, Theo could see their drawn guns.

"Don't shoot!" Theo screamed.

He squinted in the beams of their bobbing headlamps.

Distracted, Theo didn't notice the suspect grabbing at the sand. With a full hand, the man threw it into Theo's face, blinding him. Theo blinked furiously while swinging his arms around, trying to feel for the suspect.

"Get on the ground! Get on the ground!"

The shouts of the other agents echoed closer, almost there.

"Hold!" one of the agents screamed over the rest, just as Theo sensed them beside him. Backup was here and the suspect was outnumbered. But the panic in the agent's voice told Theo that something was very wrong.

Theo's eyes watered profusely but gradually his vision was coming into focus. Pulling at his waist, Theo untucked his shirt to wipe his eyes clean. His hand grazed his holster.

It was empty.

His vision sharpened and Theo saw the danger for himself.

Five FBI agents, minus himself, stood with guns drawn in front of the suspect.

The suspect faced them, pointing Theo's gun directly at the suicide vest.

Theo's stomach dropped. If the man pulled the trigger, every one of them was dead.

"Put down the gun and we'll bring you in without further harm," Theo said, his voice far more steady than he felt.

"Further harm," the suspect repeated, a small smile on his lips.

"That's right," Theo said. "You have my word."

The man chuckled, his increasingly crazy smile showing bloody teeth. His weight slumped to the right, favoring his left leg, the one Theo had shot. He turned his head to the ocean for a moment before looking up at the stars with a deep, relaxed inhale. "Your word . . ." he said. "You know, where I come from, we have a saying. 'No friend but the mountains.' Do you know what that means?"

"I do not know what that means," Theo said slowly. "But why don't you put down the gun and we can talk about it."

The man laughed. He mumbled something under his breath.

"Sorry?" Theo said.

The man's face erupted with rage and he began to scream, "I get why you're doing this but it doesn't justify what you're doing!" He shouted it again and again until his voice grew hoarse. Tears had filled his eyes and they began streaming down his face.

Theo didn't reply. No one did.

The suspect looked around at the agents and then down at the vest he wore and the gun in his hand. It seemed to be dawning on him for the first time where he was, what was happening. A look of regret flashed across his face, just for a moment, before he seemed to mentally pivot again, like something else had just occurred to him. He laughed again, but not in the same maniacal way. It was a soft, disbelieving huff.

"All this, and *I'm* the one with a choice."

His brow furrowed as he considered the situation. After a moment, he let out an amused sigh. He looked up, his eyes locking onto the stars, and carefully placed the barrel of the gun under his chin and pulled the trigger.

CHAPTER TWENTY-NINE

THE PILOTS COULD HEAR THE CHAOS AND COMMOTION IN THE VAN from the other side of the call, but could see nothing, the phone's camera still angled up at the ceiling.

"Ma'am. Are you hurt? Are the children hurt?" a voice said. A body climbed over the camera.

"We're fine," Carrie said. "We're okay."

The camera jostled and filled with light as someone outside the van picked it up off the floor. A woman appeared, her grimly triumphant smile taking up the whole screen.

"Captain Hoffman? I'm Michelle Liu with the FBI, sir. Your family is—"

The faint sound of a single gunshot rang out, and she broke off as Bill flinched.

The camera angle dropped as Liu scrambled to figure out what was happening. There was confusion and commotion, boots running. The scratchy sound of a radio broke in with a breathy voice. "Suspect is dead," a man reported. "Self-inflicted gunshot."

The phone moved and the woman's jubilant face returned.

"It's official! We got him, sir. It's over."

She breathed heavily with excitement into the camera before squinting for a better look at the scene in the cockpit, her smile fading.

"Is that a gun?" she asked.

"Cut them off," Ben said, his voice shrill. "Cut them off!"

Bill heard Carrie scream his name as he slammed the laptop shut, the call disconnecting.

Bill didn't move a muscle. He could sense the gun beside his head. But the threat barely registered and a warmth spread through his body.

His family was safe.

Slowly turning, he looked at Ben.

The young man's blank expression betrayed nothing. Tears flowed freely from his vacant eyes as he stared at the closed laptop. His best friend was dead. He was alone in the world. It seemed as though Ben had stepped out of who he once was into something entirely new. The paradigm had shifted and Bill was afraid of what that could mean.

Bill didn't want to speak first, and he needed to tread lightly. His family might be safe but the barrel of the gun told him this was far from over. Bill still needed to get the plane on the ground.

Without taking his eyes off the computer, Ben finally spoke.

"Actions have consequences, Bill. We told you . . ."

He trailed off, turning to the right of his seat. Bill heard a zipper open. Ben rummaged through his shoulder bag for a moment before turning back to the captain.

Bill looked down at the man's hand and felt his nostrils flare with the sharp intake of air. It was another canister.

Bill couldn't speak. Finally he found a single word: "No."

Ben leaned over. The gun almost touched Bill's head.

"*No?*" Ben said. "I don't think 'no' is an option anymore."

"I am not gassing them again. This wasn't part of the deal."

"Neither was you telling the crew. Or the authorities. Or killing my best friend. We told you: actions have consequences. Now take this, and pay for your mistakes."

Bill leaned back, pulling away from the canister and the gun. He raised his hands in the air.

"I absolutely will not—"

Ben unbuckled his harness. Stepping over the center console, he towered over the captain, the barrel of the gun shaking as it pressed into Bill's forehead.

Bill could feel his own arms, still spread wide, beginning to shake as well. Ben had the literal higher ground. He had a gun. And Bill had to stay alive because Ben *would* crash the plane.

"Okay," Bill whispered. "Okay."

Moving slowly, Bill brought his hands forward to accept the canister.

Ben pulled back and the gun left Bill's forehead.

Bill shot upward, grabbing the hand that held the gun by the wrist. He wrenched his own hands as hard as he could, but from a seated position he had no leverage. Ben grunted and his grip on the gun slipped, his finger leaving the trigger—but he managed to keep it in his hand.

With his fingers still locked around Ben's wrists, Bill torqued his own wrists violently.

Ben slammed Bill's head with his other hand, the one clutching the canister. Every time his fist struck Bill's body, the agitator ball inside the canister clanged. Blow after blow, the sounds of metal on metal and flesh on flesh filled the cockpit.

Bill pulled down hard and then pushed up harder, feeling Ben's grip on the gun loosening each time. One more—

Ben cracked the metal canister against the side of Bill's temple.

Bill's vision went fuzzy with pain but he kept his hands clenched tight on Ben's wrist.

Ben brought the canister down again on the exact same spot.

This time Bill's vision went black. Dazed and disoriented, instinct took over, and he brought his hands up to protect his head. Released from Bill's grip, Ben staggered backward.

Bill cursed and began to swing his arms behind him, trying to grab at Ben. Light and shadow returned to his vision, but it was all a blur.

The agitator ball clanked. Bill heard the hiss of the canister being unlocked, immediately followed by the door opening. Ben gave a small grunt and the air whistled as he chucked the poison out of the cockpit and into the cabin.

CHAPTER THIRTY

CARRIE WATCHED DIRECTOR LIU PACE WHILE SHE BARKED QUESTIONS into the van.

"What do you mean the first officer was in on it the whole time?" she demanded.

Agent Rousseau cut the rope around Scott. The boy collapsed into Carrie and wrapped his arms around her body, Elise sandwiched between them. He squeezed his mother hard and the baby whimpered.

"Gentle," Carrie said. "It's okay, baby. We're safe."

"I need to know—"

"Liu," Rousseau said softly. "Give them a minute."

"We don't have a minute!" Liu screamed.

"She's right," Carrie said, climbing out of the van awkwardly while holding Elise. Turning, she took Scott's hand before he jumped out. "What do you need?"

"The first officer—"

"Is friends with Sam." Carrie motioned down the beach. She thought for a moment before thinking better of what she was about to say. Sighing, she kissed Elise and held the baby out to Rousseau. "Would you?

I think they've seen enough today." She dropped down level to her son. "We're safe now, baby. But Mommy still needs to take care of some things to help Daddy. So I need you to stay with your sister and go with the agents, okay?" She kissed him on the top of his head, and watched them walk out of earshot before turning back to Liu. Wiping her face, she was suddenly exhausted. "His name is Ben. He's Syrian too. Or Kurdish . . ." Her voice trailed off in embarrassed uncertainty. "And he has a gun."

"Why didn't he just crash the plane himself, then?" Liu asked.

Carrie shook her head. "Because that wasn't it. They wanted to make Bill choose. Us or the plane."

"And now that there isn't a choice? Is he still going to make Bill crash?"

Carrie looked down the beach. In the distance she could make out agents circling Sam's body, taking pictures, making marks, documenting, recording.

"I don't know," she said. "But we just killed the only family he had left. So I'd imagine anything's possible."

Carrie couldn't decipher the look on Liu's face as she turned away, bringing her phone to her ear. Carrie strained to hear what she was saying.

The young man with the gun who had chased Sam and allowed Carrie to escape approached, extending his hand. He introduced himself and asked if Carrie was all right.

Carrie took his hand in both of hers. "I will be once the plane lands." She was about to thank him for what he'd done earlier when Liu returned. The two FBI agents stared each other down silently.

Finally, Liu spoke. "Don't say 'I told you so.'" She stuck out her hand.

The man looked down at it for a moment before extending his. They shook hands—but both their faces remained stony and guarded.

"Theo," Liu sighed. "We're not done here. There's a problem."

Carrie thought the woman seemed slightly hesitant as she explained that the first officer was involved. Theo's face twisted painfully as he realized the plane was still in danger. Carrie was confused by how personally the young agent seemed to take the news. He put his hands on his knees for a moment before shooting upright, reaching into his pocket.

"She doesn't know," he said, typing furiously on his phone.

"Who doesn't know?" Carrie asked.

Liu ignored Carrie's question. "Do you know the specific location in Washington that's the target?"

Carrie shook her head. "They never said."

"And the gas attack," Theo broke in, pausing his typing. "Did it happen?"

Carrie dropped her gaze and nodded. "The camera was in the cockpit, so we couldn't see what happened in the plane. But we could hear it."

He stared vacantly for a moment before turning back to his phone. "They need to know about the FO," he muttered, frantically resuming his typing.

"Who's he texting?" Carrie asked, growing impatient.

"The crew," Liu said. "The flight attendants. His aunt Jo is one of them. She texted Theo. That's how the FBI got involved."

Carrie turned to Theo in disbelief. "Jo Watkins?"

He looked up.

"You know my aunt?"

Carrie couldn't believe it. She told him that Bill and Jo had been flying together for years, and that she and Jo were friends. A new degree of anguish washed over her at the realization that Jo was on the flight. "Bill's never going to be able to live with himself," she said. "He gassed his own cabin, he gassed *Jo* . . ."

"With all due respect, ma'am," Liu said, "we don't know that's all he's going to do."

Carrie's head tilted slowly, her eyes narrowing.

"You think he'll crash the plane."

Carrie said it not as a question or a statement, but as an accusation. Liu looked up.

"He's got a gun to his head, I don't think we can—"

"And I had a gun to my head," Carrie said. "I knew exactly what Bill would do."

"You don't know what—"

"I know *exactly* what choice my husband would have made, and will make." Carrie's body shook with rage. "You don't know my husband. I do. He will land that plane."

Liu studied Carrie. Flicking her head to Theo, she said, "Get her out of here."

Theo guided Carrie away, his arm wrapping around her shoulder. As they walked off, they were almost out of earshot when Carrie heard Liu say quietly to another agent, "Get me the Situation Room. I'm recommending secondary protocol."

Carrie whipped around before Theo could grab her.

"What's the secondary protocol?" she demanded.

Liu refused to make eye contact. None of the agents would.

Carrie wheeled around to Theo. "Tell me. What's the secondary protocol?"

Theo held her gaze, but didn't speak. She could see the muscles on the side of his neck twitching.

Carrie was the wife of a seasoned airline captain, a pilot who'd been flying on September 11th. She understood the situation at hand; she knew what the military's response was supposed to be.

She knew. She wanted to hear them confirm it.

Theo looked away, toward Liu, his eyes burning with betrayal.

Carrie understood.

"You are *not* going to shoot down that plane," she said, her voice rising with each word.

"Ma'am, you need to let the professionals handle this. Ma'am—" Liu indicated to agents to restrain her.

"You have to give him a chance!" Carrie screamed, hysterical now. Two agents fought hard to pull her away. "You don't know him! He'll land the plane! I swear on my children's life, he'll find a way!"

CHAPTER THIRTY-ONE

JO STOOD AT THE FRONT OF THE PLANE, SURVEILLING THE CABIN.
The businessman in row one, the first to go after the
canister, was fiddling with his mask. He tightened the
straps and adjusted the cup before taking it off his face
entirely. Putting it back on, he took a deep breath and
his eyes widened in alarm.

Jo's pulse raced. The twelve minutes was up.

She could feel the air still flowing in her own mask
and it brought a twinge of guilt. She reminded herself it
was simply protocol. *Put your mask on first before assisting others.* She preached it every day, in every safety
demo. She'd even driven it home to Daddy and Kellie:
*You two know this plane and you know what to do in an
emergency. The passengers are going to need you alive for
this.* Jo knew she was of no use to anyone if she was
dead, but it was impossible not to feel ashamed at having a tool the passengers didn't.

"My mask broke," the businessman said, his panic
evident. "I'm not getting any air."

"Sir," Jo started cautiously, "I think that—"

She didn't hear the cockpit door opening behind her. It was the sight of a silver canister sailing over her head into the main cabin that told her a second attack was underway. Jo spun on her heels just as the cockpit door slammed shut.

Turning back to the cabin, she watched the container land with a puff of white residue mushrooming above before it rolled down the aisle toward the back. It was now well beyond the bulkhead, nearly to the over-wing.

Jo froze. Should she run after it? Or should she maintain her defensive post in case another canister appeared? But if she—

A jarring boom in the back reverberated all the way to the front of the plane as the retractable jump seat slammed against the wall. Daddy appeared a split second later, sprinting up the aisle toward the canister.

A woman in an aisle seat unbuckled her seat belt and skittered toward the window, trapping her seatmates. Other rows followed suit. Someone kicked the canister and Daddy's head bobbed as he tried to locate where it went. Passengers jostled as the canister rolled toward them underfoot until moments later when it reappeared, flying through the air after someone tossed it out of their row. Everyone scrambled to get away from the thing or to get it away from them, but the whole time, a steady stream of white poison snaked out of it, filling the enclosed cabin that now had no secondary oxygen.

Jo's heart beat so fast it was painful. She alternated focus between Daddy and the cockpit door, desperately wanting to assist. *Stay put and protect the front,* she told herself. *Let them handle the back. They got this.* But the urge to help was overwhelming.

With a glance back, Jo saw the canister drop in the

middle of the aisle just ahead of Daddy. He lunged with a grunt, his outstretched body completely airborne before he fell onto the floor with a thud, trapping the canister underneath him. Daddy curled himself into a ball, wrapping his arms around his shins. The stream of white residue ceased—the poison canister was trapped inside his awkward fetal position.

He stopped moving and yelled something and a moment later a wad of red fabric was tossed in his direction. Jo thought it looked like a sweatshirt.

Daddy laid the sweatshirt open beside him on the floor before he outstretched his legs and rolled on top of it as fast as he could. Jo wanted to cheer. She got it now. The canister was now lodged in between his body and the sweatshirt. Awkwardly, with the oxygen bottle sliding across his back, he shimmied his hands under his body to grab at the fabric, wrapping it around the canister. Jo could see him trying to press his body into the floor with all his weight as he maneuvered. *That's right, baby,* she thought proudly. *Smother it.*

He was fighting brilliantly, but his movements began to slow and look uncoordinated. Jo fought the urge to run to him. She knew it was the poison. He needed help. She could hear Kellie in the back galley opening and closing carriers with a slam. Jo knew she was looking for the trash bags and wished Kellie would hurry the hell up.

The canister was now rolled up tight in the sweatshirt and Daddy clutched it to his chest. He struggled to get to his feet before a man across from him stood up and took him under an arm. A woman on the other side did the same in spite of her relentless, involuntary cough. The whole cabin was filled with screaming and coughing.

Damnit, Kellie, c'mon. Daddy needs—

Jo's stomach turned as she remembered.

Catering had shorted them on trash bags. What few they had, Jo had taken for the attack. They didn't have any trash bags in the back. Jo and her ABPs had them all up front.

"Josip," Jo yelled, pointing to the bag dangling from the seat-back pocket in front of him. "Take that and—"

Kellie burst out of the back galley, extending something to Big Daddy as she ran up the aisle toward him. Daddy shifted and Jo could see the coffee carafe Kellie held out. The plastic vessel had a wide mouth—but most importantly, it sealed up airtight. Jo didn't know if the canister would be small enough to fit inside, but if it did, the carafe was perfect.

Daddy held out the rolled-up sweatshirt and went to unfurl it, but he stopped, looking around at the passengers. Jo saw them breathing through their shirts, covering their mouths with their hands, coughing compulsively. They had no clean oxygen.

Daddy ripped the container out of Kellie's hands and squeezed past her, sprinting toward the back of the plane, the sweatshirt tucked into the crook of his arm like a football.

Kellie yelled something after him, seeming to understand his next move.

He stepped to the side. She passed him and yanked open the door to the lav. Daddy ducked inside and she slammed the door closed behind him.

Jo kept looking from the cockpit door to the back galley. Kellie stood outside the lav, waiting, her heavy breathing apparent all the way in the front. Kellie turned forward and, seeing Jo looking back, ripped the interphone off the wall. Jo answered before the green light

even lit up. Kellie's voice was high-pitched and panicked.

"We didn't have any—"

"I know," Jo said, trying to sound calm. "You're doing
great. What do you need?"

"I don't know. I don't know. Nothing. I think—"

The lav door flew open and Daddy came tumbling
out of the bathroom backward. Tripping himself up, he
fell against the cabin divider before falling to the floor.
He kicked at the door and it slammed shut, the coffee carafe and poison canister inside. Kellie let go of
the phone and ran to him, dropping to her knees at
his side. She recoiled instantly, her hands flying to her
mask as she scrambled back up and ran to the other side
of the galley. Jo could hear a carrier opening and closing through the open line as the interphone dangled
off the hook.

With the phone pressed against her ear, Jo looked
back and forth between the front and the back. Afraid
another attack would come. Worried they wouldn't have
the tools to fight it if it did.

Kellie reappeared holding a large water bottle. Jo
kept the phone pressed to her ear, barely able to hear
what was happening. Kellie squatted beside Big Daddy.

"Take a deep breath and hold it," Jo heard Kellie say,
"then lean your head back and open your eyes."

Daddy did as he was told. Kellie pulled off his mask
and poured water all over his face. His body tensed in
response. Kellie placed the mask back on his face and
Jo could see Daddy react to the fresh air. She knew the
relief he felt, but from the noises he was making, she
could only imagine how much pain he was in. He'd
taken a massive hit of the poison and she knew he
needed medical attention. Jo wondered if they should

put an ABP in his jump seat and have him take a passenger seat for landing and the evacuation. Was he no
longer able to fulfill his duties? Was he incapacitated?
She prayed her friend was okay, that he could hold on
until they landed.

Daddy looked to Kellie and took a labored breath.
Jo waited. His voice was ragged and frail.

"Are we there yet?"

CHAPTER THIRTY-TWO

"TAKE THE PLANE OFF AUTOPILOT," BEN SAID.

Bill stared out ahead of him, his body pressed against the seat belt harness. He reached up to the panel over his head, punching a button labeled "AP1," and the green light above it went out. Three chimes rang through the cockpit. The autopilot had been disengaged. Bill wrapped his fingers around the joystick to his left, the plane coming under his total control.

His vision had returned but his head was still woozy, the struggle to focus made worse by the sounds that replayed in his head.

The sounds from the cabin during the second attack.

The first attack, the crew had expected. The noises were awful, but they were restrained and controlled; the sounds of a difficult, but fair, fight.

The second had been different. The suffering was palpable.

Goddammit, Bill. Be a pilot. Shut it out. Compartmentalize, goddammit.

Compartmentalization was the only way to remain

in control during a crisis. Tackle the issue with logic and reason—deal with how you feel about it later. It's a mindset drilled into every pilot from day one.

But all the training in the world couldn't completely drive the sounds of the attack from his head. And along with those sounds came a single voice that called up a possibility he didn't want to consider.

Today you will fail, the voice said. *Your family, Jo, the crew, the passengers. You already have failed them and you will continue to.*

Bill clenched and unclenched his fist repeatedly.

Compartmentalize, Bill.

Gradually, his shoulders dropped. He began to breathe through his nose instead of his mouth. The cacophony in his head softened until only the hum of the engines remained.

The day was not over.

They were still on their original path, approaching New York from the southwest, flying over New Jersey suburbs. Homes with a view of the city. A vantage from which, all those years ago, people had stood in their backyards watching gray smoke rise off the downtown skyline against a perfect blue-sky morning. In the distance, directly in front of them, the island of Manhattan glimmered in the night.

It was cruel of Ben to wait this long to direct Bill to the next step. Washington felt so far away now that their original destination was within view.

"Hand fly to the target," Ben said.

Bill furrowed his brow. "Navigationally speaking, how do—"

He stopped himself.

No.

No, no, no . . .

Bill cursed himself. How could he have been so stupid? So blind?

"We're not diverting to DC, are we?"

Ben's face held no emotion.

"Of course." Bill put it together out loud. "Why would you tell me the real target? You assumed I'd talk to the ground. Why would you give them five hours to prepare?" Bill shook his head and stared at New York City out the window in front of him. The looming potential targets seemed to mock his shortsightedness.

"Enough already, Ben. What's the real target?"

The Empire State Building was lit up blue and white, the iconic landmark rising up out of the heart of midtown. Below, at the city's southern tip, the tallest building on the island: One World Trade. The Freedom Tower.

"Don't tell me," Bill said.

The first officer shook his head.

Ben stared out the window straight ahead. A smile crept onto his face. He nodded in front of him.

Bill followed the direction of his gaze. Out the window, up the island of Manhattan. Past One World Trade, beyond the Empire State Building, to a cluster of bright lights in the Bronx.

Under his breath, Ben began to sing.

"Take me out to the ball game . . ."

CHAPTER THIRTY-THREE

THEO AND CARRIE STOOD ACROSS THE PARKING LOT, IGNORED BY THE other agents. They both paced anxiously, trying to figure out what to do.

According to the chatter in Theo's earpiece, preparations to enact secondary protocol had been put in motion in Washington, DC. The FBI issued an official public statement, and the media was now flooded with images of tourists and government officials running for cover. The lights at the White House had been shut off, leaving pundits to speculate that the president had been taken to the bunker. Across town at the Pentagon, armed soldiers in tactical gear streamed in and out of the building. Listening to the reports come in was disorienting. This had been their crisis, but now it spanned coast to coast. It was growing into something else entirely.

Liu and the LA team had been relaying everything they knew to the authorities on the East Coast, but they didn't have much to offer. They'd given what information they had on the two suspects and were conducting background searches as rapidly as possible. The findings would most likely be moot at this point, but after learning of Ben's involvement, they weren't taking any chances. Any potential lead was to be pursued—and that included intelligence on Bill. Theo knew Carrie couldn't hear what was being discussed in his ear, but it made him shift on his feet anyway. She was practically a stranger to him, but somehow the Hoffmans already felt like family. Hearing the FBI discuss her husband as a potential threat felt like a betrayal.

Theo had immediately texted Jo to let her know about Ben. But Jo hadn't replied. Theo and Carrie looked down at his cell phone, waiting.

"It says 'Delivered,'" Carrie said.

"Sure, but did she see it?"

Carrie had no response.

Theo stared at his phone, praying those three dots would pop up on Jo's side of the text. He tried to block out the dark thoughts, but they crowded into the silence. No one knew what the poison was. They had no idea what had actually happened up there. For all they knew, Jo never got the text because . . .

Theo handed Carrie the phone and shook out his hands.

"She's just busy," Carrie said in a way that was meant to reassure them both. "She got the text. She's fine. She just can't respond. Have we heard anything else from Bill?"

Theo shook his head. Bill hadn't communicated via Morse since his last message regarding the family's location. That didn't bode well for the argument that he remained uncompromised.

"Well, he's busy too," Carrie said. "Aviate. Navigate. Communicate."

Theo angled his head. "What?"

"Aviate, navigate, communicate. It's the pilots' . . . motto? I don't know what you'd call it. It's their list of priorities. Aviate—fly the plane. Navigate—know where you're going. Communicate—talk to who you need to about what you need to. It's usually not a problem to do all three. But in an emergency?" Carrie shrugged. "They do what they can. I think communication is a luxury Bill and Jo can't afford right now."

Theo's mind went to the "Miracle on the Hudson." He remembered looking online for the recording of the conversation between Air Traffic Control and the cockpit because he'd been perplexed by how little Captain Sullenberger had said during the incident. The entire flight was only three, maybe four, minutes long. And the controller kept giving the pilot options—but Sully hardly responded. And when he did, it was short and direct. "Unable." And then finally, "We're gonna be in the Hudson." Aviate, navigate, communicate. It now made sense.

Bill wasn't compromised. He was occupied.

"You know you're right. Right?" Theo said.

She looked up.

"You need to tell them."

"They won't listen to me."

"But you're right."

Carrie shot him a look of admonishment. "Since when does being right mean you get heard? You should understand that better than most."

Theo shook his head. "But you *are* right. And Jo's right. But no one's going to listen to either of you in time."

Theo rubbed his face in frustration, his eyes landing on the phone in Carrie's hand.

The same phone he'd watched his aunt speak from earlier in the video the whole world had seen.

"Carrie," Theo said slowly, as the idea in his head became fully formed. "We gotta go."

Jo spread her legs for balance and grabbed on to opposite sides of the bulkhead as the plane began to tremble. She refused to leave her position in front of the cockpit door. There was no indication that a third attack was coming, but then again, there had been no indication for the second.

Behind her, the cabin had grown eerily silent. She glanced back quickly to check on the passengers and the small movement sent cold streaks of pain down her neck. She felt something on her leg and looked down. Her pantyhose were corroding, burning away as painful sores blossomed on her skin beneath.

She ignored it all.

Daddy was coming out of the bathroom, drying his hands. His sleeves were rolled up, the dark-gray uniform wet at the cuffs. Jo assumed he had been trying to rinse the poison off his skin. Kellie had spent the last ten minutes passing out bottles of water to the passengers, instructing them to pour the water in their eyes, on their hands, down their faces. Anywhere the poison had touched. She told them to pull their shirts up over their mouth and nose, anything to filter the air, even just a little. Jo didn't know if the passengers were succumbing to the poison or if they just didn't have any fight left—but no one resisted, no one asked for an explanation, no one demanded a thing of her.

My god, she was proud of them. Chance had thrown these strangers together and they had responded magnificently. Same with the crew. Jo couldn't imagine better flight attendants to have been paired with than Kellie and Big Daddy. They weren't on the ground yet, but because of their actions, 144 people sat in their seats injured and struggling—but alive.

This was where their role in the plan ended. It was up to Bill now.

Bill.

The captain. The man whose family had been taken. For all Jo knew, Carrie and the kids were already dead. Jo's stomach sank at the same time that the plane dropped.

Her world rocked from side to side as the downward pitch increased. Her abdominal muscles clenched as she worked to maintain her balance. Squatting, she glanced out the small porthole window on the door to her right. The lights on the ground were growing brighter, blurring as the plane moved faster and closer to the ground. She'd put it off as long as she could. It was time to get in her jump seat and strap in. Just like she told Kellie and Daddy—the passengers needed her alive.

Buckled in, the oxygen tank sandwiched against her back, she leaned forward to look out the window again. Jo had flown into JFK countless times. She knew the approach well.

She knew they were deviating from it.

Bill.

What was it he had said to her? *You have my word that I am not going to crash this plane. But how I accomplish that I haven't figured out yet.* His statement came to Jo like he was whispering it in her ear. He had assured her he wouldn't crash the plane. But at what cost? Her heart ached for her friend and the burden he carried, the choice he had to make.

The back of her head smacked against the headrest

as her feet left the floor. She tried to look confident, like the plane's shuddering was all part of the plan. But their speed at this low altitude and the wild, off-course descent was telling her something else.

"Bill?" she whispered quietly to herself, the passengers unable to see her lips under her mask. The dim cabin hid her tears. The evidence was mounting—something was wrong. Her voice cracked as she issued a second plea: "Captain?"

Did he need help? She wanted to do something, she wanted to get up and fix it, she wanted to control the outcome. Moving to unbuckle her harness—to do what, she had no idea—she felt her phone in her pocket. She realized she hadn't checked it since before the first attack started.

The bright digital display bounced in the turbulence as she struggled to hold it still enough to read. She had several unread messages from Theo.

Carrie and the kids are safe. Bad guy dead.

Jo kicked the bulkhead in front of her with both feet. Strapped to her jump seat with her hands full, it was literally the only physical reaction she could have. Jo had never felt an emotion as pure as the feeling of relieved victory that raced through her body after reading that message. She squinted through a smile that ran over the sides of her oxygen mask as she read Theo's next text.

THE FIRST OFFICER IS IN ON THE PLAN. HE HAS A GUN. BILL MAY NEED HELP.

The human psyche wasn't meant to sustain highs and lows of this magnitude in this short a period of time. The news ran through her body like an electric shock. The phone slipped from her fingers and landed on the galley floor.

The backup plan was Ben. The threat they had been looking for this whole time . . .

. . . *was one of them.*

She stared at the plexiglass bulkhead in a slack-jawed stupor. In all of their preparations the first officer hadn't crossed her mind. Not once did she wonder how Bill would manage an attack on the cabin—with another pilot sitting beside him. The flight attendants had enough to deal with. Everything that was happening on the other side of the door she'd simply left up to Bill. But now, Jo felt like a fool that something so obvious hadn't even occurred to her.

As the plane jostled beneath her, she tried to piece together what it meant, what they were now dealing with. She numbly unbuckled her harness and reached over to pick up her cell phone off the floor. The oxygen tank slid around her body, shifting her center of gravity. Catching herself against the bulkhead, she grabbed the phone and pulled herself back upright. Her hands shook violently.

She was losing control.

Jo stopped. Closed her eyes. Took a deep breath.

Young lady, this is not over yet. Now sit deep and put your spurs on.

As she yanked the interphone off the cradle, a high-low chime rang through the cabin.

"Daddy. Get up here. We've got a new problem."

CHAPTER THIRTY-FOUR

CARRIE'S PACE WAS BRISK AS THEY CROSSED THE PARKING LOT.
Scott trailed her by a few steps, struggling to keep up.

"Mom," the boy said, "where are we going?"

Carrie glanced over her shoulder. Rousseau was walking back to the other agents nonchalantly. He hadn't seemed fazed when she retrieved the kids; he merely handed Elise over and then squeezed Scott's shoulder and told him he was a brave young man. Then he turned and walked away, and that was that.

"We're going to help Daddy," Carrie said.

Scott looked back toward the FBI agents, confused. "Aren't they?"

Carrie hesitated. "Uh, yes, baby. They are. We're just going to try something else too."

They moved toward the far end of the parking lot where several rows of RVs were parked. Theo had instructed her to get the kids and then meet him over there. She didn't ask what would happen after that. She barely knew Theo, but to say she trusted him with their lives was a literal statement today.

Carrie's pulse raced as they walked around the RVs. Some had lights on and their owners sat in collapsible chairs enjoying the sea breeze from their makeshift front porches. Carrie was nearing the end of the rows when she heard her name. She whipped her head to her left, toward the sound.

Theo motioned for them to come over just as his phone started to ring.

"Agent Baldwin," he said as he answered. He listened for a beat before looking around the parking lot. Then, with a start, he began to wave his arm. "I see you. We're at the front, by the RVs. I'm waving."

Carrie turned to see a van headed toward them. It had several antennas and a large satellite dish mounted to the roof. As it got closer, she could make out the red CNB logo painted across the side. Stopping beside them, the side door slid open and Vanessa Perez, a young woman Carrie recognized from the evening broadcast, hopped out. She gave the family a warm, relieved smile before her eyes widened at the sight of Theo, all bloody and beat-up.

"What happ—"

"Later," Theo said, cutting her off. He took the baby from Carrie as she and Scott climbed into the van before he, Elise, and the reporter piled in after them. The door shut, and the van was off.

"Where are we going?" Carrie asked, bracing herself as the van made a sharp turn.

Theo paused before saying simply: "Home."

"Coastal four-one-six, come in," Dusty said, rocking his chair back and forth.

As the tower's senior controller—and as a man whose

temperament treated the extreme as blasé—he was the obvious choice for handling 416. But watching the beacon track across the radar in front of him with no response in his headphones, Dusty felt his chest squeeze uncomfortably. He assumed that was the feeling of "anxiety" that people often talked about.

He didn't like it.

All traffic into JFK, LGA, EWR, DCA, IAD, and BWI had been diverted to alternates, the airspace closed to all inbound aircraft save one: Flight 416.

Typically at that time of night, the runways would be packed with international red-eyes heading to Europe. Trans-cons coming in from out west. Commuter traffic from all the major East Coast cities. More than sixty million passengers traveled in and out of New York via JFK's four runways every year. But tonight the airport looked like a sleepy regional operation.

Inside the tower it was another story. Flashing red-and-blue lights painted the room from the emergency crews outside on the ground. It accentuated the frenetic energy, but the professionals remained focused.

"Coastal four-one-six, come in," Dusty said again.

Nothing.

He checked the clock. Eleven minutes with no response.

Leaning back in his chair, he looked across the room to the military officer sitting at another station. The metal on his uniform glinted under the lights. He wore thick, official-looking headphones that were nicer than any piece of equipment in the tower. One hand pressed to an ear, the other wrapped around a hand mic, he tapped out Morse code. Military code talkers had been deployed to the DC towers as well, just in case, although 416 had yet to communicate with any of them.

Making eye contact with Dusty, the Morse talker shook his head. Glancing at the clock, he wrote something on a piece of paper and held it up: "18."

Dusty cursed and dragged a hand down his stubbly face. Nearly twenty minutes dark. He glanced to the back of the room, where the number of stern men in uniform seemed to grow every minute.

Dusty knew it wasn't looking good for Flight 416.

He glanced at the three large televisions that hung on the wall across the far side of the room in the tower. Normally displaying weather radars and flight information, tonight they were tuned to various news stations. The only thing being covered was the unfolding crisis. Some network showed basic stock footage and information: animated displays of the flight path, departure and arrival times, aircraft specs and logistical frameworks. Other screens replayed Jo's video, which had elevated her from anonymous flight attendant to household name in record time. A picture of the Hoffman family circulated: father, mother, son, and daughter on a beach at sunset. Live feed from Washington, DC, showed traffic at a standstill as the roads in and out of the city clogged with evacuees.

On the other side of the room, Dusty could see George in his office. The ATC manager stood behind his desk and braced himself on his fists, confronting Lieutenant General Sullivan, the military commander who was in charge. George's controllers had never seen their boss lose his temper or even raise his voice, so they looked away and tried not to listen. It felt like a betrayal of the man they respected so much. But overhearing was unavoidable and it quickly became clear to Dusty and his colleagues that George was losing the argument.

"You're going to shoot down that plane, aren't you?"

"That doesn't concern you," Sullivan said. "Contingency plans do not—"

George slammed his fists on the desk. The controllers flinched. "You're going to shoot down a commercial airliner full of innocent civilians—"

"That is enough, Mr. Patterson!" the officer barked, unaccustomed to insubordinate pushback. "You and your staff are hereby ordered to commence standard operating procedures and nothing more. Anything else is unauthorized and out of your hands."

George didn't respond.

"Do you understand?" Sullivan snarled.

"Affirmative," George replied. "Your guys will have full access to whatever they need."

The door ripped open. The controllers tried to look busy.

"Dusty," George said calmly, his face a worrisome shade of red. Three uniformed officers stepped up behind him. "I'm going to need you to teach these guys the basics."

The tower was silent.

"I'm a little busy for training new hires right now," Dusty said, his eyes darting between his boss and the men.

"Couldn't agree more. Do it anyway," George said as he put his own headset on, grabbing a pair of binoculars off a desk and tossing them to one of the officers.

No one in the tower said a word. Everyone knew what the military's secondary protocol was in a situation like this. But actually facing it rendered them speechless.

Dusty shook his head, muttering to his seatmate, "Is it too late to call out sick?" He gestured for the men to come over, but stopped short and pointed at the TVs instead. Everyone turned.

Having broken away from footage in the field, CNB was now broadcasting a lone news anchor in the studio. His eyes darted between the camera and his notes. The look on the man's face said it all: he had exclusive, breaking news, in an already unprecedented moment. Someone in the tower unmuted the TV.

"—the wife of Captain Bill Hoffman, the pilot flying the hijacked flight, Coastal four-one-six. As we speak, she is with one of our Los Angeles field reporters, and I am told Mrs. Hoffman has an important message for the American public, and for the president. We'll break to them as soon as we get word that they're ready. CNB has not been told what . . ."

Dusty looked over to George and the military officers but they were captivated by the scene unfolding on the screen in front of them. He turned back to the radar. As far as Dusty was concerned, the ball was still in play. "Coastal four-one-six, come in," he said again into his mic, almost adding at the end: *please*.

Carrie's body slapped back against the seat as the news van came to a halting stop. The cameraman slid open the side door and hopped out quickly. Vanessa followed suit with Scott trailing her. Carrie jumped out next, turning back to take Elise from Theo. The camera was already rolling on the reporter as she walked backward, away from the van, speaking into a handheld microphone.

"I'm here at what remains of the Hoffman home," Vanessa said, indicating the pile of rubble over her shoulder, "with Mrs. Hoffman—Carrie—and her two children. I'm thrilled to report that the family is now safe, and unharmed. But the situation on Flight four-one-six

remains precarious, and Mrs. Hoffman has an important message she needs to share with everyone watching. Specifically, the president of the United States." The
reporter took a breath and motioned for the family, but
stopped. The cameraman glanced over his shoulder. Seeing the family's state, he turned the lens, and the view of
the world, toward them.

Carrie stood still with her mouth hanging open,
rooted in place by the sight of her home. Or what had
been her home. With slow steps forward, she moved
toward what the explosion had left behind—which
was . . . nothing. There was nothing left to their house.
She heard Scott sniffle and took his hand.

Vanessa held up the yellow caution tape and the family ducked under. The reporter didn't speak and Carrie
knew everyone watching at home was silent too. They'd
all seen the house, they knew what had happened. But
this was the family's first time coming home, seeing it
for themselves. Carrie looked across the way to the oak
tree in their backyard, thinking of how she'd stood at
the kitchen sink, just this morning, watching its leaves
dance in the breeze. The tree was now splintered and
scorched and the kitchen was simply no longer. She
shook her head slowly as she took it all in, but didn't
say a word.

"Mrs. Hoffman," Vanessa said gently. "Are you alright?" She held the microphone out.

Carrie switched Elise to her other hip before retaking Scott's hand. Turning to the reporter, her wet eyes
burned with determination as she said, "We'll be alright
once the plane is on the ground."

Vanessa smiled. "Ma'am," she said, "what do you
need us to know?"

Carrie nodded, bringing Scott in front of her and

placing a hand on her son's shoulder before taking a deep breath in.

"Mr. President," she said, exhaling her nerves. "I know you're in the Situation Room right now deciding what should be done. I know you're being presented with all the information as it comes in. I know you know that my children and I were taken from our home at gunpoint. That we were tied up and gagged. That I was strapped with explosives. That our"—her voice broke as she glanced at the smoking pile of rubble— "our home was destroyed. I know you know that the FBI rescued us. That we're now safe. And I know you've also been informed that my husband's copilot, the first officer, has a gun and that he's been a part of the plan all along."

Carrie had no idea what officials had shared with the public so far, but by the look on the reporter's face, that was clearly new information.

"I know the decision of what to do right now is ultimately up to you alone. That choice cannot be easy to make. I know that the United States doesn't negotiate with terrorists." Carrie wrapped her arm around the front of Scott's shoulders, her voice breaking again. "And I know that more likely than not you're going to choose to shoot down that plane."

Scott looked up at his mom. She tightened her grip.

"Sir. Mr. President. Before you make that decision, before you shoot down a commercial flight full of innocent Americans, I need to tell you what information I know. What you won't be told by the FBI. What won't be in your briefings."

Carrie paused as a tear slid down her cheek. A smile graced her lips.

"I know what will save that plane. I know the best

chance those innocent passengers have at survival. I know how to get them home tonight to their families." Another tear. "But it won't be the easy choice—it will be the hard choice. Because it will require you to ignore the facts—and trust in the truth. Because the truth is this: the best chance Flight four-one-six has is already on board."

Carrie bit her bottom lip, staring off for a moment, trying to figure out how to articulate what she wanted to say.

"When my family was taken and Bill was presented with the choice of us or the plane, do you know what he said? When our children had a gun to their heads, when he knew our house had been blown up—do you know what he said?" She shrugged with a smile. "He said no. He didn't make a choice. He didn't give in because he also knows we don't negotiate with terrorists."

She ran a hand through her hair. "See, that's where these guys miscalculated. They misunderstood duty. Bill—my husband, Captain Hoffman—is a man of duty. I understand that entirely. And Mr. President, as a man of duty yourself, I'm sure you do too. I am unbelievably grateful that the FBI found us in time. Because I know my husband. And I know, on my life—and today I can actually say that—that my husband would not have crashed that plane to save us. And now? Now that his family is safe and he knows that?" A small chuckle escaped her lips. She stood a little straighter. "It's not possible that my husband won't figure out a way to land that plane safely."

Adjusting Elise on her hip, she placed her hand firmly on top of Scott's shoulder.

"Mr. President. For the sake of my children's father, and all the mothers and fathers and sons and daughters on board that plane right now, I am begging you to make the brave choice to give that plane and the passengers on it a chance. If you make the weak choice, the easy choice, and you shoot it down—we know exactly what will happen. But I'm asking you to be brave and have faith. I'm asking you to choose to trust in a good man, a man of duty. I know, sir, that your faith will be rewarded."

The tower was reduced to stunned silence before a murmur of discussion began to fill the space. The air was charged with hope and Dusty clapped the controller next to him on the back.

"Would it be weird if I gave her a standing ovation?"

The controller ignored him, her face contorted with alarm. She pointed at Dusty's radar.

"Fuuuuuuuu—" Dusty muttered. "George? Four-one-six has started to fly off course."

"Quiet!" the Morse talker said. The entire tower turned at the uncharacteristic outburst. Everyone watched him listening to his headset, intense concentration painting his face. Suddenly his tight brow slackened in understanding, mouth falling open.

"It's not Washington. The target is Yankee Stadium."

CHAPTER THIRTY-FIVE

ON THE RADAR DISPLAY IN FRONT OF BILL, MULTIPLE CROSS MARKS popped up to their rear. Four F-16s were now within striking distance of Flight 416.

Bill rubbed his face in frustration. He had known it would come to this when they found out about Ben's involvement. It was exactly why he hadn't sent a Morse message to tell them. Now he had two threats to deal with.

"It's not fair," Bill said.

Ben spoke, without looking at him. "What, Bill? What isn't fair?"

The plane bounced in response to a wind pocket, twinkling neighborhood lights appearing through the window on Bill's side as the plane banked left. It was a clear night, but the wind was fierce and the plane bucked and twisted.

"Coastal four-one-six, come in."

The repeated squawk from the same controller came through both their headsets again, but neither pilot moved to respond. They hadn't since the first gas attack, and they wouldn't the rest of the flight. It was just the two men now.

"It's not fair that . . ." Bill struggled to put his thoughts in order. "That I'm here. And you're here. That I had my life, and you had yours. It's not fair that nobody seems to care about your people. It's not right. And I'm sorry."

Ben didn't reply.

Bill turned to face his copilot directly. "You have my word, Ben. I will spend the rest of my life working to right these wrongs. I can't change what's happened in your life. You can't change it either. But if we crash this plane, nothing good is going to come of it. You know this country. You know what we'll do in response. You know who will suffer."

Ben stared out the window.

"But if we don't crash this plane," Bill continued, "we can work together. I'll educate myself. I'll learn what I already should have known. And then maybe the two of us can fix some things."

The gun was directly between them. Neither spoke. Ben turned, searching the captain's face. Bill looked him in the eye, desperately hoping his sincerity was felt and believed.

"Ben. It's not too late."

Holding the mail in his mouth, Ben pulled the door handle toward him as he struggled with the key. The lock squeaked, as did the door, when he walked into the apartment, pulling his suitcase behind him. Turning on the kitchen light, a sink full of dirty dishes welcomed him home. He tossed the mail onto the kitchen table next to a half-eaten bowl of cereal.

He sighed. Exhausted from his four-day and exhausted by his life.

"I thought you were going to call the super to fix the door while I was gone," he said loudly, laying his hat on the counter, draping his uniform coat across the back of a chair. "The place looks like shit, man."

Grabbing a beer from the fridge, he sat at the table, flipping through the mail. Trashing the junk, he laid the rest next to the newspaper.

The newspaper.

He cocked his head. He and Sam didn't get the paper.

Picking it up, he found a different publication underneath from a different day. Below it, another one. All of them were dog-eared and marked with red ink. Every story was about the troop withdrawal.

Realizing Sam hadn't said anything since he'd come home, Ben turned. Sam's bedroom light was on, the door ajar.

"Sam?"

There was no response.

"Saman," he said louder, crossing the living room. Knocking to no response, he pushed the door open.

Blood soaked the mattress so deeply it almost appeared black. If there hadn't been trails of red leading from Sam's forearms down, Ben probably wouldn't have understood what he was looking at.

"Oh my god!" Ben yelled, lunging toward his friend, then pulling back, pivoting on his heels. "Fuck!" he screamed, running into the kitchen. Grabbing his phone, he dialed 911, swearing again as he ran back into the bedroom.

Sam's eyes were clear and focused despite his shallow breathing and gray skin. Ben hovered over him shouting into the phone.

"Hurry!" he screamed, and hung up, the phone clenched beneath white knuckles.

He grabbed the bedsheet and wound it around Sam's

wrists to try to stop the bleeding. The two friends stared at each other, trying to interpret what the other was thinking.

Sam's voice was weak and slow. "Remember when we got drinks that time at that place by the beach? The place with the outdoor patio. With the blankets for when it gets cold? We had oysters. You tried to hit on the girl at the bar next to you. Then her boyfriend showed up."

Ben smiled faintly and nodded.

"Right then. Right there. That's the exact moment our village was attacked."

Ben shut his eyes.

"We left them there."

Tears squeezed out the corners of Ben's closed eyes, dropping onto Sam's chest.

"I can't do this anymore," Sam whispered. "Any of it."

He groaned in pain. Ben gripped his wrists tighter.

"Why?" Sam said. "Why are you stopping me?"

Ben clenched his jaw, his breath savage with shame and anger. For the first time he admitted to himself what Sam had already decided.

"Because I'm pissed off you would leave me here. We will do this together."

"Ben, let's make a choice," Bill said, "together. Right now. Let's choose to help your people, not hurt them. We can do that."

Bill couldn't tell if Ben was seriously considering the offer, but the young man was clearly thrown off. Empathy must not have been in his calculations. Bill realized he was leaning toward Ben, trying to will him to his side, to a place where they could land the plane safely, together.

"Coastal four-one-six, this is Air Force Lieutenant

General Sullivan speaking on behalf of the president of the United States of America."

The pilots flinched at the aggressive voice that barked through the cockpit. "Be advised, we are aware First Officer Ben Miro is a threat. If you do not respond immediately, we are prepared to authorize a military strike on your aircraft. Consider this your warning."

Ben turned to look at the sky, lifting his chin, his jaw clenching.

"It was never about the crash, Bill. It was never about you or the passengers or your family. It wasn't really even about the choice." He shook his head. "It was about waking people up. Doing something dramatic enough to get their attention. Something they couldn't ignore. It wasn't personal."

He turned on Bill with dead, black eyes.

"That was before. Now? I want you to burn."

CHAPTER THIRTY-SIX

WHEN BIG DADDY ENTERED FIRST CLASS, JO GASPED.

"I know. It's gonna be one hell of a tan line," Daddy said.

Outside of his mask, his whole face was red and swollen and covered in blisters. The palms of his hands were wrapped in gauze from the first aid kit and the whites of his eyes were painted red.

Josip stood next to Jo wearing a spare portable oxygen bottle like the rest of the crew. Big Daddy looked the man up and down.

"He's with us," Jo said.

Daddy glanced back at Dave, still slumped over unconscious. "Yeah, no shit," he said. "But why's he up here?"

"Because he's blocking for me," Jo said.

"I'm sorry?"

"We figured out the mole. It's Ben. And he's got a gun."

Daddy blinked at her.

They'd both been in aviation their entire adult lives

and they both knew the only thing you could always count on was that your crew had your back. Crew was family. And family didn't turn on its own.

Big Daddy clutched the sides of the bulkhead to steady himself, searching the floor as if the explanation was stretched out before him.

"Daddy, we don't have time for—"

Bending forward at the waist, he yelled out a string of obscenities. When he stood upright again, he locked his bloodshot eyes on Jo.

"I'm fine," Big Daddy said with a depth to his voice Jo had never heard before. "What's the plan?"

She laid it out quickly and plainly. Daddy was to sit in Jo's jump seat and lead the evacuation from the front once the plane was on the ground. Josip was going to block, and Jo was going to enter the cockpit via keypad entry.

Daddy stared at her. "And do what? Ben has a gun! Jo, we didn't even discuss keypad entry as an option. Because it's *not* an option. You know they'll override—"

"I know!" Jo clenched her fists at her sides. "But I have to try. I have to get up there. To help Bill. Or stop Ben. Or . . ." Jo slapped her jump seat. "Dammit, Daddy, sit down."

Daddy picked up the phone and called the back while strapping himself into the jump seat. As he explained the situation to Kellie, Jo closed and secured a galley carrier. In her hand was a long, hard tube of red plastic with a bulbous end.

Daddy raised his eyebrows and covered the speaker of the phone with his hand. "Ben's got a gun and you're arming yourself with the ice mallet?"

"You got a machete I don't know about?"

Josip remained silent next to Jo, laboring to breathe.

The two of them had taken the brunt of the poison up front in the first attack and, while they looked nothing like Daddy, the poison's effects were showing.

Jo placed a hand on his bicep. "Mr. Guruli. It's time. Stand here with your back to me. Face the passengers. Stop anyone who tries to get past you by any means necessary. The only people in this cabin who we trust are the flight attendants." She squeezed his arm.

Josip nodded and assumed his position. Crossing his arms, he widened his stance, standing up to his full height. He was a mountainous form, rooted and impenetrable. Standing between the two immovable forces, Josip and the door, claustrophobia trickled over Jo.

She took a deep breath, focusing on the vertical display of numbers to the left of the lav. Closing her eyes, she reviewed what was about to happen.

She would enter the secret six-digit numerical code—and then wait. In the cockpit, an alarm would sound, alerting the pilots that someone was trying to force an entry. The pilots would then have forty-five seconds to override the keypad entry attempt. If they did that, the door would remain locked and wouldn't unseal until arrival. If they didn't override her attempt, a green light would appear on the keypad panel and Jo would have a five-second window to open the door. After five seconds, the door would lock again.

The three flight attendants hadn't even considered using the keypad as an option. Mainly because they didn't know Ben was a threat, but also because it was incredibly easy for the pilots to thwart if they wanted to. The whole purpose of the keypad entry was for the unlikely event of a dual pilot incapacitation, an instance where both pilots were unconscious. There was almost no chance that it would work.

Now it was the only option they had.

Jo opened her eyes and raised a hand to the keypad but something kept her from punching the buttons. Her finger wavered over the set of numbers in a maddening hesitation.

On the other side of the door was a landscape of betrayal and violence. Ben had a gun. There was no way to know what might have already happened in there. No way to know what she was going to encounter. And she was about to barge into it blindly. Armed with a plastic ice mallet.

"Jo?"

She looked down to Big Daddy, seated in the jump seat right beside her.

"It's okay to be scared."

She nodded and began entering the code.

CHAPTER THIRTY-SEVEN

A CRACK OF THE BAT.

Foul ball.

Center fielder Bobby Adelson popped up from his ready position, blowing a bubble with his gum. Taking a few restless steps, he kicked a divot of grass.

Stay focused, Bobby. It's just another game. Just another out.

It wasn't. It was game seven of the World Series. The Yankees were up, 2-1. Top of the ninth. The Dodgers had runners on the corners and their cleanup hitter was at bat. Two outs. The count was 2-2. The Yankees were one strike away from being world champions, the only accolade Bobby's long career couldn't claim.

The pitcher shook off a sign from the catcher. He nodded to the next.

Movement out of the corner of Bobby's eye distracted him.

Focus, Bobby.

More movement from the other side. Something was out of place. He looked to the left-field stands.

The fans were leaving. He turned to right field and saw the same thing. They weren't just leaving, they were fleeing, pushing each other up the stairs to the main corridor. He looked at the upper deck and watched fans stream down the rows, disappearing into the stadium's interior. The chorus of cheering was quickly giving way to angry yelling and terrified screams.

Panic swelled in Bobby's chest as he looked to the other outfielders who were equally confused. The right fielder pointed in front of him and started running in. Bobby did the same, seeing all of the players from both teams congregating on the mound.

A prerecorded voice came over the loudspeaker.

"Ladies and gentlemen, please remain calm. For your safety, we are evacuating Yankee Stadium. Please find your closest exit and secondary exit, and walk up or down the aisle toward it now. Once outside, move away from the stadium. Exit ramps and exit stairs will guide you out. Escalators and elevators will not be used during . . ."

Bobby turned to the jumbotron and jogged backward. The screen showed a video of the stadium's evacuation plan, with cartoon figures of event staff guiding and assisting fans.

When he got to the mound, he caught the tail end of the explanation from the home plate umpire. It sounded like they were supposed to exit the field through the clubhouse and head to the team buses.

Bobby turned to the Dodgers shortstop. "What's happening?" he whispered.

"That plane? I guess the stadium's the target."

Bobby's eyes widened. They all knew about Flight 416. Equipment guys in the clubhouse had told the coaches, who told the players, and all game long they'd gotten updates. In a social media world, news this big didn't go unnoticed. Even if you were playing in the World Series.

All around them, fans scrambled in retreat. Clogged aisles lined each section of the stadium as spectators clambered over the chairs and jumped over railings. Traffic at the exits bottlenecked and the wide corridors became a sweltering mess of humanity. Bobby could only imagine how bad the mob scene would be outside the stadium.

A man in a Dodgers hat ran up an aisle, pushing people aside as he went. A woman clutching her sobbing child stepped in front of him and he didn't hesitate to shove them both out of the way. As they fell to the ground, another man pulled the fan back by the neck of his hoodie and began to pummel his face. A third man rushed over to help the woman and child to their feet.

Bobby pulled off his glove and tucked it under his arm as he watched humanity at its worst. And best. Adjusting his hat, he looked around the stands and the palpable atmosphere of fear and panic began to eat at him too—and that's when he noticed the elderly couple.

Coming down the aisle, they moved closer to the field. Stopping about five rows up from the home team dugout, they turned in, the man watching his wife's feet as she stepped over discarded cups and wrappers. They sat down and looked around, soaking up the incredible view from their new seats. It was a significant upgrade. The old man wrapped an arm around his bride and she popped a piece of popcorn into her mouth with a laugh. She wore a Yankees cap that was probably older than any of the players on either team and probably half the front office too. He had his mitt, the leather aged and worn.

"Okay, let's move," the umpire said, slapping his hands together.

"Wait!" Bobby hollered. Everyone turned to him. He was the captain. His voice had weight. "How long do we have?"

The umpire looked at him quizzically. "Five minutes? Ten?"

Bobby shook his head. "You know damn well that's not enough time to evacuate."

The umpire blinked at him.

"C'mon," Bobby said. "Top of the ninth, game seven of the World Series? At Yankee Stadium? A terrorist attack? That's not a coincidence. That's a message." He looked around at the bedlam. "You're telling me you want this to be *our* message?"

The players looked at each other, at the stadium. Bobby smiled.

"I don't know about you boys, but I always prefer to go out swinging."

CHAPTER THIRTY-EIGHT

THE PILOTS FLINCHED AS A PIERCING ALARM SHATTERED THE silence. Locking eyes, they processed the meaning of the seldom-heard alert in the same moment.

Both men released their harnesses and lunged across the cockpit.

Their bodies crashed together over the center console as Ben's left hand stretched toward the override toggle that was below them, just to the right of Bill's seat belt. It was the only way to stop a keypad entry attempt. If he managed to flip the switch down, an electronic bar would slide into position behind the three spring-loaded locks at the top, middle, and bottom of the cockpit door.

Bill felt the plane lean right. He quickly hit the button labeled AP1 and three loud chimes announced the plane's return to autopilot. Struggling to reach Ben's gun with one hand, he tried to keep Ben away from the override toggle with the other. Bill leaned his body into his copilot, leveraging his height advantage, but Ben was younger and stronger.

Bill gave up on reaching the gun and went for Ben's neck instead. Careful not to hit any buttons, he put his foot up on the edge of the center console and raised himself to increase the downward force on Ben's windpipe. Ben buckled slightly, his feet shifting to take the weight. Bill felt his back brushing the buttons in the panel above him and stooped lower as a soft purple hue began to color the first officer's face.

The override window was forty-five seconds. Bill wondered how much time had passed, knowing he *had* to get the upper hand before that door opened.

Ben's face had now turned a shade of blue and his eyes were watering. As Ben's strength waned, Bill could see the gun slipping from his fingers. Ben was able to connect one desperate blow to the side of Bill's head and Bill's foot slipped from the console. Losing his grip, Bill fell over the controls.

Ben gasped for air, leaning back against the front dash. Bill picked himself up carefully, knowing every button or lever mistakenly pushed or engaged could spell a new crisis. Bill knew Ben understood that too. It was the only reason the first officer hadn't fired the gun. A stray bullet could destroy the avionics. Worse, puncture the airframe and cause a decompression. Bill knew Ben wanted the plane to crash—but on his terms.

When Ben had recovered enough to move again, he went for the toggle, and in that moment, Bill reached into his seat, wrapping his hand around the only tool he had left. Clutching the pen that had laid in his lap the whole flight, Bill spun around, grunting as he unleashed his arm in an uppercut.

Ben's eyes bulged and then blinked softly, his free hand rising to the pen that stuck out of his throat. Blood poured down his neck, turning his white uniform shirt crimson. He glanced around the cockpit in a dazed stupor before his attention landed on the weapon in his other hand. Ben leveled the gun at Bill and his eyes rolled into his head as he pulled the trigger.

Big Daddy ducked and Jo clutched her oxygen mask at the sound of the gunshot. Josip glanced over his shoulder quickly before turning back to the cabin, eyes sweeping side to side with alarm. The flight attendants listened in vain. Not another sound came from the cockpit.

Jo adjusted the strap on her oxygen tank and centered herself in front of the cockpit door. Her heart pounded against her chest like a wild animal in a cage. Left foot forward, mallet in her right hand, she put most of her weight on her back leg, bouncing slightly, waiting to pounce on the door when the green light lit up and it unlatched. *If* it lit up and unlatched.

"How long's the override period?" Daddy asked. "Thirty seconds?"

"Forty-five."

"Jesus," he whispered into his mask.

A movement caught Jo's eye and she looked down.

A thin trail of blood seeped out from under the cockpit door.

"Who do we have up there?"

A commander slid a piece of paper in front of Lieutenant General Sullivan. Dusty stepped back out of the way, tossing his headphones on the table. Walking to the other side of the room, he stood beside George and the other controllers and watched their tower turn into a command center.

"Tink, Redwood, Peaches, and Switchblade."

Narrowing his eyes at the radar, Sullivan pressed a button.

"Tink, gimme eyes on the cockpit."

"Yes, sir." The feed sounded throughout the tower.

Blinding pain seared through Bill's arm. The bullet had torn straight through his right shoulder and into his back. Holding himself steady on the dash, his vision flagged as his body went into the initial stage of shock.

Ben's body was slumped onto the center console. Gritting his teeth, Bill leaned over to try to push the first officer off the controls. His brain went fuzzy, a dizzy light-headedness impeding even the most basic of movements. He sat down, afraid he might pass out. Bill grasped at his wounded shoulder, pulling his hand back to find it coated with blood.

He needed to stop the bleeding. He needed to land the plane. There was so much he needed to do. But his body betrayed him.

As his head succumbed to a feather lightness, he slumped forward, rolling over his legs onto the floor. The last thing he saw in his peripheral vision as he slipped out of consciousness was a fighter jet pulling up alongside the plane.

"Uh, sir?"

The whole tower was waiting for Tink's report.

"The cockpit appears to be empty. I don't see anyone in there."

•   •   •

A green light lit up on the keypad. The cockpit unlocked.

Jo pushed the door open with force, the sturdy metal frame latching neatly against the magnets that held it in an open position. She braced, wide-eyed, waiting.

Nothing happened.

Cautiously stepping into the cockpit, she saw movement outside the plane to her left. Raising her mallet reflexively, she saw the nose of a fighter jet drop out of sight behind them.

Shit.

Jo looked down, surveying the scene.

Ben was slumped face-forward onto the center console, blood pouring out from under his body. The gun lay on the floor, just beyond his reach. Jo kicked it away from him.

With her hands under his shoulder and waistline, she pushed him over, his body crumpling into a pile on the floor at the foot of his seat. Rolling him onto his back, Jo raised the ice mallet with a gasp but knew instantly there was no need. He was soaked with blood all the way to his belt from something protruding out of his neck. She leaned forward, unable to tell what it was through the mess of blood and flesh.

She dropped the mallet and turned to the left seat.

In a ball at the foot of his chair, Bill didn't move. Jo scrambled over the controls with a knee on the seat, clambering after her captain.

Crying his name, she tried to roll him over. She could see blood pooling on the ground—but she also saw his back rise with breath. She screamed his name louder, struggling to get a hold on him. She shook his torso while repeating his name but he didn't respond. Her angle was too awkward to slap him, so she pinched his arm—hard. A soft groan escaped his lips. She screamed his name one more time and his eyes fluttered open to the sound. As Bill came closer to consciousness, Jo positioned herself better and began the battle to pull him upright. He was twice her size, but adrenaline gave her an assist, and somehow she was able to get him moving. Together, with Jo doing most of the work, Bill got back in his seat.

"We're not done here," she demanded. "Tell me what to do."

The commercial plane pulled ahead as Tink continued to drop her speed.

The voice in her ear said, "All units move to firing positions. Standby for the order."

"Roger," Tink said.

The porthole window on the aircraft door was too small for her to see anything. But continuing aft, she could see in the passenger windows. An unexpected lump choked her throat.

Through the purple cabin lighting, Tink could see the passengers in their oxygen masks pressed up against the windows watching her. A man near the front of the plane pushed his glasses up as they slid down on the yellow cup. A few rows back an elderly woman laid her hand against the window, a crumpled tissue pressed against her palm. In the row right behind her, Tink could see only the top of an oxygen mask as the small child who sat there struggled to see up and out the window.

The civilian aspect of war was always the hardest to reconcile. A war zone should be a place for soldiers and no one else. Too many nights she'd woken in a sweat, the eyes of that little girl or that old man haunting her sleep.

But this wasn't a war zone. This was just a plane full of innocents, trying to get to their destination. She was the one who had no place here. For the first time in her career, she felt hesitant.

As the last row of the plane passed, she saw a piece of paper pressed to a window with two words scrawled on it in large letters.

"Help Us."

CHAPTER THIRTY-NINE

THEO STOOD APART FROM THE GROUP LOOKING DOWN AT HIS PHONE. he called Carrie over.

The family and the camera crew were all huddled around the news van, glued to the coverage on the screens inside. Some of the neighbors had come out, offering water and snacks, but no one had the stomach for anything. So they all just stood around, numb with helplessness, watching what was happening back east.

Carrie followed Theo away from the van. He kept his voice low.

"Four-one-six is starting to veer off-course."

Carrie stared at him blankly. "How do—"

"Rousseau's texting me updates. Washington was a decoy. The real target is Yankee Stadium."

Carrie turned her head, looking at nothing, as though she didn't understand the words he had said. Theo's phone vibrated.

He read the message twice before closing his eyes with a sigh. He didn't want to tell her what it said and he couldn't stand the sight of Carrie waiting to hear it.

"Theo, please," he heard her say after a moment. "It can't get much worse, can it?"

He kept his eyes shut as he told her that one of the F-16s had tried to get a visual—and the cockpit appeared to be empty. According to the fighter pilot, no one was flying the plane.

Carrie didn't say anything. Theo heard her start to cry.

"Mom?" Scott said. Theo opened his eyes to see the little boy approaching, his sister cradled in his arms.

The sight of the two of them nearly destroyed Theo. Carrie had her back to the children and she wiped her eyes hastily before turning to face them. With a small smile that looked painful, she brushed the hair out of the boy's eyes and took the baby from his arms. Taking her son's hand, they walked back to the news van together.

The beacon on the radar moved further and further from the airport, heading straight toward the Bronx. The only sound in the tower was the occasional attempt to gain contact with the cockpit. But the transmissions had become rote, without hope—no one expected to hear anything from 416.

Lieutenant General Sullivan pushed a button and spoke clearly.

"Sir? We're running out of time. We need a decision, Mr. President."

The lights seemed brighter. The grass greener. The air colder. The noise more crisp. To Bobby, everything at Yankee Stadium felt amplified.

He and the other players on the field bent at the ready, slapping into their gloves. They spat on the field while the batter tapped his bat on the inside of each shoe. The batter let out a heavy exhale before stepping into the box and grinding his feet as he settled in.

The pitch—fastball, outside.

The batter hacked at the ball, dropping to a knee as he fouled it off. Bobby knew how bad the man wanted it, because he knew how bad *he* wanted it. This was no longer just the World Series. This was something else entirely. The batter stepped out of the box, pulling his jersey up off a shoulder, lifting his helmet a couple times.

All around the park, fans continued to flee, jostling each other to get closer to the exits. Parents held their children to their chests. Couples gripped each other's hands. The exits remained clogged, the staircases filled.

A high-pitched scream came from the upper decks to his left. Bobby looked over to find a woman tumbling down the stairs, her body picking up speed in its uncontrolled free fall. Bobby held his breath as he watched her approach the rail at the bottom of the section, a baseball game suddenly the least important thing in the world, but then he saw a large man brace himself and catch her at the very last moment, stopping her from falling a hundred feet to the stands below.

In the lower decks of the stadium, crowding into the rows around home plate and trickling down the baselines, Dodger blue bled into Yankee pinstripe. As the players had returned to their positions on the field, many of the fans had followed suit. It wasn't discussed and it wasn't planned. It was a collective understanding.

They yelled and jeered with each pitch, they ribbed each other and turned their caps inside out. A big guy trotted down from the abandoned concessions with a half dozen looted beer cans clutched against his chest. His buddy heralded him as the hero he was and they promptly distributed the wealth within their section, a sloppy cheer following.

A tiny section of the electronic scoreboard was reserved for the game's stats and the rest of the massive screen projected what was going on outside of their new utopia. Carrie Hoffman pleading to the president. Rescue teams flanking JFK's runways. Reporters pointing up into the night sky. Passengers wearing oxygen masks. And a roving camera inside the stadium showing the remaining faces of those lucky enough to attend game seven of the World Series.

A crack of the bat, the ball hammered to left-center.

The outfielders chased after it, the left fielder pulling back in the gap, but Bobby waved him off, his eyes never leaving the ball. When he got to the wall, Bobby leapt off his feet to attempt the impossible.

Returning to the ground, he slowly extended his glove in the air as astonishment clouded his face. His hand inside still stung from the slap of the ball.

Third out. Game over. The Yankees had won the World Series.

No one moved. Not the players, not the fans. They all simply stared at center field.

Then came a drumbeat through the speakers as victorious horns started to bleat.

Start spreading the news . . .

Bobby stood with his back to the wall, the ball in his glove. The batter, standing in the middle of the base path between first and second, stared into the outfield at his failure. Bobby stared back. After a moment, the losing runner turned and began to walk toward the winning pitcher. He was the only thing that moved in the whole park. No one except Frank Sinatra said a word.

On the mound, the batter stopped in front of the pitcher. Reaching forward, he grabbed the man's shoulders, pulling him into a hug with such force it knocked his glove off. The pitcher's fingers turned white as he clutched the man's back.

Both teams emptied their dugouts as Bobby and the rest of the outfielders ran in. Meeting the two players in the middle of the diamond, they all embraced. Most of them cried. They held their caps and bowed to the fans.

With Ol' Blue Eyes crooning the Yankees'—and the city's—iconic anthem, every person in that stadium, player and fan alike, held on to each other and made peace with their choice to stay.

In the cockpit, Jo tried not to look at the buildings in front of them that drew closer through the windshield. Everything trembled and shook.

Leaning forward in obvious pain, Bill grabbed the sidestick. Blood covered his hand.

Taking a breath, he pressed the trigger underneath.

The open line hummed throughout the tower. Not with the typical scratchiness of aircraft communication, but with the even buzz of advanced technology. The feed to the White House, to the president, played for all to hear. No one moved or spoke as they waited for the verdict on Flight 416.

The president cleared his throat. He'd made his decision.

•   •   •

The echo of Frank Sinatra's last note lingered for a second before dissipating into silence. Everyone looked up at the sky, watching, waiting, praying.

A low rumble in the distance grew louder.

Fear mounted as the players and fans shifted on their feet—but everyone stayed put.

It was the undeniable sound of an airplane closing in.

"Okay," the president began. "I say—"

A burst of static halted the order. Someone drew a ragged breath and a faint voice hijacked the moment.

"This is Captain Hoffman. I have control."

CHAPTER FORTY

HEADS WHIPPED UP AS THE AIRLINER TORE ACROSS THE TOP OF
Yankee Stadium. Everyone ducked. The plane's undercarriage was right on top of them, the wings rocking
side to side in a crazed flyover. It wasn't until the tail
cleared the end of the stadium that they realized the
plane wasn't going to crash.

The ballpark erupted with more jubilation than if
every seat had been filled. Four F-16s appeared, trailing
after the plane. The noise shook the stadium.

They were safe.

"I repeat! No strike! Escort only!" Lieutenant General
Sullivan bellowed into the mic. "Stay ready, but we're
gonna give this plane a chance."

There was no time for celebration. The controllers
still had a job to do.

"Get the fuck out of my seat, hawk," Dusty said, putting headphones on so fast they nearly broke. "Coastal
four-one-six! Welcome back! You are cleared for landing."

· · ·

The CNB camera crew hugged one another while the neighbors high-fived and slapped each other on the back. Carrie's knees buckled under the relief but Theo caught her before she could fall. She turned a teary smile to Scott, who jumped up and down.

"Dad!" he screamed, his young voice lost in the melee.

Bill pulled back on the sidestick as hard as he could. The plane shot nearly vertical, black sky filling the window. Jo fell backward, tumbling against the open door. In the cabin, passengers shrieked at the violent change of direction. Jo pulled herself up, ripping off her oxygen mask and chucking it and the tank on top of Ben's body.

She screamed out the door, "Daddy! Get Josip in his seat! And hang on!"

Turning back to Bill, Jo searched for the wound. His entire arm felt wet. Finally, she found the source: right shoulder blade. Jo looked around the cockpit before ripping Bill's uniform coat off the hanger. Rolling it into a tight ball, she pressed the mass against the wound, using her other hand to pull against his shoulder to create pressure. Bill cried out in pain. The plane banked right as his hand jerked the sidestick.

"I know, baby, but I've got you," Jo said. "Tell me what to do."

Bill's voice was weak. "I need you to be my right hand."

In the tower, everyone watched the beacon on the radar. It turned, and turned again, angling itself east until it was undeniable. Coastal 416 was on its way to JFK.

Warm relief spread through Dusty's body as George clapped him on the back. The controller next to them collapsed into a chair with a sigh.

Outside, the flashing lights of the emergency crews began to move into receiving position.

"Coastal, you are cleared for landing on three-one right," Dusty said into the mic. "Continue direct approach." He released his finger for a sidebar and spoke to George. "They're cleared for three-one right but they're starting to fly in alignment with two-two left. Switch runways?"

George thought about it. "Let's not. Three-one right is already programmed into the original flight plan. Let's keep it as simple as possible for them. But they're going to do whatever they want anyway."

Bill instructed Jo on where to find the release for the extra cockpit jump seat. She slid it out until she heard a latch click into place. Pulling the straps as loose as they went, she buckled in, scooting as far forward on the chair as possible. She was now behind the pilot's seat with a dead-center view of Queens out the window. Taking up the blood-soaked uniform jacket, she reapplied pressure. She feared Bill might pass out.

"Okay," she said. "What first?"

"Speed," Bill said, nodding at the dash. "We've got to lower it. The knob that says 'MACH.' Twist it counterclockwise until you see one-three-zero."

Jo leaned forward, searching the displays.

"This?"

Bill nodded, grimacing.

Twisting the knob, she watched the numbers descend. At one-three-zero she stopped.

"Now pull it."

Jo pulled on the knob. She immediately felt the plane slow. "Now what?"

Bill looked at the navigation display, then glanced out the window.

"Landing gear. On the right side. See that lever? No, down. Look a couple displays down." He tried to point but his right arm was useless. "No. No—yes! That one. Pull it down."

The plane vibrated. Underneath them, the landing gear slowly dropped into position.

ONE THOUSAND.

Jo jumped at the loud robotic voice. She'd never heard the altitude callout from inside the cockpit, just muffled from the other side of the door.

"Okay, above the gear—" Bill slumped forward.

"No!" Jo screamed, pulling him back. She slapped his cheek so hard she worried she might knock him back out. "Stay with me, Bill!"

He roused, looking around the cockpit, confused. Shaking his head, he opened and closed his eyes. He looked as faint as his voice was becoming.

"Auto brake. Above the landing gear—there. Push the button under it that says 'MED.'"

Jo pushed it and the spring-loaded button popped back. A blue ON appeared beneath it.

Bill looked to the navigation display and then glanced out the window. Jo followed his gaze.

The lights of JFK's runways blinked them home.

They had visual.

When the approaching aircraft came into view, dipping and twisting its way toward the runway, the tower erupted in cheers.

The plane's lights grew brighter with each second.
ETA: one minute. Everyone with binoculars tried to
get a visual on the condition of the aircraft. The landing
gear appeared, the tires stretching into position below
the airframe.

The plane banked right dramatically, then corrected
itself, tilting far left in response. It was a windy night,
but Dusty knew that wasn't the cause of the erratic
movements.

He glanced at the radar to check their speed. One
hundred and forty-five knots. Fast. Too fast for a plane
that size, that weight, at this stage. Not impossibly fast.
But they needed to land long.

"Whoa there, girl," Dusty muttered. "Flaps, flaps,
flaps."

Slats of metal on the trailing edge of the wings extended to his request as though they heard him. The
increased drag slowed the plane nearly enough and they
were in alignment with the runway. JFK wasn't a tricky
arrival, but there wasn't much open space beyond the
runway. Landing from the west on 31R meant the end
of the runway opened onto other aircraft hangars, hotels, and roads.

They were going to land short when they needed to
land long.

Jo followed Bill's instructions and watched the artificial
horizon on the primary flight display without blinking.
She could see the sidestick shake under his hand, the
plane's orientation on the display moving in response.

FIVE HUNDRED.

She glanced at their speed. "Do the flaps again?"

Bill nodded and Jo pulled down on the flaps lever. It clicked down another notch.

"Now," Bill said. "See those two levers in the center? The big ones between those wheels with the white marks."

"These?" Jo's hand hovered.

Bill nodded. "Those are the thrust levers. Put your hand on them and keep it there until I say. Once we're on the ground—I'll tell you when—you're going to pull them back. Back toward you. Do it slowly at first. And when I tell you to, you're going to pull them all the way down."

"All the way. Okay."

The plane's nose dipped. The descent was a far cry from the steady feet-first approach aircraft generally took. Each erratic flailing made the controllers in the tower hold their breath.

The plane was approximately fifteen seconds out. At this point, with the binoculars, they could see into the cockpit.

Bill. Jo. An empty first officer's seat.

Ten seconds until landing.

No one in the tower breathed, no one moved. No one wanted to be the reason the putt lipped out, the ball bounced off the rim, the home run just missed the pole and went foul.

Five seconds till landing.

ONE HUNDRED.

Jo watched the lights at the beginning of the runway. Two thick belts of red-and-yellow approach bulbs. Then a thin green line. Then a long stretch of white: the touchdown zone. In the middle, a single path. The centerline.

FIFTY.

FORTY.

Jo and Bill watched the horizon scope. It tilted. He corrected. It tilted again. He overcorrected. He struggled to keep his hand steady.

THIRTY.

TWENTY.

This was it. Jo wanted to close her eyes but resisted.

RETARD. RETARD. RETARD.

The voice calmly warned them that the ground was imminent.

In that final second, she heard Bill whisper to himself.

"One hundred and forty-nine souls on board."

CHAPTER FORTY-ONE

THE BACK WHEELS SLAMMED INTO THE RUNWAY AND THE PLANE'S nose tipped high as it rocked backward. The tail struck the ground. Jo could feel the auto-brake system engage as the plane tried to slow itself.

"Now!" Bill screamed. Jo pulled back on the thrust levers.

The plane jerked and the nose fell forward violently in response. Slamming into the ground, the nose gear collapsed, sparks and smoke spewing out from underneath the plane. Grinding into the concrete, the plane barreled down the runway.

Jo watched Bill press his feet into the pedals as hard as he could, but he was so weak that she couldn't imagine it would have much impact. He shifted his feet right to left, steering the rudder in a desperate attempt to keep the plane on the runway.

She could see flames and sparks out the window. The plane was out of control.

The end of the runway loomed in front of them, the line of red lights issuing a declaration: *Stop*.

Jo didn't know if they could.

• • •

Everyone huddled around the CNB van covered their open mouths in disbelief of what they were witnessing. The plane was moving so fast, too fast. There was no way it was going to stop in time.

There was an unexpected snap. The nose plunged downward and the tail shot into the air. Time stopped as the plane did too. A pause. The plane stood in a strange headstand, momentarily motionless. With a loud creak, she fell back onto her belly.

No one moved.

The cloud of debris and smoke dissipated moments later. A wrecked commercial airliner. Battered and beaten at the absolute edge of the end of the runway.

But in one piece.

Everyone watching reacted in the same instant. The neighbors, the media personnel; all cheered and exchanged high-fives or hugs. Vanessa went down to one knee on the pavement, covering her face as the cameraman clapped her on the back.

Carrie and Theo didn't react. Standing side by side, they never took their eyes off the plane. Until they had a visual on Bill and Jo, they wouldn't allow themselves to breathe easy.

All was still for a few seconds. Then, in jerking and robotic movements, the forward door released and swung outward. A yellow slide belched from the opening, unfurling clumsily until it touched the ground. The back exits followed suit, as did the ones over the wings. The passengers appeared, popping out of the doors and jumping down the slides. Two people stayed at the bottom of each slide, helping others climb off. Another person stayed and directed the passengers on where to run to.

Big Daddy was at the forward door, the same door the passengers had used to board the plane less than six hours earlier on the other side of the country. As the passengers leapt from the aircraft, he was visible in profile, waving his arms and shouting directions inaudible to those outside the plane. His hand, bandaged in white gauze, clung to a bar attached to the inside wall of the fuselage, anchoring himself to firm ground.

Kellie was at the back exit, her face red as she screamed. A man hesitated at the top, looking down on the bright streak of blood an injured passenger had left on the yellow slide. Kellie placed her hand on his lower back and pushed. He tumbled down to safety, his legs wobbly as he was helped up.

Emergency vehicles descended on the aircraft, blue-and-red flashing lights washing over the chaos. Firemen circled around the plane, shouting to each other with wide arm movements as they determined what actions needed to be taken. Hazmat first responders appeared next, leaping from medical vehicles in full-body protective gear. Against the darkness of the night, their white suits shone like a new pair of tennis shoes fresh out of the box. Soon enough they would be marred by the markings of conflict: smoke, dirt, sweat, blood.

The flow of passengers slowed. The evacuation was over almost as quickly as it began—model procedure under unprecedented circumstances. A few scattered passengers streamed down the back slide, but nobody else emerged from the front.

Suddenly an enormously tall man appeared at the front of the aircraft with another full-grown man draped over his shoulder like a dish towel. The large man slid the other off his shoulder, positioning him not-so-carefully at the top of the slide. He unceremoniously used his foot to start him on his descent, the medics at the bottom receiving the red-faced, portly man. Checking for injuries, they called for a stretcher, hazmat taking him away.

The tall man disappeared into the plane and soon reappeared cradling an elderly man in his arms like a baby. The old man looked out at the scene below and then up at his rescuer with relief. The tall man sat them both down on the edge of the slide as carefully as he could, checking to make sure the gentleman's feet and head were clear. Someone inside the plane must have said something because he turned back. The tall man didn't say a word, but a smile graced his face as he dipped his head in a bow. Shimmying himself to the edge slowly, he held the old man in his lap and the two slid down the slide together. At the bottom, the big guy set the old man on his feet, holding his wrinkled hands while his legs found their balance.

By now the flow of passengers evacuating the aircraft had stopped completely, but the crew was still on board. Occasionally, the flight attendants would be glimpsed through an open door as they moved about the plane. Through the little windows they could be seen moving swiftly up the aisle as they swept the aircraft to ensure no one was left on board.

When they were sure everyone was out, they ran to the front. Daddy disappeared into the cockpit. Kellie waited outside in the galley. She bobbed and weaved, trying to see whatever was going on up there. A moment later she jerked to attention and rushed forward before quickly stepping back to make room.

Big Daddy reappeared from the front. He came out

backward, hunched over and moving with slow, awkward progress. He was carrying something heavy. Stepping back toward the opening, he pivoted left as Kellie stepped right. Daddy was holding a pair of legs and, with a tremendous amount of effort, was dragging a motionless body.

As more of the body emerged, Kellie rushed forward to take hold of something. An arm, the hand flopping about limply. She attempted to get a better grip, grabbing under the shoulder as Jo appeared, clutching the body's torso from behind, her petite arms barely able to wrap themselves around Bill's chest.

Theo covered his mouth as Carrie turned Scott's head so he couldn't watch. The baby whimpered on her hip and she began to bounce her harder.

The three flight attendants worked hard to extract the large man from a room so small and full of obstacles that it was difficult to navigate in and out of under normal circumstances. Finally they succeeded, freeing the man with a final thrust of movement, all of them dropping to their knees as they released him to the floor.

Not even pausing for a moment, they conferred, nodding and making movements with their arms and hands as they formed a plan of action. Big Daddy stood and looked out the exit at the slide and the first responders who collected at the base. He yelled something to them and made wide gestures, the emergency crew responding to his commands and shouting them to others down the line.

Big Daddy and Kellie flanked Bill as Jo sat down behind him, hiking up her skirt to straddle his back, shimmying her chest underneath his limp body as all three slowly shuffled and arranged the pair for a tandem slide. As they jostled and moved toward the opening, the view was finally unobstructed and the whole world collectively gasped at the bright-red blood saturating the front of the pilot's white shirt.

Carrie turned her head into Theo's shoulder.

"Don't watch," he whispered in her ear. "I'll watch and tell you if you should."

She nodded and hid in him before turning back a moment later.

A gurney had arrived at the bottom of the slide with medics in hazmat suits. Other responders positioned themselves on opposite sides to catch the twosome when they reached the bottom. Big Daddy yelled, his lip movements unmistakably in a countdown, the pilot and flight attendant sliding down on "three" in a heavy descent. They were received at the base like children on a playground. The pilot was lifted onto the gurney and wheeled away, medics jogging alongside.

Jo accepted the hands that helped her up but fought them off as they tried to carry her away. Breaking free, she turned back to the slide, offering a hand to Kellie as the young woman fumbled to stand. Standing across from each other they waited for Daddy to slide down, helping him to his feet once he reached the bottom.

The three stood in a circle and Jo said something to the other two that made them both nod. Jo shook her head slowly and turned, making a slow gesture across the plane with her hand, her words unheard beyond the flight attendants' ears. Daddy added something and the other two chuckled before Jo took a step forward to embrace Kellie, who had begun to cry. Jo rubbed her back softly while looking off to the medics who were working on Bill. Her face glistened with tears as she watched helplessly. Daddy turned around and looked up at the plane, his bandaged palms covering his mouth.

They stood there for a minute like that, letting what had just happened sink in. Finally, they all turned together and began to limp slowly toward the medics who waited for them.

On the other side of the country, in a suburban neighborhood surrounded by yellow crime-scene tape, the assembled humans let the moment sink in as well.

It was over.

A tiny voice squeaked with emotion. It sounded so wrong, so out of place, for such an innocent observer to be present at a scene of such horrors.

"Mommy?"

Carrie looked down at her son before squatting before him. Her eyes were red and swollen and her attempt at a smile was pitiful.

"Yes, baby?"

"Is Dad okay?"

CHAPTER FORTY-TWO

AN INTERMITTENT BEEP SOUNDED FROM ONE OF THE MANY MACHINES that flanked the bed. The acrid smell of sterility filled the room and the chair Jo sat in was uncomfortably firm. Out in the hallway, a doctor was paged to another part of the hospital.

"I didn't think of them once, Bill," Jo said quietly.

Bill's chest barely rose and fell. Gray-and-purple bruises blossomed under the tubes and bandages that covered his unmoving body. His eyes were closed, the right one swollen and black. The mass of gauze taped to his shoulder was the brightest shade of white, a contrast to the stitches underneath that held the bullet wound shut.

"They say," she continued, reliving the scariest moments of the flight in her mind, "your whole life flashes before your eyes. I've read all these stories of near-death experiences. Or people who died and came back. They all say the same thing." She swallowed. "That before they died, they thought of their family. Their children. Their spouse. That it was all they could think about."

Jo walked to the window and stared at the blue sky outside. Her back to the bed, tears flowed freely. She didn't catch them and they slid all the way down her neck. Her voice broke.

"Not even then. My husband, my sons, my parents, my sister, Theo, my friends . . . none of them. What kind of woman am I? What kind of wife, what kind of mother?"

A machine beeped and another beeped in return. Jo dropped her head. Her body shook with her sobs.

"Thank you," a faint voice whispered.

Jo turned on her heels.

"Thank you for having that much faith in me."

An unexpected lightness filled her chest as the guilt she'd carried since the flight lifted. Stepping forward, she took his hand and they both cried.

Jo wiped her cheeks before grabbing a tissue to gently wipe the tears from his. "You were supposed to be asleep."

Bill's left cheek raised in a half-smile. "Sorry to disappoint. Where's Carrie?"

"At the cafeteria with Theo and the kids getting frozen yogurt."

"I hear he got a promotion."

Jo smiled proudly. "He most certainly did. He also got a one-month unpaid suspension. But after that, a promotion."

"Silver lining."

"One of many," said Jo with a comic gesture toward the massive bouquet of red and purple flowers on the table across the room.

"Coastal went all out," said Bill. "I appreciate the four months of paid time off more."

"You and me both. Did Chief O'Malley sign the card?"

Bill's face darkened. "Hard to do from prison."

The door opened slowly with a knock. Big Daddy poked his head inside and, at seeing Bill awake, thrust the door all the way open.

"Hallelujah! He is risen!" he said, raising a bottle of champagne above his head. Kellie followed him into the room carrying a small bouquet of flowers with a brightly colored balloon floating above.

The IV antidotes and topical treatments the crew and the passengers had received from the medics and hospital staff immediately after the flight were nothing short of miraculous. Daddy's face had almost fully returned to his normal color, and after he removed the oversized sunglasses, Jo could see the whites of his eyes were once again white.

Jo wasn't sure she'd ever seen Bill smile so broadly. He tried to blink back his tears but failed. Kellie lost her battle immediately, the balloon bobbing with her sobs. Jo laughed and wrapped her up in a hug. Daddy busied himself opening the bottle, his nostrils flaring in his failing attempt to not cry as well.

They were sad. They were confused. They were angry. And Jo knew they had only scratched the surface of processing the trauma they had endured. But they were also joyful. It was a joy to be together, to be in the company of the only other people who knew what the burden they had carried, as a crew, felt like. To be with family who truly understood who you were and what you'd seen.

The cork shot out of the bottle with a pop. Kellie pulled plastic cups from her purse. Daddy poured. Standing at the sides of Bill's bed, the surviving crew of Coastal Airways Flight 416 raised their cups.

"To battle scars," Jo said.

They smiled. They drank. They wiped their tears.

Bill sat at a round table with Ben and Sam. Each man had an empty teacup in front of him, and a single teapot sat in the center of the table. One by one, the men poured from the pot, each man pouring for another, the pot producing a different drink each time. Sam received a cup of English breakfast. Ben, coffee with cream and sugar. Bill, coffee as well—black—the way he took it. The men blew on their cups, waiting until the liquid was cool enough to drink. Silently they sat, just looking at each other. Waiting. Finally, they drank. And as they drank the three men slowly broke into smiles. Soon, infectiously, the smiles gave way to laughter. The three men laughed so hard they cried, and it was only when the men pounded the table and threw their heads back in ecstasy that Bill woke up.

Drenched in sweat, his chest heaved. Staring at the ceiling fan for some time, he waited for his pulse to slow, the adrenaline to run its course.

Careful to not wake Carrie, he swung his feet over the side of the bed, the movement releasing a cold pain in his shoulder, the area sensing a phantom wetness as the nerves continued to realign themselves even three months later. He knew it would take a while longer before he could get his medical back. No doctor would sign off on his current state as "fit for duty." But he'd heal, and he'd get there eventually.

Walking quietly through their rental house, he checked on Scott and Elise, finding them both asleep, unbothered, and, most wonderfully: children. Car-

rie and he had marveled at their resiliency, especially
Scott's. They knew what had happened would be with
Scott for the rest of his life, but so far the effects seemed
manageable. Most of the time he still just wanted to
play.

Bill clicked on the desk lamp in the downstairs office and jiggled the computer's mouse. The screen illuminated, displaying the dozen or so open tabs on
his browser. Grabbing a book off the stack next to the
monitor, he opened to where he'd left off, highlighter
and red circles covering the page.

An hour passed. He laid down his pen and rubbed
his eyes.

"I'd give anything to come in here and find you mes-
saging another woman."

Carrie leaned against the doorframe in her oversized
T-shirt, white tube socks on her feet.

Bill sat back, the office chair reclining. "Worse odds
of that happening than what actually did."

Carrie smiled.

"The teapot again?"

Bill nodded.

Crossing the room, she climbed into his lap, her
head resting on his shoulder as he rocked them both.
She looked at the notebooks full of scribbles, the piles
of books with Post-it notes sticking out of the top. She
pointed at one of them.

"Have you gotten to the part where she talks about
what Saddam Hussein did?"

Bill ran a hand through his hair with a sigh, recall-
ing the atrocities the book described. One hundred and
eighty thousand killed with the same poison gas as used
on the plane. Nearly every village in that area of Kurd-

istan had been destroyed. "And how President Reagan did nothing."

Carrie stared at the cover of the book. "But neither did we. I didn't even know it happened until I read it. One hundred and eighty *thousand* people, Bill." She shook her head. "I think about what we're going through. How hard it is to deal with the pain, the anger. How hard it is to deal with the trauma. But think about it: every person on that plane walked off alive."

Bill looked to the pair of silver wings that sat on the desk next to the books, the name BEN MIRO engraved with block letters under the Coastal logo.

"Not everyone," he said.

Carrie wrapped her arms around his neck. Her warm breath was moist on his skin.

"I wish he was still here," Bill said.

"I know."

"I feel like I'm trying to fix something I don't know how to fix."

Carrie sat up, laughing. Bill watched her, a smile spreading across his face. "What's so funny?"

She placed a hand on his cheek. "Bill. You grew up in rural Illinois and now you live in Los Angeles and you're lactose intolerant and you drive your car through a fancy car wash every other Saturday and you're telling me you think *you* are going to come up with the answer for how to fix this?" She motioned to the stack of research.

Bill reminded her of his promise to Ben.

"You didn't promise him you'd *fix* it. He would've laughed in your face. You promised him you'd do everything you could to *help*. And that's exactly what we're going to do. We're going to keep learning and keep listening and when we think we know enough—which we won't—we're going to look for the people who *do* know how to fix it. And we'll help them in whatever way we can."

Bill looked at her in awe. She was right. This articulate, sensitive, intuitive goddess he was lucky enough to have as his compass in life. He was not sure he deserved her.

"Do you hate them?" he asked.

Her smile faded and her eyes went somewhere else momentarily. Bill thought of the night after he'd gotten home from the hospital when they'd lain in bed together and he'd held her as she wept while telling him what it had been like for her and the kids. The image of Sam wiping his son's nose haunted him. The way Carrie had rolled up the terrorist's sleeves did too.

"I hate what they did," she said, after some consideration. "But I don't hate them. Do you?"

Bill looked at the wings.

"I haven't decided," he said.

Taking her hand, he gently kissed the tips of her fingers one by one before placing his lips into her palm, his faced covered. He didn't move for a long time. Finally he removed her hand and said, "I'm sorry, Carrie."

She frowned. "For what?"

"For being me. If I hadn't picked up the trip. If I'd stayed home—"

She placed the tips of her fingers over his mouth.

"I knew exactly what I was getting when I chose a life with you. And it was the best decision I ever made."

His face crumpled in shame. "How can you say that now?"

She smiled. "I say that especially now."

Nestling deeper into his body, she pulled her legs up

against her chest, a position he saw Scott often take in Carrie's lap. Bill rocked her in the same way she rocked the boy.

"Do you think we'll ever be okay?" he said.

She burrowed into his chest as he tightened his arms around her. "We already are."

ACKNOWLEDGMENTS

In my attempt to find representation for this book, I sent queries to forty-one agents. All of them passed. Turns out, an unpublished flight attendant without a platform is a tough sell. Who knew?

My forty-second submission was to Shane Salerno.

When I sent him my material, I was convinced of two things. One, Shane would be the perfect fit for this story and what I'd envisioned it could be. And two, there was literally not a chance in hell he would ever give it a look. I remember scribbling a note on a yellow legal pad that I included with the first twenty-five pages. I don't know why I did that. I hadn't done it with any of the other submissions. And I can't recall exactly what the note said—but I do remember laughing as I wrote it. The message was a bold and confident pitch of both myself and the story.

After forty-one rejections, trust me, it couldn't have been further from how I actually felt.

Maybe it was the note. Maybe it was something I did right in a past life. Maybe aliens played a part. Look, I don't know. I've stopped trying to figure out what compelled Shane to take a chance on me. The only thing I *do* know is that my whole life changed for the better because he did.

Shane isn't just an agent. He's a master of storytelling and craft. A Mr. Miyagi–like mentor and teacher. A fierce advocate and loyal friend. Every day, Shane's helped me discover not only the best version of this story, but the best version of myself. The work and the education have been a remarkable journey, Shane. Thank you, thank you, thank you.

Deep appreciation to the entire team at The Story Factory, but specifically, the tireless efforts of Jackson Keeler, Ryan Coleman, and Deborah Randall. When I consider the other writers represented by TSF, it's a dizzying lesson in humility—but to be welcomed and supported by them was an unexpected privilege. Adrian McKinty and Don Winslow: when I felt stuck, your insightful suggestions pointed the way out. And to Steve Hamilton: special thanks for being so generous with your time and efforts. The book is far better because of your notes, and this first-time author is far calmer because of your encouragement. Your kindness has meant the world to me.

This is my first venture into the world of publishing, and to have the skilled, meticulous, and genuinely lovely team at Avid Reader Press help me navigate it has been such a relief. I can't imagine a better home for this book. Carolyn Kelly, Meredith Vilarello, Jordan Rodman, Ben Loehnen, Lauren Wein, Julianna Haubner, Amy Guay, Allie Lawrence, Morgan Hoit, Amanda Mulholland, Elizabeth Hubbard, Jessica Chin, Ruth Lee-Mui, Brigid Black, Cait Lamborne, Alison Forner, Sydney Newman, Paul O'Halloran, Cordia Leung, and Linda

Sawicki: I see and appreciate all the hard work you did to turn this idea into a reality. And to my brilliant editor and publisher, Jofie Ferrari-Adler, your keen eye and unbridled enthusiasm left its mark on every page. Working with you has been a complete delight. Thank you.

To join the ranks of Simon & Schuster's authors is a profound honor and I want to thank Liz Perl, Gary Urda, Paula Amendolara, Wendy Sheanin, Tracy Nelson, Colin Shields, Chrissy Festa, Stu Smith, Teresa Brumm, Lesley Collins, Leora Bernstein, Felice Javit, Rebecca Kaplan, Adam Rothberg, Irene Kheradi, Chris Lynch, Tom Spain, John Felice, Karen Fink, and Sam Cohen for their support of this book. I'm humbled to be a small part of the incredible work you share with the world. And a special thanks to Jonathan Karp for words of encouragement at a crucial time that I will carry with me the rest of my career.

Indie booksellers are a special kind of magic and I feel wildly fortunate that my manuscript had an early audience with four of the best. Cindy Dach, Kyle Hague, Sarah "Buddha" Brown, and Camilla Orr, I treasured your feedback like the gold it was. And to my literary home base—Changing Hands Bookstore in Arizona—my old staff badge remains one of my most prized possessions.

The bedrock of this story is my respect for the inherent duties of those in aviation. I am in awe and appreciation of the pilots and flight attendants who safely shepherd millions of people to their destinations daily, and it's been a joy and privilege to be in your ranks for the last decade. Let there be no doubt: I am not a pilot, and this is a work of fiction. My aim was to make it accurate enough to be convincing but skewed enough that it wasn't a training manual. I'm indebted to all the pilots I flew with who entertained my endless questions and patiently helped me understand the art of flying, especially my "phone-a-pilot" friends, Mark Bregar, Fabrice Bosse, Brian Patterson, and Jaimie Rousseau. I come from an aviation family—both my mother and sister were in-flight—but my love for the industry truly took hold when I joined my first airline, Virgin America. To the crews, GSTs, supervisors, and those at Triple Nickel (even you, CSS): I'm so proud of what we built, and I miss it every day. The crew of Flight 416 was inspired by so many of the smart, brave, funny, resourceful teammates I flew with over the years, and I hope you see yourselves in their best features. You guys were always my pixie dust.

Emily and Dominic Debonis, Sarah Braunstein, David and Susan Shuff (of the ever-generous Shuff Property Management Co.), Alok Patel, Jac Jemc, Jon Cable, Beth Hunt, Kellie Collins, and Vanessa Bramlett: prepare for the in-person gratitude I intend to rain down on you all. Consider yourselves warned.

My "people" deserve more credit than I'll ever be able to give them, so I'll keep it brief. My parents, Ken and Denise. My sister and her husband, Kellyn and Marty. And the two weasels, Grant and Davis. Thank you for keeping my wheels on. I am nothing without your unconditional love.

Finally, three people deserve special mention.

When I told Sheena Gaspar that I was writing a book, her response was so supportive you'd have thought the book was already finished, published, and on every bestseller list imaginable. If everyone had a friend who believed in them as deeply and unquestioningly as Sheena does me, the world would be filled with a lot more fully realized dreams.

I've valued Brian Shuff's opinion since we were in junior high. Handing him the first draft was terrifying because I knew he would level with me. I expected the worst. (Trust me, that first draft was *rough*.) Instead, he gave me twelve pages of notes and talked to me as though I was actually a writer. I didn't believe I'd written a book until Brian told me I had, and I'm forever grateful for the respect and generosity he showed me then and always.

I applied for a job at Changing Hands because my mom suggested it. I interviewed with Virgin America because my mom thought it would be a good fit. I pushed this book from draft to draft because my mom refused to let me settle for anything less than everything I've ever wanted. My whole life, my mom has known what I needed most even when I couldn't see it. Especially when I couldn't see it. She often tells me, "Your mother is always right." I roll my eyes every time . . . but we both know I agree.

This, all of this, is because of you, Mom.

ABOUT THE AUTHOR

T. J. NEWMAN, a former bookseller and longtime flight attendant, is the *New York Times* bestselling author of *Falling*, much of which she wrote on cross-country red-eye flights while her passengers were asleep. She lives in Phoenix, Arizona.

FALLING

T. J. NEWMAN

This reading group guide for Falling *includes an introduction, discussion questions, ideas for enhancing your book club, and a Q&A with author T. J. Newman. The suggested questions are intended to help your reading group find new and interesting angles and topics for your discussion. We hope that these ideas will enrich your conversation and increase your enjoyment of the book.*

From bookseller turned flight attendant T. J. Newman, who wrote much of this book at 38,000 feet while crisscrossing the country on red-eye flights when her passengers were asleep, *Falling* is a blockbuster thriller that grew out of a terrifying hypothetical scenario that she dreamed up during a flight and then posed to a friendly pilot to see if he could come up with a solution. The scenario? *What would you do if, during a flight, terrorists kidnapped your wife and children and told you that if you did not crash the plane, your family would be killed?* When the pilot's face went pale, she knew she had the makings of a great thriller.

FOR DISCUSSION

1. How are pilots typically portrayed and perceived in popular culture? Consider the influence of *Top Gun* on the young children who dream of becoming pilots, and the sense of authority associated with Bill's classic formal uniform. When Bill can't think of a way to escape Sam's demands, he feels "like a guy in a pilot's costume." What, to him, separates a true pilot from an impostor?

2. Likewise, how are flight attendants portrayed in the media and perceived by travelers? When Kellie, a recent hire, hears about the threat to the plane, she volunteers to take over the passengers' food and drink requests for the rest of the flight while the two experienced crew members deal with the dangerous situation. Jo clarifies that as flight attendants, their sole purpose is safety, not service: "Five weeks of training and in only one of those days did they go over food, drinks, and hospitality." Did this information surprise you?

3. If you were on a flight and your plane's pilot was facing the same choice as Bill, would you want to know, or would you rather be in the dark?

4. When Jo argues that involving the passengers in the defense of the plane could endanger the lives of Bill's family, Big Daddy counters, "What . . . do you think we're flying here? Cargo? There are *people* on this plane, Jo. And every single one of them is someone's family." How does this idea echo throughout the events of the book?

5. When Bill hears the news that his house was blown up, for a brief few moments he believes that his family is dead: "Carrie. Scott. Elise. His whole world. Gone . . . Bill had failed as a husband, as a father, as a protector." How does this fleeting experience of almost losing his loved ones help him to understand Sam's actions?

6. When Bill and the flight attendants are forced to decide who on board they can trust, they rely on personal judgment. Bill tells Jo that he trusts his copilot, Ben, "Completely. But that's my intuition." Jo, Big Daddy, and Kellie share suspicions about one particular passenger, Josip, out of 144 complete strangers: "They had no reason to distrust him besides a gut feeling. But today, that carried weight." What factors influence our unconscious decision-making, and how can we see beyond these assumptions?

7. Sam makes Bill record a video statement that conveys the message behind this act of terror. Were any

points in the statement unexpected to you? How did it change or not change how you viewed Sam and his plot?

8. Sam tells Carrie, "I will walk out the front door and never come back—if you can point Kurdistan out on a map." To Sam, the obliviousness of the American public is as unforgivable as the US government's failure to protect the Kurds. Did you have any knowledge about the Kurdish conflict before reading *Falling*? Why do you think it remains a little-known history?

9. At a crucial moment, Carrie remembers the words of her father: "You don't think everyone actually lives, do you? Most people just exist and roam around. It's a choice, to actually live." What do you think he means by this statement? Do you agree or disagree?

10. Sam explains the purpose behind forcing Bill into a no-win scenario: "It's not about the crash, Bill. It's about the choice. It's about good people seeing they're no different from bad people. You've just always had the luxury of choosing to be good." What does Sam's final choice in the book suggest about his character and his humanity?

11. In cases where an aircraft is known or suspected to be hijacked by suicidal terrorists, fighter jets are deployed to surround and shoot down the plane if necessary to prevent it from crashing into a populated target. In *Falling*, the president of the United States will have to choose whether or not to order

the fighter jets to strike. How does the choice he faces compare to the choice Bill faces? How would you approach such a decision?

12. Bill's dream at the end of the book is very different from the dream that opens the book. Discuss and compare the potential meaning of the two dreams. Do you think that Bill agrees with Carrie when she says, "I hate what they did. . . . But I don't hate them"? How would you feel?

ENHANCE YOUR BOOK
CLUB

1. The experience of traveling airborne, if all goes smoothly, can be a peaceful time to unplug from the demands of life on the ground. Ask book club members to put their devices and their minds on "Airplane Mode" to be fully present and reflective in the moment.

2. Flight attendants like Jo, Big Daddy, and Kellie are trained in first aid to respond to medical emergencies on board. Have each book club member choose a common medical emergency to learn about and lead a basic first aid demonstration. Examples: nosebleed, allergic reaction, dizziness, choking, cardiac arrest, burn.

3. T. J. Newman was inspired to write *Falling* based on her real-life experiences working in aviation. If you could write a novel, what would the story be about?

You were a flight attendant for ten years. What led you to flying as a day job, and how did you ultimately start writing a book at the same time?

My mom and my sister were both flight attendants so joining the "family business" as we call it just made sense for me. But it was definitely a winding road to get there—and here.

I studied musical theater in college and then moved to New York to pursue it as a career. Which was . . . well, I'll just put it frankly: failure. Nothing but rejection and failure. So I eventually left, moved back home to Arizona, moved back in with my parents, and started trying to figure out what to do next with my life. That's when I got a job as a bookseller at Changing Hands Bookstore, which, as a lifelong reader and writer, I *loved*. But when the opportunity to fly presented itself, I knew I couldn't pass it up so I left the store to go to training.

Throughout all of that I was writing stories. I didn't

tell anyone I was. I didn't think I was smart enough or good enough to be a real writer. Plus, I was fresh off my mortifying bout of failure in New York, so I figured I'd already used up my personal quota for public creative risks.

But when I eventually had the idea for *Falling*, it was the first time my need to know what happened to the characters was stronger than my embarrassment and fear of failure. So I started working and I just didn't stop. I refused to let myself stop. I told myself I was going to finish it, and then I would make it better, and then I was going to get it published.

Did you always know you wanted to write a thriller?

Thrillers have always been the books and movies I read and watched over and over. And while I didn't set out initially to be a thriller writer, I very quickly discovered that all of the stories I wanted to tell were in the genre.

Where did the idea for *Falling* originate?

The concept for *Falling* came to me at work. I was working a red-eye to New York and I was standing at the front of the cabin looking out at the passengers. It was dark. They were asleep. And for the first time a thought occurred to me—their lives, *our* lives, were in the pilot's hands. So with that much power and responsibility, how vulnerable does that make a commercial pilot? And I just couldn't shake the thought. So a few days later, I was on a different trip, with a different set of pilots, and one day I threw out to the captain: "What would you do if your family was kidnapped and you were told that if you didn't crash the plane, they would be killed? What would you do?" And the look on his face terrified me. I knew he didn't have an answer. And I knew I had the makings of my first book.

You drafted this book over the course of many flights. Did plotting out such a terrifying threat to the plane while you were onboard make the fear more real?

Pilots and flight attendants spend a lot of time analyzing aviation accidents and incidents. We study what went wrong, why it went wrong, what the crew did right, and what the crew did wrong. We're constantly mentally putting ourselves in emergency scenarios and asking ourselves what we would do, how would we handle it. It's how we learn. It's how we're trained to think. So imagining this particular scenario on the plane didn't feel all that odd, to be honest. It just felt like a heightened and more intense scenario than what I would normally be thinking about.

How did you write while flying full-time? Did you work on the book while strapped in a jump seat?

I usually worked as a "Lead" or "A" flight attendant, meaning, I worked in first class—which meant I had the forward galley to myself. And because I worked a lot of red-eyes (flights with a light work load since everyone is asleep), I'd have a lot of time to do my own thing. So I'd stand in my galley and write by hand—calmly turning over the paper or slipping it into the drawer beneath the coffee pot in a very "nothing to see here, folks" kind of way whenever a passenger or another flight attendant appeared. Then on my layovers in my hotel room or a coffee shop I'd transfer my work to my iPad.

As a writer, landing a seven-figure book deal quickly followed by the seven-figure film rights is a lifelong dream come true. How have you been navigating this experience?

I'm so grateful and so humbled about everything that's happened. It truly has been a whirlwind experience and I don't know what I'd do without my incredible family who have kept me grounded through all of it. Plus, I've got another book due so I'm working on getting my pages in.

What can you tell us about the film adaption and your hopes for seeing your book on screen?

I know the first priority is finding the right writer and director and actors and I know that process is underway. Besides that, I'm sworn to secrecy and I'm just thrilled that there might be a movie of my book.

What do you hope readers will take away from the book?

I'd love for readers to walk away with a broader understanding and deeper respect for what flight crews do. Especially flight attendants. I think there's a common misconception that FAs are on board for service. And that's just not true. I assure you, if it was, the airlines would have stopped paying us and replaced us with vending machines a long time ago. Flight attendants are there for your safety and security. Service is just something we gladly provide. So I'd be thrilled if a reader remembers that the next time they feel the impulse to roll their eyes at the flight attendant who asks them to bring their seat back up or to stow their bag. They're not trying to inconvenience you. They're trying to protect you.

Turn the page to read a chapter from

T. J. NEWMAN's
latest sensational thriller

The term *last-ditch* is used to describe an effort that is made at the end of a long line of failures. It is the final attempt and is not expected to succeed.

In aviation, the emergency landing of an aircraft on water is called a *ditching*.

CHAPTER ONE

WILL KENT OPENED HIS EYES JUST IN TIME TO SEE THE ENGINE EXPLODE.

His arm shot up to protect the passenger seated at the window, but his daughter Shannon didn't seem to notice. The eleven-year-old girl just watched the flames spewing out of the back of the engine's tail cone and uttered an uneasy *whoa*.

Will sat up straight and looked over the tops of the seats. The emergency exit was two rows up. A flight attendant sat there in a rear-facing jump seat staring at the passengers. He could just make out her name bar. Molly. Will caught her eye.

Molly didn't say a thing. She didn't have to.

The aircraft shook. Panic gripped the cabin as everyone craned for a look out the windows. Flames. Chunks of metal ripping off, flying by.

Will leaned over Shannon for a better view. The engine was on fire. Parts of the wing were shredded. Below the plane, crystal-clear turquoise water.

Shannon looked to her dad. "Why aren't we turning back to Honolulu?"

Will had been wondering the same thing.

In the cockpit, every pilot's worst nightmare was coming true.

"We lost thrust in engine one," First Officer Kit Callahan radioed to ATC, her voice rising involuntarily as the plane dropped. "And all hydraulic fluid in all three systems."

"Say again, fourteen twenty-one?"

The air traffic controller sounded skeptical. Even the captain glanced over to see for himself. Any other day, all this second-guessing would have pissed her off.

Not today.

Kit triple-checked the ECAM, barely believing the display herself. System failures were listed in order of severity. Level 3 failures, the most crucial, were first, in red. Red filled the screen. Every time she cleared one, another would pop up. All were Level 3. The digital screen looked like it was bleeding out.

They'd been airborne for less than two minutes. Engine one was dead. So were the hydraulics. This extended beyond their training. Pilots don't run situations like this in the simulator.

There'd be no point.

"Fourteen twenty-one, ah, did you say all three? All three hydraulic—"

"Goddamn it, dead stick!" Captain Miller said.

No hydraulic fluid. No hydraulic power.

The plane was dead in the air.

Green. Blue. Yellow. The aircraft's three hydraulic lines. Two layers of redundancy in case of a system failure.

It's *that* important. The display should have shown three green lines at 3,000 PSI. Kit was looking at three amber lines with 0 PSI. Her best guess was that when the engine blew, fragments of metal sprayed like buckshot through the hydraulic lines and drained the fluid. Any moving component on the aircraft—ailerons, flaps, spoilers, rudder—everything that let them fly the plane, had frozen in place.

The pilots couldn't command the Airbus A321 to do anything. They had no control.

"We can't turn back," Kit told the controller. "Requesting an alternate in front of us."

Will ripped open one of the plastic pouches he'd just pulled from the compartments under their seats. He passed it to Shannon.

She turned the pouch over, looking at the folded yellow life vest tucked inside.

"Are we going to crash?"

Several passengers looked at her. She'd voiced their worst fears.

"Shannon," Will said, shifting in his seat to face her. "We've lost an engine. I don't know why we're not turning back. It may be because we can't."

Will pulled the vest out and shook it open, slipping it over her head before cradling her face in both his hands.

"I know you're scared. But whatever happens, I'm going to be right here with you."

Will heard a seat belt unbuckle. He waited for the refastening click after the passenger realized there was nowhere to run. Instead came heavy footsteps. He looked up just as a red-faced, middle-aged white guy in a blue polo shirt blew past their row on his way to the back. Angry male voices began to rise in the rear of the plane as the guy in the blue polo shirt yelled at a male flight attendant who was seated in a swing-out jump seat in the center of the aisle.

"Sir!" the flight attendant bellowed. "Sit down! *Sir!*"

Suddenly, the plane dropped sharply. Everything went down—

—blue polo went up.

His head smashed into the ceiling. Will turned away as the man slammed back to the floor—just in time to see Molly the flight attendant unbuckle her harness and head for the back of the plane. Another jolt made the plane thrash violently. Molly flew forward. Her head smacked into an armrest, with her chin taking the brunt of it. Crawling on all fours back to her jump seat, Molly strapped herself in while blood trickled from a split lip.

Will refocused on Shannon. "Shannon. We stay together. You understand? No matter what. We stay together."

Shannon wasn't listening to her dad. Will followed her gaze. Blue polo was on his feet again, stumbling back to his seat amid the turbulence, moaning in pain. He held his head while blood poured down his face in thick streaks. As he passed their aisle, the plane dipped. He braced himself, then continued on, leaving behind a bright red handprint stamped on the white overhead bin.

Shannon stared unblinkingly at the blood.

"We stay together," she repeated.

Molly Hernandez winced as she wiped the blood off her chin with the arm of her uniform sweater. She tried to look calm as she blinked at the passengers from under her straight-cut bangs, but her hands would not stop shaking.

Another seat belt unbuckled. Molly turned. A woman in a long floral dress got up to let the guy in the blue polo back into their row just as the plane lurched again. Floral dress lost her balance and fell into the man. Their heads smacked against one another and the woman grimaced in pain, a streak of his blood now covering her forehead. He sat clumsily, and with another jolt of the plane, she fell back into her own seat.

"Ma'am?"

I hate that guy, Molly thought, stewing. *Three people are now hurt and bloodied for no reason.*

"Excuse me—"

The only reason Molly had even gotten up was because she was worried about the unaccompanied minor. Flying all alone. Sitting in the last row of the plane. Poor kid had a front-row seat for all that screaming, all that blood—

A piece of the engine slammed violently against the plane. Everyone jerked away from the windows and Molly yelped. A few people screamed. Holy *shit* the passengers looked terrified. Holy *fuck* everything was happening so fast.

Molly closed her eyes. She was spinning out. *Calm down*, she thought, taking a breath. *Just review your commands. Heads down, stay down. Heads down, stay down. Release seat belts. Leave—*

"Excuse me! Ma'am!"

"What? What do you want?" Molly snapped at the woman sitting across from her. She immediately regretted it. "I'm sorry."

"Where's that vest?"

"Under your seat."

The woman bent over and her waist-length braids pooled on the floor. She struggled with the compartment under her seat until the plastic seal broke off with a snap. The woman sat up with the plastic pouch, ripped it open, shook out the bright yellow life vest, and threw it over her head.

"But don't—"

Grabbing the red T-handles, the woman yanked down like it was a parachute, inflating the vest with a loud hiss. Everyone watched the woman try to lean back in her seat. She now looked more like a raft than a passenger.

In the cockpit, Kit looked to the controls overhead. The whole panel was lit up. Every button in the hydraulics section glowed amber with a single word: FAULT. Above that, a large rectangular button labeled ENG 1 with FIRE printed on its plastic guard burned bright red. She double-checked the smaller buttons flanking it. They *should* have shown a glowing white SQUIB, meaning the primary and backup fire-suppression systems had been armed. Instead, the buttons were dark.

"Push button didn't activate," Kit said.

The pilots had no way to fight the engine fire or cut off the fuel that was feeding it.

Kit cleared the engine failure and a new Level 3 fault popped up on the ECAM explaining why the fire-suppression system hadn't activated. There, like a bright red, all-caps middle finger: ENG 1 FADEC FAULT.

"FADEC fault."

"Goddamn it," Captain Miller mumbled.

The Full Authority Digital Engine Control was a

small computer affixed inside the engine that acted as the link to the pilots. Any action in the cockpit went *first* to the FADEC, *then* the engine responded. Engine one's FADEC was dead. Without it, there was no communication between the two. The pilots couldn't tell the engine to do anything—and they also had no idea what the engine was doing.

"I need eyes," Captain Miller said.

Kit punched a button.

Three high-low chimes sounded throughout the cabin. A red light lit up on the ceiling above the emergency exit row. Will watched Molly rip a phone from a cradle and press it to her ear without saying a word.

Shannon took her own phone out of airplane mode, brought up a text thread, and began typing. Will noticed the contact. MOMMY, with a pink heart emoji.

There was a loud bang. Will grabbed his armrests as the plane dipped to the left. The phone flew from Shannon's hands, dropping to the floor with a thud. Just as she bent to get it, the plane dove, and the phone slid forward.

"No!" Shannon cried, reaching out. Like every eleven-year-old, her phone was her life. Being without it was unthinkable. She grabbed at her seat belt but Will's arm pinned her down.

"Leave it," he said.

"I want to tell her—"

"You'll tell her in person."

He was firm. He wanted her to take it as confidence that they were going to be okay.

But he also knew she was smarter than that.

• • •

Further up, strapped into his jump seat in row eight, Kaholo Kapule did what all the flight attendants were doing: holding the interphones to their ears and not saying a word.

In emergencies, flight attendants are trained to wait. The pilots will be busy. They'll communicate as soon as they can, *if* they can. Do not distract or interfere by calling them. They will call you.

While Kaholo waited, that nice young couple was watching him with wide eyes, so the flight attendant gave them an easy half smile. They held hands, knuckles turning white next to shiny new wedding bands. Another couple up in first class was celebrating their fifty-fifth anniversary. Colleen, the lead flight attendant, had made an announcement for both.

"Who can see the engine?" came Kit's voice through the interphone.

"I can," Kaholo said, unbuckling his harness and standing for a better look. The passengers leaned back so he could see. The Hawaiian native could surf before he could walk, so even in an uneasy ride, he never had to hold on to anything. But as he bent and saw what was on the other side of the window, he instinctively grabbed a seat back.

Will stared at Molly.

She'd had that phone to her ear for a nearly a minute now but hadn't said a thing. She was just sitting there. Listening.

Will leaned into the window. It was hard to assess the engine since he was sitting behind it, but flames had now covered all that was left of it. Most of the outer cowling had been blown off or ripped apart by the airstream.

Mechanical inner workings were exposed. The inlet cowl, the massive circular section of metal covering the front of the engine, clung to the bottom, swaying precariously, looking like it might fall any second.

Suddenly the plane dropped like a brick thrown off the roof of a building. A baby started to wail. The mother held her tight and sang a soft song into her ear. No one had a clue what was going to happen. Uncertainty brought fear. Fear created anxiety. They prayed. They cried. They texted goodbye to their loved ones.

But Will's attention had turned back to Molly. And so he was the only one who saw the blood drain from her face at something said to her by someone on the other end of that phone.

Molly's jaws parted. She blinked a couple times. Then, without saying a word, she hung up the phone and just sat there very, very still.

Will reached over and took Shannon's hand. He knew what came next.

A chime rang throughout the cabin.

"This is the captain. Prepare to ditch."